TEMPER THE FLAME

AN MM BEAUTY AND THE BEAST RETELLING

BEAUTIFUL NIGHTMARES
BOOK FOUR

ANNA FURY

AMY PENNZA

COPYRIGHT

© Anna Fury & Amy Pennza 2023

E-Book ASIN: B0C3JTYJ4C

Paperback ISBN: 978-1-957873-45-9

All rights reserved. No part of this publication may be reproduced, stored or transmitted in any form or by any means, electronic, mechanical, photocopying, recording, scanning, or otherwise without written permission from the publisher. It is illegal to copy this book, post it to a website, or distribute it by any other means without permission.

This novel is entirely a work of fiction. The names, characters and incidents portrayed in it are the work of the author's imagination. Any resemblance to actual persons, living or dead, events or localities is entirely coincidental.

If you read this book ANYWHERE other than Amazon, it is a pirated copy and we are not being reimbursed for our work. Don't be that person. Please.

Cover - Miblart

Cover Photo - DepositPhotos

CONTENT NOTICE

Temper the Flame is intended for mature audiences due to adult themes that might be triggering for sensitive readers. These include on-page murder, battle scenes, mention of parental death, torture, and violence.

While the themes of this retelling feel dark, the deep love between our characters is a beautiful light at the end of the tunnel. This book ends with a happily ever after.

Take care of yourself, and email us with any questions.
author@annafury.com
amy@amypennza.com

CHAPTER 1
FUOCO

I sit in the vaulted Great Hall thrumming bejeweled fingers against the glossy black armrest of my chair. The cavernous space rings with music and laughter as my court gathers for the evening meal. Dragons and other creatures of the Myth line the tables, each courtier garbed in dazzling colors and dripping with jewels.

Servants wend their way through the crowd carrying trays of food and mead, stopping occasionally to fill a goblet or replenish a plate. A siren harpist plucks sweet melodies from the corner. A fire blazes in the hearth, its crackling flames sending sparks up to the ceiling to mingle with the smoke of incense that burns in braziers along the walls.

My court is a marvel of grandeur and revelry—and it never, ever changes. Day after day, week after week, month after month, it's the same. The same conversations circle round and round like a never-ending carousel. The same music plays in my ears. The same people laugh at the same jokes and drink the same drinks.

"Are you enjoying yourself, my lord?"

I turn to find my enforcer, Varden, watching me with curiosity in his amethyst eyes. He lifts his wineglass and gestures toward the crowd, saluting the merriment. "It's an exciting evening."

Exciting isn't the word I'd use, but I nod. "A night like no other."

Varden sips his wine. On my other side, my second enforcer, Nazzar, digs into a dessert stacked with so many layers of chocolate and cream it threatens to topple over.

Lirem, my third enforcer, is absent.

As I study his empty chair, I return to drumming my fingers. It's not like him to skip dinner. He's usually back from his rounds well before the evening festivities begin.

An elderly servant appears at my side and places a tray of raw venison steaks before me. When I turn to thank her, she ducks her head, obscuring her face and leaving me staring at her white cap. I swallow the sigh that rises in my chest. My human servants never willingly meet my gaze. Most of the time, they avoid looking at me altogether. It's been this way since I accepted the role as leader of the Fire Syndicate. Even in human form, I terrify the humans who dwell in my territory.

It could be my sheer size. I tower over every one of them. It could also be the demi-form I take when my temper rises. When emerald-green scales slide down my arms and my hair turns the same shade, my servants scatter.

I try to keep my temper at bay. But dragons are passionate creatures. Our fire always simmers just beneath our skin.

"Your meal, sir," the woman says, backing up a step. She keeps her gaze down and folds trembling hands in front of her. "Freshly hunted and uncooked just the way you like it, sir."

I shove down the irritation that bubbles whenever the servants act petrified in my presence. I've done everything I can to make them comfortable. They're handsomely paid. They enjoy plush living quarters. I even provide magical healthcare right here in the castle.

Still, they're afraid. Always afraid.

Even in my current humanoid form, the sour stench of the woman's fear burns my nostrils. Her heart gallops in her feeble chest. It's on the tip of my tongue to remind her how much I've done to maintain peace on this plane—how much effort I invest in making sure humans can live in harmony with various creatures of the Myth.

But I swallow my explanations along with my sigh. Reminding your subjects why you lead them doesn't inspire loyalty—or love. *Actions speak louder than words.* It's a distinctly human phrase. In the Myth, words work just fine, especially if you can imbue your words with magic. But I've adopted the human saying. I've tried to fit in.

"Thank you, Ellen," I say, arranging my features in what I hope is a reassuring smile. Rheumy eyes dart to mine and drop quickly to the ground. Before I can say anything else, she turns and scurries away.

I release my sigh.

Varden snorts, drawing my gaze to him. He gives me an exasperated look as he lowers his wine. "When will you learn, Fuoco? The help will never see us for anything other than the monsters we are. They're not going to be your friends."

"I don't want them to be my friends," I say tightly. *I'd settle for them not wetting themselves when I glance in their direction.*

My enforcer shrugs. "Humans are narrow-minded, clannish creatures. It's hardly surprising they blew up their civilization."

I grab my glass of wine and swirl it, inhaling the musky tannins that were once popular in the California region of the United States. That whole area was reclaimed by the sea after the humans' nuclear wars "blew up their civilization" as

Varden calls it. In truth, they destroyed the planet. The explosions were so powerful, they ripped the Veil between the human plane and the Myth realm. Magic poured into the human world, devouring technology and wreaking havoc. Even with all of our powers combined, the creatures of the Myth only possessed enough magic to mend one plane. We had a choice: repair our world and let the humans die out, or fix their plane and abandon the Veil to the mists of history. We chose to save the humans.

And now we're all one big, happy family.

Suppressing a snort of my own, I bury my nose deeper in my glass. The cabernet's rich, herbal bouquet releases the knot of tension between my shoulder blades. Wine is one of the pleasures of this plane. The humans got that much right, at least.

Maybe I could start a winery here in the North, in what was once known as "upstate New York." The Fire syndicate covers nearly a hundred thousand square miles. The weather is temperamental, especially in the winter, but I'm a dragon. Surely I can think of a way to keep grapes warm.

The castle has a greenhouse. That might work...

"I've angered you, my lord," Varden says in a low tone.

I set my wineglass down and turn to him. Rings glitter on his fingers. A stack of priceless bracelets adorns his wrists. His linen shirt is bespoke, sewn by my court tailor. Like all dragons, Varden loves fine things. And like most of my people, he finds it difficult to relate to humans.

"I'm not angry," I say. "Merely frustrated. The Veil between this world and ours fell nearly two hundred years ago. Humans should be accustomed to seeing dragons by now. I'd like to be able to walk among the people. Maybe talk to them."

Varden frowns. "But...why? What could they possibly have to say that's important?"

Irritation sparks in my chest. "They're unlikely to speak to me if I approach them with that attitude. We are not the dragon houses of old, lording our rule over beings we deem lesser." I lean toward him as I warm up to a topic near and dear to my heart. "The humans may appear weak to you, but I have found them to be—"

"They will never be *us*, Fuoco." Varden's purple eyes glint in the candlelight. "They will never shift into great beasts and take to the skies. I would not call them lesser, but we are certainly not the same."

My sigh returns. Varden and I have had this discussion so often I sometimes feel like I'm cursed to forever repeat it. We're unlikely to see eye to eye. But he's actually more liberal in his views than the majority of dragons. Unlike most of the Myth, my kind rarely ventured through the Veil before it fell. Not even the strongest glamour can conceal a dragon in flight. So we mostly kept to the magical plane—until the humans destroyed the Veil and sent the two worlds crashing into each other.

But Varden was born after that cataclysm. This plane is all he's ever known, and he's more at ease around humans. Still, his insistence on *othering* them hinders my goal of a truly integrated society.

"You don't shift, either," I remind him. "And if you don't find your *selsara*, you'll *never* shift." As his mouth tightens, I let a hint of my beast seep into my tone. "We're not so different from the humans, Varden. As my enforcer, you work closely with all of my people, including the humans who live in this syndicate. It will benefit everyone if you at least attempt to understand them."

And I *need* him to understand them. I need him to serve as an intermediary between me and the people. Like the rest of the dragons in my court, Varden hails from one of the lower houses, which means he won't take beast form until he finds his fated mate. All dragons are tall and powerfully built, but those from the lower houses blend more easily with humans than I ever could. Varden is several inches shorter than my own seven feet. No one could ever mistake me for anything other than a dragon. My enforcers don't suffer the same impediment.

For a moment, Varden seems like he wants to argue. Then he sits back in his chair and runs a beringed hand through his short, dark hair. He falls silent for a moment before saying, "You're right, of course. It's difficult to undo generations of ingrained thinking."

"If I didn't think you capable of change, I wouldn't have chosen you to serve as an enforcer." Varden has been by my side for six decades. I couldn't run the syndicate without his steady presence. I put a hand on his shoulder. "You bring honor to my house and yours, Varden of House Forza."

He opens his mouth, but whatever he might have said is interrupted by the Great Hall's double doors flying open. The glossy panels crash into the stone, making every head in the Hall turn toward the entrance. I rise and prepare to shift.

An elderly human male falls through the opening and onto both knees. Lirem appears behind him, his face twisted into a sneer. My enforcer's pale blond hair tangles around his broad shoulders. His eyes glitter red as he stares down at the human. One of Lirem's sleeves is torn at the elbow, revealing the shimmering red scales of his dragon. He lifts his head and locks gazes with me. The look in his eyes tells me everything I need to know.

This human is a thief or a killer. Maybe both.

I round the high table with Varden and Nazzar on my heels. Except for the sound of our boots on the flagstones, the Hall is silent as we approach Lirem and his prisoner.

The human is filthy. He remains in a crouch at Lirem's feet, his white hair streaked with more than a month's worth of dirt. His clothing is full of holes, his shoes falling apart.

A highwayman, perhaps. The Fire Syndicate is isolated in the North. The road between my territory and the rest of the syndicates is long and often treacherous. My enforcers and I do our best to provide protection, but we can't be everywhere at once. My syndicate is a haven for monsters and humans alike. All are welcome. But not everyone wants to live peacefully. Thieves prey on the humans who travel the road from the Fire Syndicate to the other three territories. This man is likely one of them—a degenerate who would rather steal than do an honest day's work.

Lirem kicks the man in the side, making him grunt. "Stand before Lord Fuoco."

The man gets to his feet. He lifts his chin and meets my gaze with a brazen stare. Eyes the color of the sea pierce me. My nape prickles as an odd awareness settles over me. If I didn't know better, I'd think he was unafraid. He's either too stupid to be intimidated, or he's lost his mind.

I look at Lirem behind him. "His crime?"

"I caught him stealing from the apple orchard." Lirem crosses thick arms over his broad chest. Red scales peek from under his collar. When he finally meets his selsara and shifts, his dragon will take the same brilliant shade. Until then, his inability to shift makes him more approachable to the humans in my territory.

Although, the man in front of me probably wishes he'd never crossed paths with Lirem.

He continues to stare me down, his sea-colored eyes unflinching. His hands are balled in fists at his sides. His muscles tremble.

Definitely insane. I'm nearly three hundred pounds of muscle. I could flatten him with one blow.

If only it were that simple.

I let my beast rise. The human's pupils reflect the green flames that dance in my eyes. "You know the punishment for stealing," I tell him. "Do you wish to say anything?"

At last, the man begins to sweat. It trickles down his dirt-streaked forehead and pools in the purple hollows beneath his eyes. His chest rattles as he draws quick, shallow breaths. Death is a shadow just behind him. Regardless of tonight's outcome, he's not long for this world.

I give him a minute, then two, allowing silence to stretch. Behind me, the Great Hall stays quiet. My court watches. And waits.

Lirem gives me a meaningful look. "Let's take this outside, shall we, my lord?"

I nod and gesture toward the door.

He grips the human by the scruff of the neck and steers him out of the hall. As Varden and Nazzar follow, I face the court. A range of expressions greets me. Irritation. Boredom. Impatience. The last is the most prominent. My court is comprised of Myth creatures. The execution of a human thief is hardly compelling entertainment. If an activity doesn't involve wine or fucking—or some combination of the two—my courtiers generally want nothing to do with it.

I raise my voice. "Everyone, please return to your dinners."

Almost immediately, chatter resumes. Knives and forks clink against plates. Laughter rises from one of the tables. I turn to head outside, but a flash of white stops me.

Ellen stands in the shadows in the far corner of the Hall hugging an empty serving platter flat against her chest. Her face is a mask of horror, her eyes sheened with tears. Suddenly, her eyes flick to me. With a startled gasp, she turns and flees.

I don't sigh this time. Instead, something else rises in my chest. Disappointment?

Or is it shame?

Laughter rings out again. Pushing the feeling aside, I stride out the doors and into the courtyard. I've ruled the Fire Syndicate for almost two hundred years. My subjects know what to expect. My rules are simple.

No theft. No murder. No assault.

And no exceptions.

That's the way it is. The way it *has* to be. When monsters and humans mingle, the rules must be crystal clear. It's the only way to maintain peace. I can't allow the emotions of one human servant to cloud my judgment.

The courtyard is vast—large enough to accommodate my dragon form and the fire I spew when I mete out justice. Lirem drags the thief to a thick metal post and fastens chains around his waist. Then he yanks the man's arms above his head and locks them in metal cuffs.

"Not iron, eh?" the man says, his raspy voice almost shocking after his previous silence.

His words are a taunt. Everyone knows creatures of the Myth despise iron. The metal hurts us and weakens our magic. An iron spear, crafted by an early human I encountered, is responsible for the tiny scar that runs down my stomach.

I step close to the human. "I don't tolerate thieves. If you have any last words or family I should care for, now is the time to say so."

The old man sneers, sea-colored eyes darting over my shoulder to where Lirem stands behind me. "Don't tolerate thieves, huh? What about those under your own roof?"

My enforcer snarls and moves past me. He raises a hand, but I grab his arm before he can land a blow.

"Hold, Lirem," I say quietly, meeting his red gaze. "There's no honor in venting your frustration on a dead man."

There's a tense moment of silence. Then my chief enforcer gives a curt nod. "Yes, my lord. My apologies."

I release him and turn back to the human. "Dragons didn't steal from you, *thief*. None among the Myth have taken from your kind. On the contrary, we've given you everything, including your world. We didn't ask for the Veil to fall, and we certainly didn't ask to be pulled into this plane. Believe me, ours was far nicer."

As he did in the Hall, the man holds my stare. Vitriol burns in his eyes. Dirty lips press tightly together.

Which is why I don't anticipate the glob of saliva he launches at me. It lands on my cheek with a disgusting splat.

"You dragons with your fancy clothes and shiny jewels can fuck off!" he shouts. "Treasure-hoarding thieves, the lot of you. Burn in hell!" His blue eyes are wild as he jerks against the cuffs securing him to the post.

"Only one thing will be burning tonight, old man," Lirem snarls as I wipe the saliva from my face. My enforcer's fangs appear between his lips as his red eyes glow more brightly.

"Enough," I growl, hearing the anger in my voice. Lirem hears it, too, because he shuts up and turns to me with a chastened look.

I loosen my mirrored tie, remove it, and place it in his waiting palm. When I turn, Nazzar is behind me, his quick fingers unlacing my black corset. I shrug out of it, and he catches it before it can fall.

My shirt goes next, then my pants, and then I stand nude in the courtyard with moonlight streaming down on me. But I'm not unadorned. My jewelry remains, the metal enchanted to shift with me when I take beast form.

Lirem and Nazzar jog toward the safety of the castle. The human thief casts a dismissive gaze down my body.

I know what he sees—and I know his dismissiveness is an

act. Even in human form, I'm not easily dismissed. Seven feet tall and packed with muscle, green scales glitter like emeralds from my shoulders to the tops of my thighs. More emeralds decorate my jewelry, from the stud in my ear to the rows of bracelets around my wrists. The Prince Albert piercing through the tip of my cock glitters with tiny diamonds. The barbells in my nipples are plain silver tonight, as is the barbell that nestles under the base of my dick. The guiche piercing behind my sack includes a rare blood emerald from the Old Country.

The man says nothing, but he licks his cracked lips as he yanks on the cuffs.

He's nervous now. I'll make sure he's not nervous for long.

Stepping back, I let the fire overtake me. It spreads through my mind like a trail of embers igniting. The blaze explodes in my chest, and then I'm standing in dragon form in the courtyard staring down at the tiny, chained man.

He cries out, his bravado evaporating.

I take no pleasure in it, nor do I relish this task. But I can't allow the lawless to ruin the syndicate for everyone else. Opening my mouth, I call my fire, feeling it mix with gas from the sacks just inside my cheeks. It sizzles hot in my throat as I drag in a breath to give it oxygen.

"Wait!" the man calls out. "I've got a wife, a fam—"

A stream of fire silences him, his skin bubbling and cracking. He shrieks as his flesh melts from his bones. Within seconds, bone disintegrates into dust. Fire flows from my mouth as sorrow spreads through me. Taking a life is the worst thing I have to do for my syndicate. Each death is a stain on my soul, and some days I wonder just how black it can get before it's as dry and worthless as the remains before me.

Now-empty cuffs clink and jangle against the post as I call my fire back and let it die in my throat. The stones around the post glow bright orange. But they'll cool quickly. I built my castle with my duty in mind, choosing granite strong enough to withstand hot temperatures.

Lirem jogs back to me as I shift. He offers clothing, but I wave it away. "You're getting slow, old friend," I say, pointing to his torn sleeve. "Did the human have a weapon?"

"A knife," Lirem says, his voice gruff. "He surprised me. Popped up from some bushes on the side of the road. He was obviously lying in wait for one of us." Lirem scowls. "These fools never change. You'd think the humans would greet us with gratitude. Instead, we get knives."

"It will come with time. Most of us lost everything when the Veil fell. But we've built something good here. Perhaps one day, the humans will see it as we do."

Lirem looks unconvinced, but his scowl fades as he glances toward the castle. "Tell me there's fresh venison for dinner so I can forget this entire sordid night."

"I left a platter on the table. It's yours."

"You dined already?"

I shake my head. "I'm not hungry." I look at the stars just beginning to emerge in the night sky. "I think I'll go flying."

His scowl returns. "Don't tell me you're upset over killing a thief."

I look to where the dead man's dust now swirls in the early evening air. The breeze picks up, spreading it over the cooling stones. In an hour or so, no trace of him will remain.

"Fuoco—"

"I'll return by morning," I say, striding away from my enforcer before he can accuse me of being sentimental. Or weak.

∼

An hour later, I streak down the coastline of Old New York City—now known as the Hallows. Electricity is scarce in my territory, but there's enough of it here to illuminate the syndicates below.

The Statue of Liberty slumbers on her side in the bay, the wounds she gained during the humans' war hidden by the seabed. Her head rests in the Sea Syndicate, which is ruled by Triton. He and his mermen are unlikely to be near the surface, so I wheel and glide down in a lazy spiral. Flapping my wings once, I alight on one of the spikes of the statue's crown.

The ocean is choppy, its waves frigid and restless in winter. Water crashes against the statue's face and drips down her cheeks like tears. I watch the tide as I catch my breath from the long flight. The waves are murky and black, the crests tipped with foam. A thick wave builds, smashes against the statue's shoulder, and sends an icy spray across my leg.

I shake the moisture away, then look at the ocean and raise a brow. *Settle down, would you?*

At once, the water retreats.

That's better, I say in my mind, my communication limited in this form. *No need to be rude.*

The waves crest more slowly, the sea's cadence less violent. After a moment, I twist around and face the statue's feet. One sandal rises above the waves, its toes pointed toward the shiny towers of the Air Syndicate. Ruled by the gargoyle Gothel, the Air Syndicate is the only part of the Hallows that resembles what used to be New York City. Like all gargoyles, Gothel loves buildings. Over the years, he's purchased properties and raised new skyscrapers, restoring Old Manhattan to its former glory.

But I'm not here to admire the buildings. I want to talk to their master.

Lifting my snout to the sky, I let out a roar. Then I settle more comfortably on the crown and wait.

Half an hour later, a winged figure appears at the edge of the tallest tower. He lingers for a moment, then disappears. Amusement curves my lips. *Admission granted.*

Shoving off the crown, I swoop across the bay and flap my wings. Currents buffet me as I approach Gothel's tower. Light flashes, guiding me to the spinning glass window at the top of his library. Dozens of panes retract, creating an opening large enough for me to sail through.

Snapping my wings close to my body, I streak toward it. Wind screams in my ears as the opening looms larger. I dive through it, pull up fast, and shift as I drop four stories to the ground.

It rears up and meets me far sooner than I'm ready for it. I land with a heavy grunt and wince at the sting that reverberates up my legs.

Gothel leans against his desk in human form, his powerful body wrapped in an expensive three-piece suit.

Another power play. He shifted and dressed. I know without asking he won't offer me clothes. Not that I'd deign to wear anything he offers. Gothel's wardrobe is pricey, but his taste is woefully uninspiring. Aside from a pocket watch, he doesn't even wear any jewelry.

"Rough landing," he murmurs, smiling as he puffs at a cigar. Big, dark horns swoop up and away from his head. Whiskey-colored eyes glint in the electric light.

"Smoother than most of yours," I say easily.

"It's been a while since you visited, Fuoco. What do you want?"

Straightforward and to the point. This is why I prefer Gothel over the other syndicate lords. Triton is too dramatic and self-righteous. Wotan is a brooding asshole. Gothel is reasonable. Most of the time.

I stalk naked across his office and grab a cigar from the box on his desk. When I turn, he stands at the ready with a lighter. Sucking in a deep hit, I sigh when pleasure spreads warm and tingly through my gut.

"Your girl gets better with every batch," I say, raising my cigar in salute.

Gothel smiles. "True. She outdoes herself."

We smoke in companionable silence. When he doesn't push me to state my business, I take a moment to study him. He looks different. Sated and happy. Peaceful. I've heard rumblings as to why that might be, but I'm curious to confirm it.

"You haven't answered my letter," I say as I exhale.

Golden eyes narrow. "I can't take a student, Fuoco. I'm a mated male now. My teaching days are behind me."

So the rumors are true. I suppress a growl at that less-than-fortunate news. "Tell me more, my friend."

A smile touches his lips. "I took him as a student and he wormed his way into my heart. He hasn't left."

I raise my brows. "I wasn't aware you had a heart." But now that I listen for it, I hear the slow, steady beat. The sound is irrefutable evidence that Gothel speaks the truth. He's heart-bound, as the gargoyles call it. Mated for life. "Congratulations," I add. "I'm happy for you."

"I can recommend other teachers," he offers.

Sighing, I examine the tip of my cigar. "I'll take you up on that. I'm being hounded daily by a dragon who believes his daughter would make the perfect consort for me."

"You don't want a bedmate?"

"Not at the moment." This is hardly the first time some enterprising father has pushed a daughter—or son—at me. I've taken consorts in the past. Under the right circumstances, it can be a beneficial arrangement for both parties. But lately, I long for something more than a warm body in my bed. I long for my fated one. *The* one.

I look at Gothel. "I was hoping to dump her into your capable hands and get her father off my back in the process."

"Noble of you," he says. "What's wrong with her power?"

"We're not sure. It manifests so sporadically, we can't tell if she possesses foresight or compulsion. But the latter is so rare among my kind, I suspect it's foresight and she simply doesn't want to see the future."

Gothel smiles. "Maybe it's something else altogether." He flicks ash into a cut-glass ashtray on the edge of his desk. "Something a bit stronger, perhaps?"

Now he's just fucking with me. Like all gargoyles, his power is that he understands power. He undoubtedly understands mine—and my reluctance to discuss it.

"I feel confident it's foresight." I offer him a lazy smile of my own. "I highly doubt it's anything more than that."

Golden eyes glint with something that might be amusement. "I'll send a letter of introduction to two others who might be able to help."

"Many thanks." Remembering her father's latest visit—and the *three-hour* dinner I sat through—I shudder. "The sooner the better."

Gothel's smile gleams in his eyes. "You heard Wotan is recently mated as well?"

"Yes." News travels slowly to my syndicate, but that particular bit of gossip spread like wildfire. "I can't imagine any male taming him. I think I'd like to meet this enigma."

"Maybe you will," Gothel says, puffing at his cigar.

Unlikely. At least not any time soon. Winter is always a tense time in the Fire Syndicate. More than any other season, it seems to produce crime and disruption. And after tonight, I'll have to keep a close eye on the road and the villages around it. Where there's one thief, there are inevitably more.

"Thanks for this," I say, waggling my cigar. "And for the help with the female."

Gothel inclines his dark head. "Any time."

After a few more pleasantries, I thank him again and head for home. As I fly north, my thoughts drift back to the courtyard and the ashes I left behind. The thief is gone, but his accusations ring in my head.

Treasure-hoarding thieves, the lot of you.

I snort, sending smoke rolling from my nostrils. He dared to call *me* a thief after Lirem caught him red-handed in the orchard. To an outsider, death for stealing apples might seem overly harsh. But rules are rules, and mine exist for a reason. I planted the orchard with seeds from the Myth. The fruit there grows wild and uninhibited. The magic it contains can wreak havoc in the wrong hands.

My subjects know my laws. No theft. No murder. No assault. *No exceptions.* Opening that door invites disaster. The Fire Syndicate is the most peaceful and prosperous of all the syndicates. In the two centuries that I've ruled the North, I've worked hard to build a community where everyone feels safe. It's a refuge. I'm determined to keep it that way.

But as the spires of my castle appear in the moonlight, my head fills with visions of sea-colored eyes and a woman's white cap.

Chapter 2
Beau

I leave my sack of bread against the wall of my father's workshop.

Whirring sounds greet me as I open the door and step inside. No surprise, Dad is hunched over his worktable, his shoulders rounded as he tinkers with his latest contraption. My greeting dies on my lips as I let my gaze wander over his shoulders.

He's lost weight. And he can't afford to lose more. A lump forms in my throat as memories of last winter wash over me. The electricity in our cottage hasn't worked in five years. Firewood is great and all, but only if you have access to it. The dragons ration it the same way they do bread. Dad wept when I chopped up the machine he invented to feed the birds that sometimes frequent the patch of grass behind his workshop. But it was either that or watch him shiver under a mound of threadbare blankets. I watched my mother die when I was ten years old. I might be pushing thirty now, but I'm not ready to lose my father.

Suddenly, Dad lifts his head and looks over his shoulder.

Brown eyes framed by gold wire spectacles fill with worry. "Beau? Has something happened?"

Forcing cheerfulness into my voice, I smile and cross the short distance to his worktable. "Nothing at all. I'm getting ready to make deliveries, and I thought I'd check on you before I go."

Instantly, my father frowns. He casts a fearful look at the open door behind me and lowers his voice. "You won't take any bread to Robert, will you?"

The sack of bread outside the door weighs on my conscience like an anchor. "I won't take any to Robert," I say carefully. It's *technically* true. Robert doesn't keep the bread.

Dad's gaze sharpens. "Beau—" His words cut off as he lapses into a coughing fit. His once-broad shoulders shake violently as he curls forward and wheezes. The pencil tucked behind his ear threatens to tumble to the scuffed floorboards. His hip bumps the table, setting his tools and instruments shivering and clinking together.

"Here," I gasp, shoving his chair away so I can grasp his arms and guide him away from catastrophe. Or at least a really big mess. Tools of every shape and size litter the table. Glass beakers hold a colorful assortment of liquids of questionable origin. Dad loves working with magic, but magic doesn't always return the favor. The last time his worktable got upended, it cost three hundred dollars to repair the hole his "experiment" blew in the workshop's wall. I worked fourteen-hour days and slept in my apron to avoid paying interest on the money I borrowed from the village blacksmith.

Dad's cheeks turn red as he continues coughing. His arms under his ratty, patched sweater feel like twigs ready to snap. Alarm beats a loud drum in my head. "Let's go inside—"

"No." Dad pulls from my grip as he speaks between rattling

coughs. "I'm...almost...finished"—he sucks in a breath—"here."

Exasperation rises. "Can't it wait until tomorrow?" I fight the urge to reach for him again as he leans heavily against the table. White hair wreaths his head, the wispy strands defying gravity as they stretch toward the beamed ceiling. The cough subsides, and the brilliant red in his cheeks fades to a dull pink. Weak sunlight streams through the shop's window and slants over the beakers, making the liquid inside sparkle like gems. As my father's gaze falls on a bright green beaker, a smile touches his lips. He points at it and turns to me with excitement dancing in his eyes.

"You see that, son? It's a new type of fuel I've been working on." He holds his forefinger and thumb an inch apart. "I'm *this* close to perfecting it. A few more tweaks and I could heat the whole village for the winter!"

My exasperation rounds a familiar corner. For as long as I can remember, Dad has been "this close" to some kind of breakthrough that will transform our lives. When I was a kid, I got excited right along with him. As a teen, I endured my peers' taunts about my "batshit crazy" father. Now that I'm an adult, I do my best to shield him. It took me a long time to understand my father—and to accept his quirks with the same grace my mother wielded so effortlessly. Maurice Bidbury is never going to heat the whole village. But Mom couldn't tell him that, and neither can I. His inventions fuel his soul. Snuffing that flame would stomp out *his* fire, and I'd rather pretend than ever see the light in my father's eyes wither to ash.

"Sounds great, Dad," I say softly. "I can't wait to see it."

His smile turns wry. "I know you don't believe me." He waves a hand as he faces the table. "Old Man Bidbury up to no good again. Crazy as a fox." He turns his head and shoots me a knowing look over the tops of his thick lenses. "Isn't that what they say in the village?"

I fold my arms over my chest. "I think it was crazy as a loon."

He gives a bark of laughter as he begins tinkering again. "Not one soul in the village knows what a *loon* is. They've been extinct for a hundred years." His spectacles slide down his nose. Rather than stopping his work to adjust them, he wriggles his nose to force them back up.

Shaking my head, I step close and gently nudge his glasses into place. Then I pull a bundle wrapped in wax paper from inside my jacket and set it on the corner of his table. "Promise me you'll eat, okay?"

He pauses his work. Slowly, he places a hand on the wrapped bread. He rests it there for a moment before lifting his gaze to mine. "Only if you promise to be careful when you venture out."

"I always am."

Dad's expression turns skeptical. Anxiety floats in his gaze, and I can see him shuffling through replies in his head. Finally, he sighs. "You're twenty-eight years old. I can't stop you from doing what you're going to do. I just..." He glances at the window. "If they catch you..."

I cover his hand with mine. "They won't." When he opens his mouth, I move my hand to his shoulder. "Eat, Dad. I'll be back within an hour." The green liquid begins to bubble. As Dad and I look at it, sparkles shimmer above the surface. I squeeze Dad's shoulder. "Looks like something is happening."

"It is." He fumbles at his scattered instruments, clearly seeking his notepad. "I have to record the levels," he says as he searches, knocking over an empty beaker in the process.

I reach across him, snag the notepad, and settle it at his elbow.

"Ah! There it is." As he begins rummaging for a pencil, I pull it from behind his ear and slip it between his fingers. "Thanks, son," he murmurs, scribbling furiously. He darts a look at the bubbling liquid as his hand flies across the notepad. "Fifty-nine! That's more promising than I expected!"

I rescue the toppled beaker and set it out of the path of danger. As I go to the door, the whirring starts up again. "Sixty!" Dad exclaims. When I turn in the doorway, he pumps a fist in the air. "We're nearly there, Evangeline! Nearly there, indeed."

My heart squeezes. Sometimes when I squint, I can almost see Mom standing at his shoulder like she used to, her lovely face beaming with pride. Maybe I'm wrong. Maybe Mom believed Dad would heat the whole village one day.

"I hope it works, Dad," I say.

He waves a hand without turning around. "It will, Beau. Just you wait."

I slip out the door and close it behind me. Then I grab the sack of bread and prepare to break the law.

TEN MINUTES LATER, MY HEART POUNDS AS I PRESS MY BACK AGAINST the exterior wall of Robert the bookseller's shop.

Sweat trickles down my spine and soaks into my waistband. In this part of the village, the buildings are so close together it's difficult to see the sky. My vision is limited to a narrow strip of washed-out blue.

But the sky is the least of my concerns. The only dragons I'm likely to see today are the kind stuck on solid ground. Lord Fuoco's enforcers can't take beast form. Dragons adhere to a rigid social order, with those capable of shifting sitting at the top of the pecking order. So-called "lesser" dragons—the non-shifters—take orders from their more powerful counterparts.

That doesn't mean the lower-ranking dragons aren't dangerous. The enforcers who patrol the village are tall, hulking males who move faster than the eye can follow. A few months ago, the one with red eyes followed me home.

Lirem. He accused me of cheating on my taxes. When I showed him my records with his signature at the bottom, he broke the front window in my shop. Lesson learned: next time, just pay the extra taxes. It would have been cheaper than replacing the window.

Wind gusts down the alley, sending icy fingers burrowing under my coat. With a quick look left and right, I gather my courage and dart around the edge of the shop. A dozen breathless steps later, I wrench open Robert's door. Bells tinkle as I duck inside and pull the door shut behind me. The scent of old books fills my nose. Tension drains from my shoulders.

"Beau Bidbury," a feminine voice drawls.

The tension snaps back into place. I squeeze the knob as my heart pounds harder. For a second, I consider opening the door and walking into the street, dragons be damned.

The heady scent of rosewater replaces the smell of books. A second later, the voice sounds at my shoulder. "Aren't you going to say hello?"

Steeling myself, I face Gastonia Legum, the blacksmith's daughter. Wide blue eyes fringed with thick, dark lashes take my measure. Gastonia's plump lips curve in a sensual smile. "You look even more handsome than the last time I saw you."

"Thanks." I lower my gaze and find myself staring at her breasts. Heat enters my cheeks as I jerk my eyes back up. "Um, you look...nice. Also."

She touches a glossy, dark ringlet that drapes over her shoulder. "Me? Please, I look *dreadful* today."

Confusion drifts through me. Gastonia looks the same as always. Black hair. Nice clothes. Pretty face. The unmarried men who enter my shop wax poetic about her curves. Some of the married men do too.

"I'm a total mess," she adds, a glint in her eyes.

That glint lifts the hair on my nape. At the same time, my confusion grows. Does she want me to...agree?

A shuffling sound makes me look past her, and my confusion turns to relief as Robert bustles from behind a curtain in the back of the shop.

"Beau!" The bookseller beams and rounds the counter that holds a cash register and stacks of books. His gaze drops to the sack in my hand as he nears. His smile fades, replaced with caution. In a lower voice, he asks, "Extra delivery today?"

"Yes." I hand him the sack and speak in the coded language we use for this particular transaction. "I baked too much. I thought maybe you could use the bread."

Robert nods. "It won't go to waste."

"Glad to hear it."

He looks at Gastonia, who watches our exchange with a shrewd expression. "I'll just take this to the back." He gestures at the shelves. "Help yourself to whatever you want, Beau."

Joy leaps in my chest. "You sure?"

Robert tosses a grin over his shoulder as he moves to the rear of the shop. "Of course. But good luck finding something you haven't already read."

I chuckle as I walk to the shelves. Unfortunately, he's right. I've probably read every book in the store. Robert doesn't get new shipments very often. Paper is expensive, and books are difficult to come by in the Fire Syndicate. When I was a kid, the dragons burned most of the village's books as a punishment for a bad harvest. Back then, Robert's father ran the shop. The dragons threatened to burn him, too, but Robert threw himself in front of his dad. Robert still bears scars from the knife the dragon slashed across his forearm during the scuffle. That was years ago, but the dragons haven't aged. No matter how much time passes, they remain strong and unstoppable. And merciless.

Shoving the bad memories aside, I trail a finger over a row of worn spines.

"Why do you like books so much?" Gastonia demands at my shoulder.

Startled, I turn and find her frowning at the stacks. "You don't like to read?"

"No." She flicks her blue eyes to mine. Her smile reappears as she dips her gaze to my chest. She snags her bottom lip between white teeth, then slowly releases it. "I have other interests."

My stomach knots. I know where her interests lie. She's made it abundantly clear. Six months ago, she cornered me in the bakery and pressed her body against mine. When I disentangled myself from her arms and pushed her away, she looked like she wanted to slap me. Instead, she drew herself up and gave me a scathing look. *"Really, Beau, it's like you're not even trying."*

The thing is, I *have* tried. For as long as I can remember, I've tried to be like other men. I'm not sure when I realized I was different. It was early on, though. Before Mom died.

I never told her. What would I have said? *Mom, my stomach felt sick when Winifred Matherby tried to kiss me behind the school. Also, I can't stop thinking about her brother's chest when he changes his shirt after gym class.*

"Do you have any other interests?" Gastonia asks now. She drifts closer, her shoulder brushing mine. Her eyes glint again. "Besides baking and"—she glances out the shop's window and lowers her voice to a purr—"risking death by giving food away?"

I suck in a breath. "Gastonia—"

"The dragons will kill you if they find out." Her eyes drop to my mouth. "You're a very bad boy, Beau Bidbury."

My heart clatters against my ribs. "I'm n-not trying to be. I just want to help." As she steps into me, I take a hasty step back. "Little kids are going hungry." Gods, would she *tell* on me?

She stops her advance. Rosewater thickens in the air as she tilts her head, sending more glossy ringlets spilling over her shoulder. "You're a good man. I admire that. Any woman would be proud to stand at your side."

The knots pull tighter. "I should go." I look at the door, which suddenly seems like a portal to happiness instead of a gateway to danger. "I, um, have a lot of work to do."

"No, you don't." She moves forward again, her breasts in serious danger of brushing my chest. "You bake first thing in the morning and sell all of your bread by noon." Rosewater clogs my lungs and makes my eyes sting. "It's three o'clock. This is the time of day when you sit in the window of your shop and read."

My jaw drops. "You watch me?" My ass bumps into something hard and solid, halting my retreat. She's backed me all the way to the counter.

A teasing note enters her voice. "If you put yourself in the window, Beau, don't be surprised when customers ask how much you cost."

Heat sears my nape. Discomfort crawls through me as I grip the edge of the counter and grope for a response. My parents raised me to treat women with respect. But Gastonia never fails to render me tongue-tied.

"Everything okay?"

I turn and find a frowning Robert in the curtained doorway. His brows pull more tightly together as he looks from me to Gastonia.

She flashes a winsome smile. "Beau and I were just chatting about the price of goods. Everything is more expensive these days."

Robert nods but his frown stays put. "That's true." He moves around the counter, and Gastonia backs away as he steps close and offers me a book. "I forgot I had this. It's new from an author in the Hallows. Epic fantasy. I thought you might like it."

Gratitude wells as I accept the book and flip through the first few pages. "No dragons, though, right?"

Robert laughs softly. "No dragons."

I smile as I tuck the book inside my jacket. "Thanks. I'll return it as soon as I can." Robert has always been kind to lend me books. He does the same thing for the poorest families in the village. Tomorrow, he'll fill a cart with books and my bread and make his rounds, delivering food and knowledge to kids who can't leave the fields to attend school. If the village produces a substandard harvest, the farming families will suffer the most. Dad thinks I take too great a risk baking extra bread for hungry kids. But Robert is the real risk-taker. Without him, the farmers' children would starve body and mind.

"I should get back," I say. "Dad is waiting for me."

"No problem, Beau. Thanks for stopping by." Robert turns to Gastonia. "If you wait here a moment, I'll grab the books you ordered."

"Another time," Gastonia says. "I need to get home, too."

Several new knots form in my stomach. She's going to tag along, and there's no easy way out of it. Her father's blacksmith shop is one street over from the bakery. On the bright side, she can't accost me in public. Gastonia is bold, but even she draws the line at groping men in front of an audience. At least I think so.

I mumble my goodbyes to Robert and head for the door. The bell tinkles merrily as I gesture for Gastonia to precede me. We step into the street, and I grit my teeth as she falls into step beside me. The village shines under the winter sunlight. That's nothing new. From the outside, everything looks clean and well-maintained.

But as every villager knows, the *inside* tells a different story. For every fresh coat of paint and sparkling clean window, there's a bare pantry and cold hearth. The dragons only care about the village's exterior. Dad says Lord Fuoco doesn't want interference from the other syndicate lords, so he takes care to keep up appearances. Personally, I think the dragons simply don't give a crap about anyone other than themselves.

"Afternoon, Beau!" someone calls, and I turn my head and make eye contact with Mrs. Pepperdine as she's pulled down the street by several of her children. They flap around her legs like goslings, each one towheaded and dressed in patched clothing. Just before they round the corner, she cranes her neck and shouts, "Can you have six loaves for me in the morning?"

I'm running low on wheat—and everything else—but I raise my voice. "Not a problem, Mrs. Pepperdine."

A smile blossoms over her frazzled features. "Thank you!"

Gastonia gives me a look as we continue down the street. "You don't have enough wheat for six loaves, do you?" It's a question, but her tone tells me she knows the answer.

"I'll make do."

"With what?" Gastonia links her arm with mine and gives a dainty laugh. "Air?"

The urge to shake her off is so overpowering I almost stumble. But I cling to my composure as we move toward the bakery. When I don't answer, she leans more heavily on my arm. Wind whips across the town square, stirring dead leaves.

"Someone should pick those up," Gastonia mutters. "Those thugs will blame us if the streets aren't spotless."

Nerves prickle over my skin as I dart a look around. "You shouldn't call them that."

She makes an angry sound. "Why not? It's the truth. The dragons are nothing but bullies."

I can't argue with that. But it's dangerous to say such things out loud. Lord Fuoco's enforcers have eyes and ears everywhere. Insults don't go unpunished.

"He burned John Robinson last night," Gastonia says in a low voice.

A gasp lodges in my throat. I pull her to a stop and search her face. "You're certain?"

Gastonia nods, her expression grim. "Fuoco summoned my father to the castle this morning to replace the manacles on the post."

Pain stabs my heart. Resignation follows in its wake. It was only a matter of time before John got caught. After one particularly brutal winter, he took to robbing travelers on the road that connects the North to the other syndicates. He distributed the food he stole to the villagers.

Gastonia's mouth tightens. "My father says Robinson was a fool."

No. He was brave. Far braver than I could ever be. Without John, children would have died last winter. Dad will be devastated when I tell him.

Gastonia takes my arm again. "Come on. We shouldn't stand in the street."

She's right, so I let her pull me forward, and I keep silent as she launches into gossip about various people in the village. The weight of John's death—and all the other executions—is so heavy, I don't pay much attention to her chatter until she says, "My father will lend you the funds to restock your supplies."

"Thank you, but no." I'd rather work around the clock than owe Gastonia's father again. The blacksmith is almost as bad as the dragons when it comes to collecting payment. Tall and strapping with a chest like the horses he shods, Gastonia's father carries his hammer when he knocks on doors for money. According to the history books, blacksmithing wasn't an affluent profession before the Veil fell. But factories are a thing of the past. Magic won't tolerate the technology required to keep something that big running. Someone has to make everything from nails to door hinges. Gastonia's father is busy—and rich.

Gastonia strokes her free hand down my forearm. "Of course, if we were engaged, it wouldn't be a loan. Daddy would just give you the money."

I stop in front of the grocer's shop. Through the window, a fruit display holds a shriveled apple and two blackened bananas. I barely notice as I fix my gaze on Gastonia. My heart pounds, but it's not from nerves this time. Now, anger kindles in my veins. I've been polite. I won't be polite to a fault. "Gastonia, we're not getting married."

She lifts her chin. "Every man in the village wants me. Why should you be any different?"

You have no idea. I draw an even breath. "It's not you. I don't want to marry anyone."

Irritation flashes in her eyes. "So you're going to sit alone in your bakery for the rest of your life?" She sweeps a dismissive gaze over the shops around us. "Don't you want more for yourself than this backwards village?" She's tall for a woman, and our faces are nearly even as she steps closer and tips her head toward the window of the grocer's shop. "Look at us." When I turn toward our reflections, her expression in the glass becomes triumphant. *My* face looks shell-shocked, my brown eyes wide and my cheeks flushed under the dark stubble I didn't have time to scrap away this morning. A chilly breeze ruffles my brown waves that never cooperate. As if to prove a point, an errant lock flicks over my forehead.

Gastonia's blue eyes track it as she takes my hand and lowers her voice to the silky purr the men in the village rave about. "We're the two best-looking people in this provincial town. Imagine the children we'd create."

Everything within me recoils. Facing her, I tug at my hand. "I don't think that's a good reason to have children."

"You're right," she drawls, her grip surprisingly strong as she refuses to release me. "There are much better ones."

Gods. I tug harder. "Gastonia—"

"I could change you, Beau." She licks her pink lips. "You don't know what you're missing."

Panic bolts through me. "I d-don't know what you mean."

Her eyes glint. "Oh, I think you do." She tightens her grip and jerks me forward so our hips collide. When I draw back, she does it again.

"Gastonia..."

Just as our tug-of-war becomes a true battle, a teenage boy stumbles around the corner. "Beau!" He doubles over, his hands on his knees as he speaks through choked breaths. "Dragon...in the...bakery!"

My insides turn to ice. One thought replaces all the others in my head.

Dad.

I don't think. I just run. Wind whips through my hair as I race to the bakery, my feet flying over the pavers. Villagers leap out of my path, their faces a blur and their exclamations following me. I ignore them as the ice spreads to my limbs and numbs my senses. When I reach the bakery, I grapple with the latch a few times before I manage to seize it. I fling the door open, making the hinges squawk in protest.

Lirem turns from the counter with a bun in his hand. As his red, glittering gaze falls on me in the doorway, he rips a bite from the bread. Chewing, he advances toward me, his long, embroidered coat flaring around his polished boots.

Dimly, I'm aware of Gastonia behind me. *Go*, I tell her silently, but of course she doesn't. The bakery is empty, thank the gods, but that doesn't mean Dad is safe. Images flash in my head in rapid succession. Dad lying in the workshop in a pool of blood. Dad slumped over his table with a knife in his back. Dad burnt to a crisp, nothing but ashes left for me to bury next to Mom's lonely grave in the village cemetery.

"Stop it," I whisper.

Lirem lifts a blond brow. His shadow falls over me as he halts a few paces away. Still chewing, he runs a deliberate gaze down my body. He swallows, and his deep, raspy voice fills my tiny bakery. "Who will stop me?" His lips curl in a slow grin, exposing sharp-looking fangs. "Not you, surely." Red eyes flick to Gastonia over my shoulder before returning to me. "Courting, baker? It's not very responsible of you to leave your store unattended." He lifts the bun, his long fingers sinking deep into the butter-glazed bread. "Someone might rob you while you're away."

My throat is so dry, I have to swallow a few times before I can speak. "Can I help you with something? Sir," I tack on hastily. The title sets my teeth on edge, but humiliation is better than death. I'll call Lirem whatever he wants as long as Dad is okay.

The dragon looks around my shop, his shoulder-length blond hair brushing the high, stiff neck of his collar. Jewels the same ruby-red as his eyes glitter among the silver embroidery.

His coat probably costs more than everything I own—or ever will. *"Don't you want more for yourself than this backwards village?"* Gastonia asked. Yes, but not like she meant it. I don't want things. I just want to live without fear.

I want that for my father. I want him to have a warm bed and medicine that will cure his cough.

I keep one hand on the latch. My other dangles at my side, my fingers curling into a fist as I wait for the giant of a male to make his next move. When my father was young, Lord Fuoco didn't have enforcers. Before he grew tired of dealing with humans, he ruled alone. A handful of older villagers remember seeing him. They say he's even bigger than Lirem and the others. One farmer's voice shook as he described the syndicate lord as "taller than a tree with hair like green fire."

But I'm not sure I believe it. Lirem is several inches taller than my own five-foot-ten. His shoulders are so broad they could take out my shop's doorway. His clothing obscures his red scales, but I've seen them in the past. If Lord Fuoco is bigger, I don't ever want to meet him.

Lirem settles his gaze on me. "You're short on your taxes this month."

Outrage burns my chest. I should have expected this. He's had it out for me since the broken window incident. "I believe there's some mistake. I'm current on my taxes, sir. You collected them yourself, remember?"

In a blink, the dragon's fist grips my sweater. Red eyes burn less than an inch from mine, and the scent of my bread wafts over my face as he hisses, "Insolent human." He hauls me onto my toes, his knuckles lodged against my throat. "If I say you're late, you're late. And you'll pay the fine."

My heart gallops in my chest, each beat pumping fear through my veins. But there's misery, too. The fine is fifty coins. That's my entire profit for this month. Without that money, I can't buy wheat or fruit or any of the other supplies I need to stock my shelves.

"Sir—" My plea cuts off as bread fills my mouth. He moved so quickly, I couldn't track it. I gag on the half-eaten bun as he shoves me into the door and stalks to the cash register. Rosewater hits my nose, and Gastonia is at my side, her fingers gentle as she pulls the bun from my mouth. Her blue eyes meet mine briefly, a warning in the sapphire depths.

A sharp crack splits the air. I bite my tongue as Lirem smashes the register open and scoops coins from the drawer. He drops my profits into a velvet bag and cinches it tight. In another blurred move, he sweeps an arm across the counter, knocking stacked plates and a glass cake dome to the wooden floor. Gastonia backs us against the door as he rounds the counter, his boots crunching over broken glass.

He pauses in the middle of the shop. With a fang-tipped grin, he scoops the base of the cake dome from the floor and hurls it through the window I replaced.

Gastonia screams as glass shatters, shards scattering over the floor and skidding to a stop at the tips of our boots. More heavy footsteps, and then Lirem's broad chest fills my vision. He grips my jaw and forces my head up.

"I don't like liars, baker. Remember this lesson, hmm?"

I hold his stare as fury simmers under my skin.

His fingers dig into my jaw. His lips curve in a smile that doesn't reach his red eyes. "You and I will meet again soon." With a final hiss, he shoves me hard and leaves the shop.

For a long moment, silence reigns. Then the distant sound of whirring drifts through the ruined bakery. I sag against the door as relief swamps me. If Dad's working in his shop, he's okay. Lirem didn't touch him. That's all that matters.

Gastonia flings herself against my chest and twines her arms around my neck. "Oh you poor thing," she breathes in my ear. "Don't worry about the money. I'll talk to Daddy." She strokes my nape. "I'll take care of everything."

I stand woodenly, my arms limp at my sides. I don't need to look at the cash register to know Lirem took everything. How am I going to tell Dad? Forget supplies for the shop. Now I don't have enough coin to buy groceries for the cottage.

Weariness settles over me as Gastonia continues murmuring in my ear. Her breasts press against my chest. In a minute, I'll gather the energy to push her away so I can check on Dad. But right now, the only thing I can do is stand still as my head fills with a single, burning thought.

I hate dragons. And that will never change.

CHAPTER 3
FUOCO

It's late as I sit before the fire in my bedchamber with a glass of wine at my elbow.

Outside my window, a bright moon hangs in a pitch-black sky. This plane is so much darker than the Myth. Those lands are long gone, but they're vivid in my memories. Even at night, the sky there sparkled gold and pink. The human world is plainer. It certainly doesn't sparkle.

Behind the Veil, the dragon realm was dotted with volcanoes wreathed in mist. The lords of the great houses built their castles from cooled lava flows, and the obsidian spires glittered opalescent in the sun. My father's castle was the grandest. House Drakoni thrived, our influence stretching from the elven lands all the way to the Lathendriel Sea.

Homesickness sours my gut.

Or maybe it's the bite of jealousy. Gothel's relaxed, happy face swims before my eyes. He looked so pleased with himself—a newly mated male eager to return to his beloved.

With a grunt, I pluck my wineglass from the table at my

side. Before the rim touches my lips, the curdled stench of fear burns my nose. The scent signature is elderly and female.

Ellen. The servant from last night. She must have brought wine to my bedchamber before she finished her duties this evening.

Sighing, I set the glass on the table and stretch my legs before me. Flames snap and blaze in the hearth, their sinuous dance beckoning me like a lover. But I long for another kind of companion—one made of flesh and blood. Someone who doesn't tremble at my countenance or quake when I glance in their direction.

If a male as forbidding and ancient as Gothel can snare a mate, surely Fate won't keep me waiting much longer. Even Wotan managed to find a male willing to tolerate his cantankerous disposition. And just an hour ago, news arrived from the Sea Syndicate. Not to be outdone by the other lords, Triton recently took two mates: his long-time lover, Ari Razorfin, and a young sea witch.

"Show off," I mutter, drumming my fingers on the plush velvet arm of my chair.

Why not me? I've dreamed of my selsara—my fated one—for hundreds of years. I've been preparing for him even longer, filling my mountain lair with a hoard of jewels, costly furs, and priceless treasures. I've spared no expense readying the place where I'll woo and spoil my mate. Marble veins the walls. The ceilings drip with crystal. Elven craftsmen constructed a sumptuous sunken lounge area big enough to fit my frame and accommodate hours of bedsport.

I built my lair a day's flight from syndicate headquarters. The castle is always bustling with activity, and privacy is difficult to come by. By contrast, my lair is a peaceful retreat where I can pamper and seduce my fated one. Just as soon as I find him.

And he is a *him*. Dragon mates can be either sex. In some cases, Fate matches a dragon with two or more selsaras. But polyamory isn't my destiny.

No, Fate has paired me with a male. Like all dragons, I've dreamed of him since I was a fledgling. Until recently, those dreams have been so hazy, I couldn't tell if my mate was male or female. But the past few years have brought clarity. Not only is my mate male, he's *here*, somewhere in the North. Out there in the darkness beyond my window, my mate's heart beats in his chest. When I meet him, I'll press my claiming jewel into his flesh and bind him to me forever.

My cock tightens as I rest my head against the back of my chair and let my mind wander into the flames. *Dragon dreams.* Shadowy snippets of my future dance in the fire. As the flames leap higher, my mate appears.

His frame is muscular but smaller than mine. Wavy chocolate-brown hair dances on a breeze as he turns to me with a throaty laugh. His face is unfocused, his features too blurry to make out. I let my gaze roam the rest of him, searching for exposed skin. I find it on his forearm, where his sleeve is rolled to his elbow. *No scales.* But that doesn't matter. Whoever—and whatever—he is, he's perfect for me.

But his shirt is worn, the fabric thin and patched. Even as blood pumps to my cock, a growl rises in my chest. No mate of mine will wear rags. The first thing I'll do when I find him is take him to the court tailor. My beloved will wear the finest silks and velvets. I'll drape him in jewels befitting his station.

In the fire, he walks ahead of me, his lean hips and firm ass turning my growl into a moan. "Show yourself," I murmur, palming my cock through my trousers. I grip my length and squeeze. Pleasure rolls up my dick in a warm wave and settles hard in my stomach. "Come to me."

Lately, I speak that command aloud. In the morning before

the castle wakes, I stand on my balcony and send my entreaty into the wind. My father would dismiss it as whimsy. My mother, who has always been loving but practical, would tell me I'm wasting my time. Dragons believe things happen when they're meant to and not a moment before. I can no sooner summon my mate than I can snap my fingers and make him appear. If I could, I would have done it long ago.

My cock pushes painfully against my trousers, so I yank them open and free my shaft. My hot length fills my palm, my Prince Albert winking in the firelight. Pearlescent moisture pools at my slit and drips over the curved ring. The flames roar higher as I swipe the bead and bring it to my lips.

I'll feed him my cum one day. When I find my selsara, I'll train him to crave my taste. He'll beg for it on his knees, his beautiful mouth watering. Breath hitching, I lift my shaft and toy with the curved bar that pierces the base of my cock. My beloved will know every hard, throbbing inch of me. And I'll return the favor.

"Fuck," I gasp, fire spreading under my skin. Arching my back, I stroke my dick and stare into the crackling flames. My dream fades, but I don't need it. My imagination supplies me with a parade of possibilities. The nameless, faceless male crawls nude across a beautiful carpet. He nuzzles my thigh, then turns and lifts his ass. His hole winks at me, calling for my cock. Heavy balls swing between his thighs. He's pierced in that soft spot behind his sack, the jewel in the silver ring the same green as my scales.

"*Selsara*," I moan, entranced by the vision.

My chair creaks as I jerk my cock faster, my hand flying up and down my pulsing length.

In the vision, I kneel behind my mate. Bending forward, I lick at his sack, then suck one soft globe into my mouth. I tug gently, swirling my tongue over the smooth skin. A groan floats back to me, letting me know my beautiful mate likes my attention. I release his tender flesh with a *pop* and run my tongue up his taint, swirling over the piercing that marks him as mine.

A ragged moan joins the crackle of the flames. I don't know if it's real or part of the daydream I'm conjuring. And I don't care. My balls draw tight as I stroke faster, slicking moisture from my tip to my base. My hips jerk, and I grunt as my mind returns to my selsara. We're fucking now, pleasure threatening to boil over as I watch my dick plunge between his firm, round cheeks.

Orgasm overtakes me, blackness blotting out the vision as I clench my teeth and spurt into my hand. Pleasure batters me and then recedes. I bring it back with a few quick tugs, my head spinning with visions of chocolate-brown hair and a tight ass.

"Selsara!" I cry hoarsely as waves of ecstasy crash against me a second time. When I come down, I sprawl in my chair with my spent dick in my hand. The soft chirp of insects drifts from outside. Moonlight spills over the carpet, reminding me that duty will come far too early in the morning. I should go to bed.

The problem is, I'm tired of sleeping alone. The fireplace crackles on, the flames indifferent to my longing. Absently, I lift my hand and let fire build under my skin. In a flash, the cum burns away from my fingers, leaving clean, whole flesh behind.

I'd much rather watch my mate lick it off. Propping my chin on my hand, I stare into the flames.

Where are you?

∽

After a restless night, I stalk through the castle's greenhouse. Winter sunlight streams through the glass, the pale rays falling on rows of pumpkins, corn, and tomatoes. The syndicate's villages don't always produce plentiful harvests. When the humans' crops fall short, Lirem and my other enforcers distribute food from my own stores. The only part of my lands off-limits to the humans are the enchanted orchards.

But the humans are welcome to everything else. If I add some grapevines, I could start making wine. It'll take a few years to create the first vintage, but it would be nice to bring the process in-house instead of purchasing wine from the Hallows. And if anything is likely to endear me to the villagers, it's free alcohol.

Winemaking plans dominate my thoughts as I leave the greenhouse and approach the East Tower. Its pale stones reflect the sun, which is unseasonably warm for December. An arched door framed by scrolling masonry marks the entrance to the castle's underbelly. I enter and descend the spiral staircase, my knee-length coat flaring around my legs.

Heat rises, caressing my skin and making my beast stir in my chest. I take the stairs two at a time, excitement swirling as the temperature soars. At last, the staircase opens into a cavern supported by broad pillars that stretch twenty feet overhead. Massive fireplaces line the walls, each one housing a roaring fire.

But it's the workstations that draw my gaze. Dragons sit at each one, their skilled fingers molding jewels and metal into precious works of art. Gems of every size and color twinkle as the metalsmiths and jewelers labor at their craft.

I wander down the line, returning nods and greetings. The male I came to see stands at a large table at the very last station, the muscles in his broad back rippling as he bends over his task. He straightens and turns at my approach, his handsome face spreading in a smile.

"Good morning, my lord."

"Zayek," I say, clasping his shoulder. He's shirtless, his black scales reflecting the fire. "Any progress?"

Garnet-colored eyes crinkle at the corners as my head jeweler turns and plucks something from his table. When he faces me again, he holds a golden, jeweled vambrace. "You have good timing, Fuoco." He taps a pair of long metal tweezers against a small hole in the metal. "I was just about to place the last gemstone."

Anticipation flutters in my chest. "May I see it?"

He hands the vambrace over, his smile in place as he watches me examine the jewel-studded armor, which starts in a golden cuff and grows broader to accommodate a male's forearm. In ages past, a piece like this would serve as protection rather than adornment. Any serious knight would have skipped flashy gems, which would have inevitably been knocked from their settings by a sword or lance.

But this vambrace isn't meant for protection. No, this beauty is for pure pleasure. *Mine.* Because I have every intention of seeing it on my mate. Ideally, he'll wear this piece and nothing else.

The vambrace is gorgeous, its golden surface engraved with my house crest depicting two dragons. Their tails intertwine. Jaws stretch wide as they spew fire into the sky. Small, round emeralds wink in their eyes. More green gems scatter over their bodies, forming tiny scales that must have taken hours to set. Zayek is a master of his craft, which is probably why my father was so furious when I swiped the jeweler from under my sire's noble nose.

"It's breathtaking," I murmur, turning the piece in reverent hands.

Zayek points to the spot where the cuff begins to flare. "I thought about adding a row of chocolate diamonds here. Something a little different. What do you think?"

Visions of soft brown hair flit through my mind. "Perfect." I meet Zayek's gaze. "This is your best work yet, old friend."

Satisfaction gleams in the jeweler's eyes. "I hope your selsara will love it as much as you do, my lord."

My heart sinks. "Yes." *When I find him.* I chat with Zayek a moment longer before taking my leave. As I head down the line of dragons, my gaze snags on a necklace spread over one of the tables. Thick, square-cut rubies march down the silver chain. The dragon working on the piece shifts his elbow, revealing a medallion bearing the crest of House Lastri.

Lirem's house. The dragon in the center of the medallion clutches arrows in its claws. A ruby dots the beast's eye.

Treasure-hoarding thieves, the lot of you.

The dragon at the table lifts his head. His bright eyes fill with polite curiosity as he meets my gaze. "Is there something you need, my lord?"

"No. No, thank you." I turn to go, only to swing back. "How many pieces have you made for Lirem this month?"

"I believe this is the tenth, sir." The jeweler hesitates. "Is that...all right, my lord?"

"Yes," I say at once. "Yes, of course." With a wave and a smile, I go to the stairs. An odd apprehension prickles over my skin as I recall the man I burned two nights ago. *Treasure-hoarding thieves.* He meant it as an insult, but there was truth in his words. From our first flight, my people build hoards. Every dragon creates a lair—and then fills it with treasure.

But we don't accumulate these riches for ourselves. As much as we enjoy the finer things in life, our hoards are strictly for our mates. To a human, I suppose it looks like greed. But instinct drives us. Dragons long to please our mates. When I find the male from my dreams, I'll carry him to my lair and lay him in a bed of coins. I'll pledge my body and soul to him. Promise to see to his every need for all time. I'll surround him with gold so he'll know I can deliver on my promises.

Lirem and my other enforcers do the same. I don't draw lines of distinction between the upper and lower houses. My enforcers are free to avail themselves of my jewelers' services. When the jeweler finishes Lirem's necklace, my enforcer will add it to his hoard. His treasure.

The thief's words shouldn't bother me. And yet they continue to ring in my head as I reach the top of the stairs and exit the tower. I pause, my gaze on the greenhouse shimmering in the sun. The humans harvested their crops two months ago. According to Lirem, the yield was plentiful. He and Varden have yet to tap into the castle's stores.

But the post-harvest season is just as important. If the humans don't prep their fields for planting, next year could be a lean one. Lirem and the others check the fields, but they can't see things as I do. It's one thing to walk rows of dirt. It's quite another to view it from fifty feet in the air.

Turning on my heel, I head for the courtyard. It's still early. I can strip, shift, and take to the sky without anyone noticing. It's been too long since I patrolled my territory. I'll view the fields and check on the villages. At the very least, I'll be able to identify any roofs in need of repair.

And maybe I'll sense my mate.

As soon as the thought enters my head, I push it away. After so much time, I can't get my hopes up. My dream man is out there, but I'm unlikely to find him today. Everything happens in its own time.

I simply have to be patient.

Chapter 4
BEAU

I'm running low on patience. Scratch that, I'm running low on *everything*.

Heat blasts my face as I thrust a wooden paddle into the brick oven built into the bakery wall. My stomach sinks as I withdraw the first—and only—loaf of bread I baked this morning. Although, "loaf" isn't the right word. More like "lump."

Biting back a growl, I deposit the doughy, misshapen mess onto a cooling rack and lean against the battered counter behind me. The heel of the lump slides lower as it cools, making the unfortunate-looking bread look like it's frowning.

Yeah, well, join the club. I used the last of the fruit and wheat for Dad's supper last night. I'm out of milk and sugar, and I scraped flour from the bottom of the bin to make this loaf. It wasn't enough. I can't sell this to anyone. I certainly can't fulfill Mrs. Pepperdine's order. And after Lirem's visit, I don't have coin to buy even the most basic supplies. I'm out of options.

That is, unless I swallow my pride and go to Gastonia's father.

Instantly, my stomach knots. It wouldn't be a loan this time. It would be a betrothal. My chest tightens as the lump begins to spread over the cooling rack, half-cooked dough dripping through the gaps in the wire mesh. Can I really sell myself that way? Because that's what it would be—a cold-blooded transaction.

It would also be unfair to Gastonia. After a lifetime of trying not to be different, I know I can't grin and bear my way through a wedding night—or any of the nights that would follow. Mom told me I'll recognize true love when I see it. *"You'll just know. It won't even be a question."* I was too young to understand what she meant. But looking back, I saw true love shining in her eyes whenever she looked at Dad. I don't know if I'll ever find someone who looks at me like that, but I know it's not Gastonia.

A dry, rattling cough interrupts my thoughts. I move without thinking, my feet carrying me across uneven floorboards to Dad's room. He's sitting up in bed, his cheeks bright red in his gray-tinged face. His shoulders shake violently as he coughs into a scrap of cloth.

"Dad!" I fly to the bed. Leaning a hip against the thin mattress, I slip an arm around his shoulders. "Deep breaths, remember? Just like the doctor said." But that was over a year ago. And I'm not even sure he was a real doctor—or even human. Not that the latter makes any difference, but some species of the Myth enjoy tricking humans.

"It's...all...right," Dad says between coughs. He catches his breath and slumps against me. "I pulled you from your work. I'm sorry, son."

"You didn't. I'm just about finished for the morning." I ease him to the pillow, trying to ignore how frail he feels under his nightshirt. He releases a reedy sigh as he settles into the bed, his white hair like cotton candy on the pillow. I smooth it back.

"Can I get you some water?"

His brown eyes twinkle. "No, but I'll take whiskey if you're offering."

"Maybe for dinner."

"With shepherd's pie," he says, playing our old game. "And one of your fruit tarts."

"Strawberry or apple?"

"Apple. With whipped cream on top." His lids slide to half-mast, but his smile remains as he keeps the game going. "Your apple tarts are better than your mother's." One eye pops back open. "Don't tell her I said that."

I return his smile even as my heart squeezes. "I won't."

He pats my hand. "You're a good lad, Beau. The best son any parent could hope for. Your mother is proud of you. She'd tell you herself if she were here, but..." His eyelids droop, and he finishes his sentence on a sigh. "You'll just have to trust me."

"I do," I murmur. I watch him fall asleep, my fingers entwined with his. When his breathing stays even, I rise and pull the quilt to his chin. The scrap of cloth falls to the floor, a bright-red splotch of blood in the center.

My hand shakes as I retrieve it. He's dying. The knowledge sinks into my bones. But maybe it's been there for a while. Since last winter, when his cold became pneumonia and then settled in for good. If I could keep him warm, maybe it would go away. If he had enough to eat or the right kind of medicine. But I don't have access to any of those things. Medicine is impossible to find. It would be easier to raid Lord Fuoco's apple orchard than to find—

I jerk my head up.

Options. Marrying Gastonia isn't the only avenue open to

me. The apples in the Fire Lord's orchard have magical properties. John Robinson smuggled me some about six months ago. I baked them into a pie and for two weeks, Dad walked with a spring in his step.

But the orchard is forbidden land. For all I know, Lord Fuoco executed John for stealing from it. If I get caught...

Dad lets out a sudden cough, his whole body jerking. His eyes stay closed as he gasps for breath. After a tense moment, he settles down again. His chest rises and falls steadily.

But now blood flecks his lips.

One apple. How hard can it be to grab one apple?

Bending, I stroke the cloth over Dad's mouth, wiping away the blood. Then I tuck the quilt more snugly around his shoulders and rush from the room with new determination pounding through my veins.

It's a twenty-minute walk to the orchard. By the time I reach the hedge that grows tall around the rows of trees, my heart pounds so hard I think it might burst from my chest. One silver lining? I'm sweating so much the cold doesn't bother me.

I walk quickly, pausing every few steps to glance at the sky or look over my shoulder. The village is a blurry collection of buildings on a slope in the distance. If Lirem or Varden catch me, they'll probably kill me on the spot. The yellow-eyed enforcer, Nazzar, always has a knife on him. Rumor has it he carves his initials on his victims before putting them out of their misery.

Sweat trickles down my spine as the hedge looms. The road is deserted. No footprints mar the the dirt. *Because no one is stupid enough to come here.*

The sweet scent of apples teases my nose. Between a gap in

the hedge, a thick ribbon of green grass stretches into the distance. Trees line either side, their branches teeming with fat, red apples. Dozens lie on the sun-dappled ground. Even at a distance, the first signs of rot are visible. Anger kindles in my gut as I approach. All of this fruit going to waste when people in the village are starving.

Right on cue, my stomach rumbles. My mouth waters uncontrollably, and the orchard darkens at the edges as a wave of dizziness sweeps me. Swaying, I stop and brace my hands on my knees as I fight to stay on my feet. I skipped dinner last night—and lunch before it. But if I can pull this off, Dad and I will dine on stewed apples tonight. And maybe I can sell enough to buy wheat and other supplies.

The dizziness passes, and I straighten, the determination I felt at Dad's bedside propelling me forward. Just as I reach the gap in the hedge, a shuffling sound makes me freeze. A second later, a white head appears in the gap, and a horse with a platinum mane stares me down.

No, not a horse. Awe spreads through me as I fix my gaze on the mother-of-pearl horn protruding from the center of the beast's forehead. It's a unicorn.

Without warning, it opens its mouth and releases a wet burp. A tiny rainbow-colored cloud puffs in the air.

I blink, my feet rooted to the ground. Did it...? Did it just burp a rainbow?

The beast snorts and tosses its head. It shuffles around, a pair of stubby wings flapping in the center of its back. A snow-white tail swishes as it clip-clops down the strip of grass between the trees. A moment later, a wet squelch splits the air, and a rainbow puffs from its hindquarters.

My awe shifts to amusement. A smile tugs at my lips as I walk forward. I hesitate at the break in the hedge, then hold my breath and step through it.

Nothing. Lirem doesn't appear. Dragon fire doesn't rain from the sky. A gentle breeze picks up, stirring the apple trees' leaves and sending the scent of fresh fruit into my lungs.

The unicorn's broad hips sway as it meanders the path in front of me. Moments later, a second beast noses its way from between a pair of trees. It gives me a bored look as it chews rhythmically. Its pale wings flap, and if I didn't know better, I'd think it was happy to see me. Or maybe just happy to see anyone.

Another wet squelch echoes down the rows of trees. Ahead, the first unicorn pauses and releases a long, thin rainbow-hued stream of flatulence.

"Oh, *really*, Cornelius," a deep voice scolds.

The air leaves my lungs. My brain screams at me to run, but I can't move. I stand frozen as a cloaked figure shifts at the base of one of the apple trees. His legs stretch before him in a casual pose. His hands are folded in his lap. His cloak is brown like the bark at his back, the long folds of cloth covering him from head to toe. Maybe that's why I didn't see him. I'm so stupid. I was distracted by the unicorns, and now I'm going to die. Any second, the man is going to spring up and slit my throat.

"I'm not going to hurt you," he rumbles. Bright green eyes study me from inside the hood of his cloak. Sunlight slants over him, illuminating features that loosen my knees.

And tighten my cock.

Oh gods. *Not now.* Of all the times to be attracted to a man... But *this* man is gorgeous. There's no other word for it. High cheekbones shaded with dark stubble lead into a firm jaw. Sensual lips curve at the corners. Something about those corners makes me want to move closer. They're mysterious and perfect—little hollows I want to explore. He's big. His position on the ground makes it hard to tell just how big, but he's not a small man. His cloak stretches over wide shoulders and a broad chest. Heat snakes through me as I continue to gawk, every teenage fantasy I tried to suppress flashing bright in my mind.

The ghost of a smile plays around his mouth as he studies me. "There is nothing to fear." A languid hand gestures to the first unicorn, which is busy tugging an apple from one of the trees. Green eyes gleam with humor. "Unless you're afraid of intestinal discomfort."

"I..." My throat is so dry, I have to gulp a couple of times. "I'm not."

His smile spreads to his eyes. "A fortunate coincidence, then." He looks at the first unicorn. "Honestly, Cornelius."

The beast pauses its tugging. Its pot belly trembles, and it releases another rainbow-sheened belch. The second unicorn sidles up to a tree and drags its flank over the bark. Its deep-blue eyes go half-mast as it releases a sound somewhere between a honk and a purr.

"Terrible manners," the stranger murmurs. He meets my gaze with something like exasperation in his eyes. "They're supposed to guard the orchard. But I'm afraid they're quite drunk."

"Drunk?"

"Mmm. Apple juice will do that to unicorns." He keeps his eyes on me as he raises his voice. "Especially when they can't control themselves."

The first unicorn snorts as it snaps an apple off the tree.

The stranger and I continue our staring contest. When he seems content to simply watch me, I blurt, "Who are you?" He's not a dragon, thank the gods. If he were, I'd already be dead. Probably, he's some kind of Myth creature. An incubus, perhaps. Or maybe one of the elves. Although, the books I've read say the elves mostly live in Europe.

Green eyes sweep down my body, raising goosebumps on

my skin. As they travel back up, I swear I can feel their caress. My breath hitches, and my erection pushes against the front of my pants. For once, I'm grateful for my oversize coat, which conceals the effect the stranger has on me.

"A passerby," he says in that low, rich rumble.

It takes me a second to realize he answered my question. Partially answered it, anyway. Maybe he doesn't want to give a proper name.

Maybe he's here to steal too.

"Do you have a name?" he asks, green eyes making another lazy trip over my chest. As they linger, my nipples tighten. My heartbeat pounds in the taut peaks the same as it throbs in my dick.

"Beau," I rasp. Right away, regret sweeps through me. *Stupid.* So stupid to tell him my name. He could be a spy or—

"Beau," he says, rolling the vowel like he's tasting it. Sensual lips curve, those tempting hollows growing deeper. He tilts his head and his hood gapes, exposing a strong, brown neck and the graceful arch of his cheekbone. "That means handsome, does it not?"

Somehow, I will my tongue to move so I can say, "Yeah."

"It suits you." His eyes darken, the green as rich and deep as the leaves on the apple tree above him. "It's perfect for you."

My heart slams against my chest. My cock aches, the tip wetting the front of my briefs. Gods, I have to get out of here. It's been a long time since I lost control like this. Years ago, when denial and confusion swirled like poison in my veins, I avoided touching myself. At night, I lay in bed and ignored the images of broad shoulders and thick biceps that tried to rise in my thoughts. All that denial led to a few close calls—one too many scenarios that nearly exposed me to everyone in the village.

I feel exposed now, desire burning so hot I wait for smoke

to waft from my skin. The stranger is definitely an incubus. There's no other explanation for my lust.

"I..." I back up a step. "I have to go."

"So soon?" The man frowns, his disappointment so seemingly genuine I almost believe it. Almost.

I jerk a thumb over my shoulder. "I'm needed—" I suck in a breath. "Someone is waiting for me."

Green eyes sharpen. His voice dips dangerously low. "A man?"

"M-My father." Fear spikes then wanes as his eyes soften once more. "Um...nice meeting you." I turn, my eyes on the gap in the hedge and the tiny view of the village beyond it.

"Hold."

The stranger's deep command wraps around me like a whip, jerking me to a stop as surely as if he'd clamped a hand on my shoulder. Heart in my throat, I slowly turn.

In one graceful movement, he rises from the ground and steps away from the tree.

My heart skips beats as I crane my head back...and back some more so I can meet his gaze. Even with the distance between us, he *towers* above me. In his hood, his glittering eyes appear to dance with green flames.

Not an incubus.

My knees loosen as he slinks forward, moving with that same inhuman elegance. Because he's not human. He's a dragon. Bigger and taller than the enforcers. The voice of the elderly farmer echoes in my head. *"...taller than a tree with hair like green fire."*

The dragon's hood conceals his hair, but as he advances toward me, the two halves of his cloak part, revealing golden-tan skin covered in emerald-green scales.

Green fire.

Lord Fuoco.

"Please," I croak, nausea rising as death stares me down. "I-I'm so sorry…" Speech deserts me as tears burn my eyes. *Dad.* He'll be alone in the world without me. Who will make his tea exactly the way he likes it? Who will tug him away from his workbench when he falls asleep in the middle of scribbling notes?

Lord Fuoco's shadow falls over me. Unable to face the flames in his eyes, I drop my gaze to his chest. A spicy scent wafts around me. It's dark and masculine, like expensive cologne mixed with herbs and incense.

No. *Smoke.* He smells like smoke, I think dumbly as I stare at the scale-covered skin exposed by the gap in his cloak. Against my will, my gaze travels down, and my breathing stutters as I take in rippling abs and a line of dark hair that leads to…

Oh gods. He's nude under the cloak.

As I struggle to catch my breath, he curls a finger under my chin and forces my head up. Burning green eyes capture mine. Then his expression shifts, something like wonder dancing among the flames in his stare.

"*You.*"

I blink. He doesn't sound like he wants to kill me. He sounds…enthralled.

Slowly, he rotates his hand so he's cupping my chin. One big thumb strokes my cheekbone, the tender touch raising goosebumps on my skin. Inside his hood, his eyes soften. His voice gentles. "You *never* apologize to me, selsara."

The strange word trips around my mind. His scent floods my senses, crowding and overwhelming until every breath is drenched in dark, smoky spices. His thumb continues its sweeping caresses, each brush of his skin against mine streaking a frazzled path to my throbbing dick.

His touch welds me to the ground. Holds me immobile. But

I'm no longer frozen. Now, a delicious warmth spreads through my limbs, loosening tense muscles and sapping tension. My lips part and my breath shudders out.

"There you are," he whispers, eyes glittering. "Beautiful."

Beautiful? People have called me handsome. Good-looking. But no one has ever called me beautiful. No one has ever looked at me like this. Like I'm a diamond they unearthed from the dirt. Confusion swirls, joining the fog of desire in my head. Before I can puzzle it out, he steps back. In another elegant move, he bends and retrieves an apple from the ground. Then another. His big hands gather half a dozen, then he straightens and tucks them into my pockets.

"What...?" I drag in a breath. "What are you doing?"

Tenderness and humor mix in his gaze. He pats my laden pocket with one hand. With the other, he runs his thumb across my lower lip. "This is what you came for, yes?"

Fear pierces the thick, spice-scented cloud of desire. "I'm not supposed to take anything." As if he doesn't know that. This is his orchard. The one I'm forbidden to enter upon penalty of death. Fear spikes higher. "I'm s-sorry—"

"No," he rasps, big palm cupping my cheek once more. Glittering green eyes sear mine. "Whatever is mine is yours. Anything you need, *selsara*, you come to me. Understand, Beau?" The flames in his eyes flare higher. "Tell me you understand."

The spices in my lungs form a hook that sinks deep into my soul. It tugs, drawing me closer. Making me want *more*. "I understand," I breathe, unsure what I'm saying. My head spins, the heat in my limbs curling into pleasure.

A rustling sound is my only warning. Before I can react, Lord Fuoco whips his head up and blurs. One second he's in front of me, the next he's gone, leaving me swaying. I stumble, regain my balance, and spin around.

The spike of fear becomes a lance that pins me in place.

Nazzar stands in the gap in the hedge, his bulk obscuring the view of the village behind him. He moves forward, pulling a long, wicked-looking blade as he enters the orchard. Bright yellow eyes fix on Fuoco, who stands between us.

"My lord," Nazzar says, inclining his dark head. His citrine stare flicks to me, and his mouth twists in a sneer that exposes his fangs. "Allow me to remove this vermin from your sight."

My blood freezes in my veins, all the hazy heat evaporating. *It was a set up.* Fuoco toyed with me. Now he'll let Nazzar chop me into pieces. I take a swift step backward, the primitive part of my brain kicking into overdrive. Urging me to turn and run.

"No," Fuoco says, stopping me. But he doesn't turn around. Instead, he advances on Nazzar, his brown cloak flaring around his ankles. The enforcer's eyes go wide, surprise flitting through them as he furrows his brow.

"My lord, you shouldn't concern yourself with filth from the village—"

"He's not *filth*," Fuoco says sharply, and I can't see his face but his tone is enough to make terror slosh in my gut. "This one is off-limits. No one touches him. Is that clear?"

Nazzar ducks his head like he's a marionette controlled by a puppet master. His frown stays put but deference enters his voice as he rasps, "Clear, my lord."

Fuoco turns, his emerald eyes latching onto me with a predatory stare. He jerks his head toward the hedge. "Go," he says, his deep voice touched with a little of the tenderness from before. "Quickly now."

I don't hesitate. Clumsy and inelegant, I lurch forward. Steering a broad path around the dragons, I rush to the gap in the hedge. Fuoco's stare burns in the center of my shoulder blades as I scramble through the gap and rush into the street.

No one touches him. Somehow, I know he tells the truth. Nazzar won't hurt me. At least not this time.

But I don't wait around for Lord Fuoco to change his mind. I sprint toward home, apples bobbing in my pockets. The village looms larger but I hardly see it.

My vision fills with a pair of burning green eyes. The rhythmic pounding of my footfalls disappears, replaced with a deep voice rumbling a foreign word wrapped in a tone that shivers into the deepest, most secret corners of my soul.

Selsara. I don't know what it means. I don't know what just happened. But I'm alive. That's good enough for now.

CHAPTER 5
FUOCO

Nazzar clutches his knife tighter, his yellow eyes trailing Beau through the hedge. His predatory focus yanks my dragon to the surface. When I snarl, flames curl out of my lips. Nazzar's gaze flits back to me, and his pupils blow wide. He offers a respectful nod, but his fingers twitch on the knife handle.

I saw Beau enter the orchard and knew he was mine.

And Nazzar seeks to take that from me.

My blood boils knowing my selsara is running, slipping farther away by the second. Nazzar was going to hurt Beau. My Beau. Fierce anger heats my skin, flames dancing just beneath the surface as fury and protective instinct take over. I *need* to ensure my selsara's safety. To eliminate the threat Nazzar poses. I stride across the grass and tower over my enforcer.

He's careful not to show me his throat as he lifts his chin to meet my gaze. Confusion clouds his citrine eyes. "Why did you stop me? You burned a human for stealing from this orchard this very week, Fuoco. If you allow it once—"

I shove him, knocking him backward a step. "That *human* is

my selsara. You will not touch him!" The words come out on a roar. Frenzied outrage rises, urging me to rip Nazzar limb from limb for even thinking of pointing his knife at Beau.

Nazzar's yellow eyes go wide as his mouth drops open. He raises his knife. "No, it can't be! He's just a—"

I lurch forward and grab his throat, digging my claws into his neck as rage builds. Red descends over my vision as I squeeze, choking off the insult he was about to deliver.

"What?" I demand. "Only a human? Just a thief? Tread carefully, Nazzar. I've waited centuries for him. I wouldn't touch a hair on his head if he took every fucking apple in this orchard." I glance at the knife Nazzar still holds between us. "I won't allow you near Beau," I growl. "Not now, not ever."

Anger flashes in my enforcer's eyes. The trust we've built over many decades crumbles to ash. Time slows as apprehension tingles down my nape. I look at the knife just as he slashes upward, aiming for my side. I shove him into the hedge, but the knife slashes my forearm, fire following in its wake.

Snarling, I smash my fist into his jaw, snapping his head back. He recovers quickly and comes for me again, slashing with the knife.

I dodge him easily, tapping superior speed as I grab his wrist, jerk him into me, and pin his arm behind his back. I yank up, and a sickening *pop* echoes around the orchard as his shoulder dislocates. The knife drops to the grass at our feet.

Nazzar screams. Eyes burning with anger and agony, he snaps his long fangs, missing my neck by less than an inch.

Spinning, I toss him into the nearest tree, relishing the crack of his spine when he hits the broad trunk. He lands in a heap at the base of the tree, his legs flung out at odd angles.

"You threatened my selsara, Nazzar." I stalk toward him, scooping the knife from the ground as I go. I flip it and point the tip at my enforcer. "No one threatens my mate. No one."

"You're a fool," he spits through bloodied lips. "An insufferable fool sent here to babysit beings far beneath you. And now you wish to take a human thief for your selsara? I can't serve you another fucking minute."

I stare down at him. Grief for what I'm about to do sinks in my stomach like a ten-pound stone. I trusted him for years. But that's gone now, evaporated like smoke over cinders.

Nazzar's breathing grows more labored as I lift his knife higher. Red draws my gaze to the blade. Dried blood crusts the metal. Unease buffets me as I step back and turn the knife over. It's an unremarkable piece, the blade worn and scratched. The handle is simple and unadorned. More dried blood gathers in the groove between the blade and the handle.

I look at Nazzar. "This isn't a blade for your hoard. Why would you even carry this?"

"Attacks. Highwaymen." He licks his lips, wariness flitting through his gaze. "Justice when the situation calls for it."

"Bullshit. Your job is to protect the humans. I handle lawbreakers. You've never meted out punishment." I sniff at the blade, a sickening feeling roiling my gut as the scent of iron fills my nose. "This blood is human."

Nazzar laughs—a cruel sound like he's enjoying a joke at my expense. When his laughter dies, his lips curl in a vicious sneer. "This plane is ripe for the taking, *my lord*, if one knows how to keep a secret."

Maybe it's true that some dragons are cursed to go mad, because madness threatens to overtake me. It rises in my chest as the implications of the bloody blade and his words sink in. Wrath hovers just out of reach, urging me to tear Nazzar apart.

He laughs again. "You never could see the truth, could you? Dragons are *better* than everyone else." His eyes glitter with a viciousness that steals my breath. Bloody spittle flies from his lips. "We could have ruled this plane like the kings we are had you not insisted on helping the humans. It's ridiculous. It's—"

The knife thunks into his chest, the handle vibrating just below his collarbone. The pain hits him a second later, and he screams hoarsely. He claws at the blade, but it's useless. He's pinned to the trunk.

I go to the tree and kneel at his limp knee. "How far does this rot go, Nazzar?" I ask, gripping the handle of the knife and twisting. "Is it just you who holds this opinion of humans? Or Lirem and Varden as well?"

Nazzar screams, throwing his head back against the tree as tears stream from his eyes.

"Answer me." I stop twisting, and his screams fade to heavy, labored pants. He grits his teeth and shakes his head. When it's clear he won't say anything else, I rise and cast my cloak to the ground. Glacial fury replaces the sinking realization that Nazzar isn't the male I thought he was.

He wanted to hurt Beau. It's my privilege to protect my selsara. As long as Nazzar lives, Beau isn't safe.

A trickling sensation like boiling water trails down my spine and spreads along my limbs. It climbs up my neck, a searing hand spreading its fingers over my scalp. Hot, ruby-red rivulets coat my vision as I call the orchard to attention.

Nazzar watches me, disbelief stirring in his eyes.

"I've kept a secret too," I murmur.

As my power builds, Nazzar makes a choked sound. "It can't be," he rasps. "There hasn't been an elemental dragon for hundreds of years. They died out in the Old Country!" His breathing goes fast and hard. He claws at the knife again, struggling even as his body below his waist remains limp.

Power swells in the forefront of my mind. Cool clarity illuminates the world around me. I sense every element—the fire in my chest, water that trickles in an aquifer far beneath us, the air that dances around my body in the form of a cool breeze. The ground under Nazzar.

Swirling my hands, I summon the earth, willing the ground beneath my enforcer to crack.

"It can't be!" he insists, panic twisting his features as he struggles to free himself. "We heard the rumors. We watched you for years. There's never been a single fucking sign of elemental power!" He yanks at the knife, grunting.

Snarling, I snap my fingers, calling to the air and forcing it to press the knife harder into his shoulder. He screams and writhes against the pain.

I don't bother explaining why I hid my power. Nazzar betrayed me. He wanted to hurt Beau. Nobody touches Beau.

The ground beneath Nazzar opens, and his useless legs fall into the widening crack.

"No!" he shouts. "I didn't realize! I won't touch him. I'm sorry, my lord! Please! Let's talk about this!" He scratches at the tree behind him, trying to find purchase.

I cleave the ground in front of him, creating cracks that splinter out from the base of the tree. The dirt heaves and sways. It shreds apart, the opening growing wider. Nazzar shrieks as his lower body sinks into the hollow. A crack splits the tree trunk, releasing the knife. He drops, then catches himself on the crumbling edge of earth and grass. He claws at the ground, desperate yellow eyes boring into mind. "Please, Fuoco! We're *friends*."

He wanted to hurt Beau. Unacceptable.

I wave my hand, setting the ground quaking. "Would you have made Beau plead for his life? Would you have drawn his blood?"

Nazzar's long claws scratch at the dirt as he clings to the heaving ground. Sweat dots his forehead and darkens the neck of his bloodstained shirt. He dangles over the hole, the muscles in his shoulders bunching as he tries to haul himself up. "No, my lord, please!"

"Would you have hurt Beau like you've obviously hurt others?" My dragon simmers just under my skin, ready to burst from my human form and burn my betraying enforcer to ash.

Nazzar shakes his head, clawing at the ground and tearing up chunks of grass and dirt as he slides deeper into the abyss. "Fuoco, don't do this."

Red flames streak along the cool fingers wrapped around my mind. Nazzar will never touch my mate. I bellow, the sound ripping from my throat when I think of what could have happened if I hadn't visited the orchard today.

The chunk of ground under Nazzar's claws turns to dust. He drops out of sight, his scream spiraling up until it cuts off with an abrupt squelch.

Panting, I call the dirt back, filling the holes and covering Nazzar's broken body. I smooth the earth into place until the ground is flat and whole. Exhaustion nips at the edges of my mind as I mend the crack in the tree's trunk, leaving no scar behind.

Silence descends on the orchard. The apple trees dance and sway on a slight wind. Over my shoulder, Cornelius and his brother snore. There's no sign of Nazzar. No sign that anything happened here.

He wanted to hurt Beau.

My selsara.

Grabbing my cloak, I swing it around my shoulders and sprint from the orchard. I race toward the village, instinct urging me to protect my mate at all costs. I've lost crucial minutes fighting my enforcer. The need to protect my mate outweighs every other emotion. If I can just get my hands on him, I can keep him safe. I can ask him why he needed to steal.

I can give him the *world*. I've planned and prepared for him for centuries.

I reach the village in under a minute. For a tense beat, panic rises as I think I've lost my quarry. Then I spot Beau's chocolate-brown waves and ratty coat. He dips between two tall cottages and into the village.

Too late. Godsdamnit.

Red-hot fury rises again, clouding my vision and filling my mouth with the taste of cinders. Madness beckons, its long, bony fingers scrabbling at me. I stand in the road and suck in a deep breath, willing the insanity to recede. My heart pounds. My selsara is close—so close—and yet I can't touch him. I've finally found him after so many years of dreaming and longing. By rights, I should carry him back to the castle and declare him my mate before the entire court. Instead, I cling to the shadows, fearful of being seen.

Swallowing a growl, I skirt the edge of the village. I can hardly stride into the town square wearing nothing but a cloak, yet I'm not ready to give up the chase. The need to see Beau eats at me. Frustration builds, my instincts urging me to abandon caution and go door to door until I find him. As quickly as it comes, I squash that impulse. Beau is mine. He'll still be mine tomorrow. I know where to find him. Now I need to know why he entered the orchard with theft on his mind.

Stalking along the outermost buildings, I peer down every alley, hoping to see him. After half an hour, I've rounded the entire village, but he's nowhere to be found. I slip into a dark space between two buildings and let the shadows swallow me. Huddled in my cloak, I lean against the cool bricks. Humans pass, heads down and shoulders hunched against the cold.

Dozens of homes and buildings dot the village. Shops form a circle around an old water fountain, although there's no water this time of year. At first glance, the village appears clean and orderly like any other.

A mother and several small children hurry past. The breeze picks up, ruffling their clothes and making the mother pull a threadbare shawl more tightly around her thin shoulders. The children follow like ducklings, worn boots ringing out against the pavers. A tiny girl with pale ringlets brings up the rear. Suddenly, she stops and looks down my alley. Blue eyes lock with mine and go wide.

Slowly, I lift a finger to my lips. Some wild impulse compels me to let my beast rise. As flames wreathe my head, I wink at the child.

Wonder fills her eyes. Her bow of a mouth curves into a sweet smile. Just as she starts toward me, her mother appears and tugs the child back into line with the others.

I shove my dragon down, pressing into the shadows as the mother and children hurry past.

More villagers pass. People going about their business. A few call out greetings, but no one pauses to speak. "Open" signs hang in shop windows, but no customers come and go. And every villagers' clothing is as worn and tattered as my selsara's.

Something's wrong. From above, this town would appear to be cared-for and thriving. But standing here at street level, I see another story and it sours my gut.

Treasure-hoarding thieves, the lot of you.

The memory of the thief's penetrating sea-blue eyes hits me like a punch.

Lirem, Varden, and Nazzar reported an exceptional harvest. The humans should have been ready for winter. The villagers should be relaxing before their fireplaces with full bellies and fat bank accounts.

The scene before me doesn't match my enforcers' reports. Not at all.

The sun dips behind the treeline and casts long shadows across the town's square. The number of humans crisscrossing the street dwindles until the streets are bare. My skin prickles with the need to stalk the village and find my selsara. But it's clear I won't catch another glimpse of chocolate-brown waves tonight.

With a final look at the square, I leave the alley and return to the orchard. The unicorns doze beneath the trees. A half-eaten apple dangles from Cornelius's lips. I pull it out and toss it away lest he choke. Then I find a clearing, fling my cloak off, and call to my beast.

It answers right away. The change roars through me, claws and wings replacing my weaker form. Now, the ground is dozens of feet below. Soil flies as I take a running leap and burst into the sky. On the horizon, my selsara's village sparkles with light as dusk slides into true night.

Treasure-hoarding thieves, the lot of you.

Beau's village is one of many in my syndicate. Nazzar said this plane is ripe for the taking. What has he been taking from my people? Are Lirem and Varden party to his deception?

As I beat my wings against the frigid wind, icy resolve fills me. Nazzar was right about one thing. I've been a fool. I kept my distance from my people, and now it looks like they've suffered for it. My *selsara* has suffered for it. The wind gusts harder as I wheel in the sky, my gaze on the distant lights that mark the next village. Before this night is through, I'm going to find out just how big of a fool I've been.

CHAPTER 6
BEAU

The scent of cinnamon and nutmeg fills the air of the bakery. Humming, I pull a sheet of hot cross buns from the oven. The golden-brown crusts glisten, the butter-and-sugar glaze sparkling in the morning sunlight.

Perfect.

Bits of diced apple peek from the bread as I place the sheet on a cooling rack. Whirring sounds drift through the bakery's back door, which I propped to release some of the hot air from the oven. Shuffling backward, I look through the doorway to Dad's workshop on the edge of the cottage's tiny garden.

The whirring echoes across the short distance. Worry gnaws at me as I stare at the shop's closed door. Although, maybe I shouldn't worry. Dad woke at dawn and practically skipped from the cottage. One bowl of spiced apples cured his cough and restored his energy.

"Where did you get apples, son?" he asked when I handed him the bowl last night. A tremor went through him, and he glanced at the window before lowering his voice to a whisper. "You didn't go to the orchard, did you?"

"*Of course not,*" I said, the lie like acid on my tongue. I nodded toward the bowl. "*Eat before it gets cold.*"

As the whirring continues, I return to the buns. The oven pops and creaks as I grab a knife from the counter and scoop a dollop of frosting from a mixing bowl. As I spread frosting over the cooling buns, I eye the bowl that holds the apples I diced when I returned from the orchard yesterday.

I made twenty batches of stewed apples last night, and the bowl never emptied. As cinnamon wafted from the bakery, neighbors appeared. Within minutes, I had enough coin to buy flour and butter. The ten pies I baked sold in under an hour. After another trip to the grocer's, I filled the bakery's shelves with cakes, apple muffins, and loaves of bread.

And the bowl of apples stayed full to the top.

Glittering green eyes appear in my mind. Lord Fuoco's words echo through my head. "*Whatever is mine is yours. Anything you need, selsara, you come to me.*"

The orchard is a forbidden place. The dragon lord executes people for taking apples, yet he stuffed six of them into my pockets. He stood between me and Nazzar when the yellow-eyed dragon would have carved me up—or worse.

And Fuoco called me that strange name. *Selsara*. What does it mean? He didn't look like he wanted to kill me yesterday. He looked like he wanted to...devour me—and not in a way a dragon might ordinarily devour someone.

Frosting splats on the counter. Shaking myself, I grab a rag and wipe up the mess. *That's my Beau*, my mother always said. *If his head's not in a book, it's in the clouds.*

I have no business daydreaming about Lord Fuoco. Whatever his reasons for giving me the apples, he didn't...desire me. My cheeks heat as I dip the knife and spread more frosting on the buns. But even as I work the sugary confection into the grooves, phantom hands brush my legs. When Fuoco touched me, I forgot to be afraid.

The oven creaks, but I ignore it as I finish the buns and load them onto one of my mother's round serving platters. The "old beast" as Dad calls it has been temperamental today, heating up too quickly and taking forever to cool down, but I've got too many orders to fuss with it now.

"Hello?" a voice calls from the front of the bakery. Grabbing the platter, I hurry from the kitchen and into the main part of the shop.

A slender young man with pale hair and bright blue eyes stands before a shelf of muffins. He's dressed head-to-toe in black leather that hugs his lean but muscular body. His black, fur-trimmed coat looks like it was tailored just for him. Slits in the fabric allow a pair of iridescent wings to rise gracefully from his back. His ears are pierced, and a studded choker circles his neck. He turns as I enter. Immediately, his jewel-bright eyes drop to the platter of hot cross buns in my hands.

"Buns!" Smiling, he strolls to me, plucks a bun from the platter, and holds it up. He gives it a squeeze and winks at me. "And they're glazed. You naughty boy, you."

"You're a pixie," I say stupidly. He's beautiful. Ethereal. But not my type. As quickly as the thought comes, I shove it away.

He turns slightly, showing his wings that flutter and stir the air. "Guilty as charged." He peers at the bun in his hand. "Are these apple-flavored?"

Words stick in my throat. I curl my fingers around the edge of the platter as my heart beats faster. "Yes." *I did nothing wrong.* And I have no reason to fear this stranger. Pixies are known for mischief, not murder. I nod toward the shelves. "I have other flavors, too, if you don't like apples."

"Oh, I love apples." He waves his bun toward the broken window, which I tacked a sheet over. "Kid throw a rock?"

"Something like that."

"Bummer." He waves his bun again, gesturing around the shop. "Looks like business is booming, though. Kind of unusual for this neck of the woods, huh?"

"We had a decent harvest this year." Face flaming, I heft the platter. "I should put these out for display."

He steps aside. "Be our guest."

I start forward. A beat later, I stop as his words register. "Our?" My nape prickles. Fun-loving party-goers they might be, but pixies are part of the Myth. And no creature from the other side of the Veil is completely trustworthy.

Something squeaks. Before I can locate the sound, the pixie bends and scoops something from the floor. As he straightens, small, dark eyes peer at me from between his fingers.

"It's all right, little guy," the pixie says softly. "Beau is a friend."

I startle at his use of my name, which I definitely didn't tell him. Before I can puzzle it out, he opens his hand to reveal a small, gray mouse perching on his palm. Long whiskers twitch, and a pink nose wriggles as the mouse appears to take my measure. Abruptly, it turns to the pixie and releases a series of high-pitched squeaks.

The pixie raises sculpted brows. "Well, how should I know?" Another squeak, and the pixie gives the mouse a stern look. Behind him, his wings flutter rapidly, the delicate edges turning red. "No, and it's rude to ask."

The mouse sticks its head in the air and curls its tail tightly around its furry body.

"Fine," the pixie sighs. "Be that way." He looks at me. "I'll take some raisin bread if you have it." The mouse perks up, its whiskers twitching once more. A smile plays around the pixie's mouth. "Raisin bread is Bert's favorite."

For a second, I can only look between the pixie and the

mouse. Then I clear my throat. "Of course." Nodding, I back up a step, bump into a display of muffins, then turn and go to the shelves where I keep the bread. I grab one, then look over my shoulder at the duo. "Uh...do you want the whole loaf?"

"Yes, please." The pixie angles his free hand against one side of his mouth and speaks in a stage whisper around it. "Bert's doing one of those low carb diets, but I know he'll bitch later if I don't buy the whole thing."

An angry squeak splits the air as I pull the loaf from the shelf and go to the cash register. After a few more bewildering moments, the pixie smiles as he accepts the paper bag of bread. "Thanks, gorgeous. This will come in handy when I'm waiting to speak to Lord Fuoco."

My stomach does a flip. "Fuoco?"

The pixie nods. "He was supposed to give me an audience yesterday, but he never showed up. And his courtiers were all sleeping off hangovers, so they were no help. Dragons, am I right?"

Curiosity blossoms inside me. I push the register drawer shut and will myself to keep my mouth shut too. But then I open it and ask, "Why do you need an audience?"

"Flight arrangements." The pixie jerks a thumb at his wings. "These are pretty, but they won't get me to Europe." He rolls his eyes. "And let me tell you, if I hear one more dragon make a joke about *endurance*, I will hex the everloving shit out of Fuoco's princess castle. A bunch of stand-up comedians, those metal-gazing nerds. And they have a lot of nerve because those horny fuckers..."

As he prattles on, my head fills with images of what Fuoco might look like in flight. Dragonback is the only reliable way to cross the ocean. After the Veil fell, human airplanes could no longer fly. The magic in the air warps the metal.

"Would Fuoco take you?" I blurt, interrupting the pixie's

tirade. For some reason, the thought of the elegant male on the dragon lord's back fills me with a heavy, uncomfortable heat.

"Doubtful," the pixie says, tucking the mouse in his front shirt pocket. He points a manicured nail decorated with a tiny pink heart at the rodent. "Stay in there this time. You know you can't tolerate the cold." The pixie meets my eyes, and something twinkles in his. "Fuoco isn't one to give rides. But you never know. He might make an exception for the right man."

My heart pounds, the heavy heat streaking to inconvenient places.

The pixie's wings beat the air, shedding glitter that sparkles in the sun. "Gotta run. Dragons get so shitty when you keep them waiting." He goes to the door. On the threshold, he turns and gives me another wink. "Thanks again for the bread, gorgeous." With a final swish of his wings, he leaves.

I stand at the counter, staring blindly after him. The right *man*, he said. Not person. Is Fuoco...gay? The pixie certainly was. Although, maybe I shouldn't assume. But something tells me the leather-clad male would be perfectly fine with the assumption. He wasn't ashamed. He definitely wasn't interested in hiding. A smile pulls at my lips as I picture him strutting through the village with his painted nails and a mouse in his pocket. I look at my hand on the counter—at my plain, square fingernails and my hand covered in tiny, waxy burns from various oven accidents. Even if I wanted to, I could never be like the pixie.

With a sigh, I turn toward the kitchen.

BOOM.

A gust of wind picks me up and hurls me backward. Time slows, and glass spins around me as I fly through the air. A second later, I land hard and sprawl on my back. For a second, I just lie there, my head spinning and my lungs trying to inflate.

The fall knocked the wind out of me. What the *hell* just happened?

"Beau!" My father's voice reaches me, and then he kneels at my side. "Beau... Oh gods." Panic fills his eyes as he shakes my shoulder. "Speak to me, son. Are you all right?"

"Fi..." I swallow, tasting copper. "I'm fine." I wiggle my toes and then hold back a sob of relief when they move in my shoes. My back isn't broken. That's a good sign, right?

My father's face crumples. "This is all my fault."

Footsteps and the crunch of glass fill my ears. Cold winter wind gusts over me, raising goosebumps on my skin. The grocer and his teenage son appear and gaze down at me with troubled expressions. A second later, the cobbler shows up, his face smeared with something bright green and sparkly. It glints in the sunlight as he shoots my father an angry look.

"This was your doing, Maurice!" The cobbler points to his green-streaked jaw, then to me. "That explosion took out the wall of my barn and almost killed your son."

Explosion?

Dread rises as I sit up. The cobbler steps back, revealing the rear of the bakery. As I take it in, nausea burns my throat.

The kitchen is *gone*, nothing but gray winter sky beyond the bakery. Smoke billows around the hole where the kitchen used to be, the tendrils floating up and into the air. Bright-green sludge covers the floorboards and splatters over my loaves, muffins, and cakes.

Bright green. I've seen that color before—in a beaker in my father's workshop.

Slowly, I turn to my father. "Dad," I say carefully, "what did you do?"

Tears fill his eyes. "I was only trying to help." As he wrings his hands, several more villagers step through the hole in the wall. Great. Now a crowd is forming.

"Dad," I say more loudly. "What. Did. You. Do?"

My father bows his head. "It was supposed to fix the oven," he says in a small voice.

My breath catches. "The fuel?" Anger surges, turning my voice into a growl. "You put *experimental* fuel in my oven? Magical fuel?"

The cobbler sucks in a breath. "We don't truck with magic around here, Maurice."

My father lifts his head and gives the cobbler an indignant look. "There is nothing wrong with magic."

"There is when you blow up my fucking bakery!" I yell. As all heads swing toward me, I clamber to my feet. Pain shoots through my skull—and just about every other part of my body—but I push it aside as I limp to the wreckage. Silence reigns, the only sound the occasional whistle of wind coming from outside—or I guess *inside* now, since my father just destroyed my livelihood.

Despair chokes me. There is no coming back from this. I can't bake without an oven. Not even a bowl of bottomless apples can save me.

I freeze, and a single word pounds through my head.

Selsara.

Lord Fuoco's voice was soft and reverent when he called me that. *"Whatever is mine is yours. Anything you need, selsara, you come to me."*

The dragons are rich. An oven is nothing to a male like Lord Fuoco. *Whatever is mine is yours.* That's not the sort of thing someone says when they want to roast you alive. Maybe he meant it. Maybe I should go ask him. What else do I have to lose? Because right now it feels like I've already lost everything. The pixie didn't seem frightened about having an audience with Fuoco. Why can't I have one too?

Anything you need, selsara, you come to me.

As bright-green sludge creeps toward the toe of my shoe, I square my shoulders. Time to find out if Fuoco is a man of his word.

A HALF HOUR LATER, I STARE UP AT LORD FUOCO'S CASTLE WITH MY heart trying to pound its way from my chest. The castle's pale stone sparkles in the late morning sun. Towers of various heights soar above a main keep so large it could house the village a hundred times over. Mullioned windows glitter like diamonds. As my gaze wanders over the imposing structure, I'm fairly certain I've lost my mind. The explosion knocked me senseless, and now I'm going to walk into a dragon's castle and ask him to replace my oven.

Hysterical laughter bubbles in my throat. I force it down as the wind picks up, its icy fingers delving under the jacket I threw over my rumpled clothes.

Clothes that are now splattered with sparkly green goop. Angling my head down, I pick at a drying spot on my shirt. I should have changed before leaving the village. Lord Fuoco might interpret my sloppy appearance as an insult.

But it's too late to turn back now. And if I do, I know I won't work up the courage to try this again. So, I run my fingers through my hair, doing my best to smooth the thick waves without the benefit of a comb or mirror. That task complete, I draw a deep breath and move forward.

The castle gates loom, the scrolling metalwork like something out of a fairy tale. Until today, I've never ventured close enough to Lord Fuoco's home to see the gates. As a child, I sometimes climbed the hills on the outskirts of the village so I could stare at the castle and dream of living in something so grand one day. That was before I realized ordinary boys from tiny villages don't grow up to live in castles.

The gates are flung wide, and no one stops me as I continue my approach. Colorful gardens border the path to the castle, the blooms as bright as gemstones. No...they *are* gemstones I realize with growing awe. Rubies curl into tight rosebuds. A few others are in full bloom, the multifaceted petals casting a red glow over their neighbors. Amethysts and sapphires mimic foxglove and hydrangea, their petals glittering in the sun. The blooms shouldn't be able to stand upright. In an ordinary world, the gems would be too heavy to wave in the breeze. But these are magic flowers. Dad would love them.

The thought of my father sobers me, and I tear my gaze from the flowers and pick up my pace. A thick curtain wall surrounds the main keep. In the center, an open archway shows a glimpse of a large, airy courtyard. My heart pounds harder as I head toward the opening, nerves prickling as I wait for guards to appear.

But no one comes, and I pass through the arch and enter the courtyard unmolested. As I stop and look around, a sense of unease lifts the hair on my nape. The castle is enormous, and the courtyard is sized to fit. Gray flagstones stretch as long and wide as one of the old football fields that dot the ruins of human settlements from before the War That Ripped the Veil.

Fuoco is rumored to command an army of servants. But no one moves about. Aside from sunlight streaming through patches of blue sky, the courtyard is deserted.

The cavernous space is beautiful but austere, with high walls made of smooth white marble. Dragon statues stand sentinel at every corner, their wings folded around bodies that glint with jewels. The nearest statue depicts a blue dragon with wings veined in gold. I don't need to venture closer to know the gold is real. As I wander deeper into the courtyard, the beast's eyes appear to track my progress.

Blood rushes in my ears. Movement in my peripheral vision makes me whirl toward the source. On the far side of the courtyard, a thick metal post rises from the ground. Manacles dangle from a chain fastened at the top. Around the base of the post, the flagstones are solid black.

From being repeatedly scorched by dragon fire. A cold sweat breaks out on my forehead as I realize I'm staring at the spot where John Robinson died.

The spot where Lord Fuoco burned him alive.

Trap. This is a trap. And I'm an idiot. Just as I turn to run, a hand clamps down on my shoulder. I'm spun around, and then shoulder-length blond hair and a pair of glittering ruby-red eyes fill my vision.

Lirem's mouth twists in a malicious smile. He holds my stare as he lifts his voice. "Look what I caught."

Booted footsteps ring out. A second later, a dragon enforcer with dark hair and bright purple eyes appears next to Lirem. My heart stutters. It's Varden. He's even bigger than Lirem, with a broad chest and a square jaw shaded with stubble. Dark-purple scales peek from the collar of his shirt, which strains over thick biceps. His gaze is cold and hard, and his voice drips with contempt as he rakes his gaze down my body.

"This one looks like he got into some magic."

As I bristle at being spoken about like a misbehaving dog, Lirem tightens his grip on my shoulder. He hauls me closer and uses his other hand to flip my coat open. He gives a vicious chuckle as he takes in the green mess staining my clothes. "What happened, boy? You wander into the path of a spell gone wrong?"

"It's nothing," I grind out. And I'm an even bigger fool than

I thought. If they find out Dad was using unauthorized magic, there's no telling what they'll do.

"Looks like something to me," Varden says. He widens his eyes and places a gloved hand over his chest. "You wouldn't lie to us, would you, human?" He turns to Lirem. "I think our friend here is lying to us."

Lirem's red eyes gleam, little fires dancing in the ruby depths. "We don't like liars, boy."

I'm not a boy. The words stick in my throat as fear sinks its claws deep. Swallowing my pride, I lower my gaze. "I-I'm sorry. I didn't mean—"

"Didn't mean to lie? Or didn't mean to trespass?"

I jerk my head up. "I'm not—"

"Yes, you are," Varden says. "You entered the castle grounds."

"Without permission," Lirem adds.

Varden heaves a put-upon sigh. "I think we have to teach him a lesson, Lir."

"No," I gasp, tugging at Lirem's grip. "No, please—"

"Shut up," he growls. As if they rehearsed it, he and Varden hook their arms under mine and drag me between them, sweeping me off my feet as they hustle me backward. I can't see where they're taking me, but I already know. Seconds later, my back hits the post. Metal clanks and then Lirem yanks my arms above my head. Cold steel burns my wrists. My bowels go watery as visions of fire and torture dance in my head. These two can't burn me with dragon flame, but they're capable of hurting me all the same.

They step back, their eyes burning with hatred. Varden yanks one of his leather gloves off and slaps me across the face with it. I cry out, not from pain but the sheer humiliation of it. I'm not good enough—not man enough—for a punch.

But that comes a second later. Lirem's arm blurs. Pain

explodes in my gut. I jerk, instinct driving my shoulders forward as I try to curl over the pain. But the manacles bite into my wrists, keeping me upright. Before I can catch my breath, my head snaps back. Metal clanks as my vision blurs and numbness spreads through my jaw. It's going to hurt later. Everything is going to hurt so much.

The blows keep coming, fists pummeling me. My feet scrabble on the blackened flagstones as I twist and turn, helplessly absorbing the enforcers' punches and slaps. Deep, masculine laughter accompanies my hoarse cries. Flashes of purple and red punctuate the bursts of agony. The enforcers' gem-bright eyes shine with hatred that sinks almost as deep as their fists.

Endure. I have to endure. This can't go on forever. Dad needs me. I do my best to dodge their fists, but the hits come too quickly. Darkness huddles at the edges of my vision. It beckons, and I want to answer its call. In the darkness, I won't feel any pain.

The dull thuds of the enforcers' fists grow fainter. My screams seem to echo, as if they come from someone else. The darkness swells, and I reach for it. A roar builds, the sound louder than anything I've heard. Louder than the oven exploding.

The ground shakes, but I pay it no mind as I stretch toward the blackness.

CHAPTER 7
FUOCO

Bulleting through the early morning sky, I focus on my castle's stony spires when they come into view. I built a territory and home where my people and the humans were supposed to coexist peacefully. After what I've seen over the past several hours, that false peace tastes like ash in my mouth.

I flew all night going from village to village, hiding in shadows to observe the human towns. Each village was more destitute than the last—empty storefronts with ragged interiors and homes that only appeared well-tended at a cursory glance. Rage simmers under my skin, fire building in my throat. The ominous black clouds overhead match the stony sensation in the pit of my belly.

Sometime in the night, I decided I'll confront Lirem and Varden in front of my court versus privately. Their demise will send a message, and I'll pick off anyone else who shares their beliefs. I'll trace the rot all the way through my people, and only those who truly believe in equality can remain.

Treasure-hoarding thieves, the lot of you.

Those words haven't stopped ringing in my ears. I don't know if they ever will—or if they should. They'll hang like a weight around my neck, reminding me of my neglect.

My shadow looms over the open courtyard as I swoop low to land. Lirem and Varden stand before the post, their fists clenched at their sides as they step away from a chained, limp man.

No. Not just any man.

Beau.

My selsara. Bloody and groaning, his head lolls from side to side.

Lirem and Varden look up as I race toward the ground. Varden waves a hello, as if beating a man is commonplace.

Bellowing, I snap my wings close to my body and land with a thud, shoving my head between Beau and my enforcers. Lirem and Varden stumble backward, twin expressions of shock on their faces.

My mate groans, a pained sound that yanks at my soul and has me spinning around. Protective instincts burst through my rage as I snuffle Beau gently, running my snout up his neck. Blood flows freely from a wound along his hairline, and I scent my enforcers' hands all over him.

Die.

As it did with Nazzar, the red madness descends over my vision. Roaring in fury, I spin and swipe my tail in an arc, knocking both Lirem and Varden to the ground. In a flash, I curl my tail behind them, trapping them where they lie.

Varden leaps to his feet and throws both hands in the air. "My lord, this man came onto castle grounds without permission."

Lurching forward, I open my mouth and let a stream of fire erupt from my throat. Varden screams as he burns, skin melting from his bones, blood dripping to sizzle on hot stones. His voice fails as his throat caves in, bone turning to liquid.

I jerk my head toward Lirem. He's burned but he moves quickly, dipping under my chin as Varden crashes to the ground. I swivel, catching sight of Lirem as he darts behind Beau. Lirem's red eyes glitter as he glances around, looking for a way out.

There is no way out for him. No survival for the sin of touching my mate. If I were in human form, I'd cackle like a madman.

Madness beckons now, red tendrils snaking into my veins. Urging me to call the elements and dispose of this vermin as I did with Nazzar. I could do it. I could call *everything*. Water and earth. Air and fire. I could make sure no one ever touches what's mine again. The rage builds, its call growing louder. *Do it*, the rage whispers. I should. I'll summon the air to cleave Lirem's limbs from his body. Then I'll present the pieces to my selsara like bloody jewels.

Beau's grunt punches through the rage. My selsara sways against the pole as he struggles to lift his head. Lirem hovers behind him, the skin on one side of his face blackened and bubbled. Fucking coward, using my mate as a shield. Growling, I whip my tail around the pole, stabbing the sharp tip into Lirem's side and knocking him sideways. The moment he's away from Beau, I slap him again, tossing him across the courtyard like a rag doll. He hits the far wall with a scream and slides to the black stones, unconscious.

I'll deal with him in a moment.

Shifting quickly to human form, I rush to Beau and rip his manacles in half. He falls forward into my arms, his head dropping to my shoulder. Chocolate hair is matted with blood. His face is swollen, his handsome features distorted.

They beat him for daring to enter my home. Knowing what

I know now about how the enforcers have treated the humans, I'm amazed he had the bravery to come here.

Fury storms through me, the red madness threatening to overtake my reason. I hoist Beau higher in my arms and turn back to the courtyard.

The spot where Lirem fell is empty. He's gone.

I roar as my beast rises, intent on finding Lirem so I can shred his muscles from his bones. He hurt my Beau, my selsara. The red tendrils of my elemental power slither up my spine like snakes.

Beau stirs, the movement drawing my attention to him. His eyelashes flutter, and I hold my breath as he opens his eyes. He stiffens, his pupils blowing wide as he stares up at me. A second later, he comes alive, pushing against my chest as he tries to squirm from my arms.

"Easy, selsara," I croon, crossing the courtyard. "I will keep you safe."

He pauses, one hand on my chest and his gaze locked with mine. His eyes are so fucking beautiful—the color of melted chocolate in the center with flecks of black and gold along the outer rim. I could lose myself in his eyes.

But he reeks of fear, the scent acrid and bitter in my nostrils.

"Y-You can put me down. I'm able to walk." His voice wavers, his lower lip trembling.

I don't slow as I enter the castle. "I don't think so, selsara. You need a healer."

His throat works as he swallows. "I shouldn't have come here. I didn't mean to cause you trouble." He keeps his hand on my chest, his skin warm against mine. I wonder if he realizes he's touching me? Seeking me.

I shift him higher, curling my arms around his lithe frame. His thighs and back are strong and supple under my palms.

"You could never trouble me, Beau. It's my pleasure to be at your service."

He does more wide-eyed staring. "But..." He clamps his mouth shut, another gust of fear lifting from him. He's clearly terrified of me. Watching me burn Varden and fling Lirem across the courtyard probably didn't help. He doesn't know how I spent last night, or the deception I uncovered. And he doesn't understand why I spared his life—or why he's in my arms right now.

I'll remedy that as soon as possible. Desire spikes as I head toward the castle's infirmary. First, I'll make sure Beau is healthy and whole. Then I'll deal with Lirem. After that, I'll court my little mate, replacing his fears and doubts with pleasure.

I hook a right down a candlelit hall and stop in front of a glossy black door. I shoulder inside, calling for the healer as I move down two rows of empty beds.

A tall dragon strides from an antechamber, surprise filling his gaze as he sees me naked with Beau in my arms.

"Dieter," I say, giving him a nod. "I require assistance."

"Of course, my lord." He moves briskly, rolling up his sleeves as he gestures for me to set Beau on one of the beds.

I lower him carefully onto a plush mattress and step back. "Dieter has served my house for hundreds of years. He's an excellent medic. In my castle, he treats not only the dragons but also my human servants."

Confusion moves through Beau's eyes as he shifts backward, propping his shoulders against the bed's metal frame. "You give your servants health care?"

"Yes." And his confusion makes sense. Now that I know the depth of my enforcers' betrayal, any gesture of goodwill toward my servants probably comes as a shock. I hold my selsara's gaze. "We have much to talk about, Beau."

Dieter clears his throat as he hovers on the other side of the bed. When I meet his stare, he looks from me to Beau and back, curiosity in his diamond-bright eyes.

"Selsara," I murmur, folding my arms.

Dieter says nothing but he lifts a brow as he finishes rolling his sleeves. When he turns to Beau, there's none of the typical dismissive, casual dragon arrogance. He's yet another excellent asset I stole from my father's court. Like me, Dieter wanted a new world with new rules.

He smiles at Beau as he sits on the edge of the bed near Beau's hip. "Many dragons are blessed with magical gifts. As you've probably guessed, mine is healing." Dieter runs an assessing gaze over Beau's face. "I can treat your injuries, but I'll need to place a hand on your stomach and another on your forehead. Is that alright?"

Beau looks up at me. My heart squeezes as I give him a nod of encouragement. He draws a deep breath and turns back to Dieter. "Yes. Go ahead." He holds himself stiffly, and he jolts when Dieter lays hands on him.

Having been on the receiving end of Dieter's skills a time or two, I know Beau will feel the heat of the magic coursing through his veins as it mends his injuries. Sure enough, his cheeks flush a brilliant scarlet, and his plump lips fall open. His brows knit together as the wound on his temple closes, but he remains still as Dieter works his magic.

A long moment later, Dieter pulls his hands away and stands. "You need rest. Healing magic takes its own sort of toll. But you'll be right as rain come morning."

Wonder spreads over Beau's face as he touches his temple. He lowers his hand and stares at his fingers. "No blood." He gives a bemused laugh as he extends his arms, moving and stretching like he expects to feel pain. Finally, he looks at Dieter with wonder in his eyes. "Can you heal everything?"

Dieter smiles. "Not everything. But most human ailments." The healer's smile fades. "Although, the servants don't come to me as often as I'd like."

My blood freezes, because the truth is far worse than Dieter knows. The humans in my syndicate avoid him because they've been taught to fear dragons. And their terror is justified. My enforcers have stolen and taken and ravaged, and it happened while I distanced myself so I *wouldn't* terrify people I swore to protect.

Beau offers Dieter a shy smile. "Well, that's amazing. I'm so grateful for your help. Thank you."

"You are most welcome." Dieter rounds the bed, a knowing look in his eyes as he claps my shoulder and makes a quick exit. Beau watches him go, nipping at his lower lip as the door closes behind the healer.

I have to touch him. Now that he's healed, the instinct to pleasure and protect is overwhelming. I settle on the mattress, my thigh brushing his. When he sucks in a breath, I plant one hand on the other side of his hips and lean forward. "Why did you seek me out today, Beau? How may I serve you?" My gaze drops to his lips. The upper one is slightly plumper than the lower.

And I'm still naked—and getting harder by the second. I'm also tall enough that he can't get away, so I surge forward until my lips nearly brush his. "Anything," I murmur. "Ask and it's yours."

He darts a look down my body, his gaze landing on my dick before bouncing right back up. A flush spreads over his cheeks. He gulps, and the bob of his throat makes me bite back a groan. "My father is sick," he blurts. "And my oven exploded." Another gulp. "I'm a baker."

A smile spreads through me. "Ah, the apples are making

sense. Tell me, sweet one, did you bake him an apple pie after we met?"

Beau's flush grows deeper, trailing down his neck into his threadbare shirt. He clutches at the bedding, twisting the sheet in his hands. "Yes."

I place my hand on both of his, stilling his nervous movements. "It's okay. Whatever you need, I'll provide for you." I brush my fingers over his knuckles and place the lightest kiss on the corner of his mouth. "*Whatever* you need," I say as I draw back.

His breath hitches. A delicious scent fills the air—something sugary and spicy all at once. I drag it into my lungs, letting it fill me up. If I'm not mistaken, my beautiful mate is just as affected as I am. His blush deepens, highlighting the tiny golden freckles that dust his nose.

He's so sweet for me. So shy. Fucking irresistible.

I put a finger under his chin. "I love the colors your skin turns, selsara. Reading your emotions is like reading my favorite book."

Black eyelashes flutter. "You can read my mind? Is that"—he sucks in another breath—"dragon magic?"

"It's not *my* magic," I say. "Mine is something else entirely, and I can't wait to show it to you. For now, let me help your father and see to your oven."

Hope fills his eyes. "You really think your healer will be able to help my father?"

I move my fingers to his jaw, stroking along the firm curve and then down the side of his neck. Soft, supple skin begs for my fangs and claws. I can't wait to introduce him to the pleasures of being mine.

But I won't lie to him either. "I can't say with certainty, selsara, but dragon healing magic is very powerful."

He licks his lips. "What does that mean? Selsara?"

I drag my thumb over his plump lower lip, touching the spot he swiped with his tongue. His mouth is so soft, so kissable. It would be easy to lean in and claim his lips. My dragon rumbles under the surface, eager to taste him. I force my beast back as I hold Beau's gaze. "Selsara is an ancient dragon word for mate."

Beau pales. "Mate?" he croaks, his jaw dropping before he snaps it shut. He presses himself against the bed frame, making the metal squeak in protest. "What, exactly, does that mean?"

Regret pummels me. He's afraid. Wariness I might understand. Few humans mingle extensively with creatures of the Myth. And mating a dragon would give most people pause. But Beau's fear stems from experience. His tattered clothing is a glaring reminder of the hardships he's endured at my enforcers' hands. And he has no reason to believe I'm any different.

I can tell him things will be different now. But words are empty vessels. They mean more when they're filled with action. I have to earn his trust before I can win his heart.

That realization brings a fresh wave of yearning. How long will I have to wait to have this beautiful, gentle man in my bed? Under my hands?

The answer comes right away. *As long as it takes.* I want to fuck him. Kiss him until he's breathless and begging. Instead, I ease back and let my longing seep into my voice. "It means we belong together," I say quietly.

His lips part. He draws a shaky breath, then speaks in a voice as low as mine. "You... You're...gay?" That fierce blush surges back, and he bites at his lip again. "You like men?"

"I like you," I rumble, staring at his mouth. When he makes a choking sound, I tear my eyes away from temptation. His cheeks are so red, I might almost think he's inexperienced. But that's ridiculous. He's not a teenager. I smile and lift a shoulder. "I suppose humans would call me bisexual. I've taken both female and male lovers over the centuries. Dragons call them consorts. But that's all in the past, Beau. Now that I've found you, I'll take no others."

His lips part again, but no words emerge. He's not recoiling in horror. On the contrary, the spicy-sweet scent of his arousal reaches me, curling into my lungs and getting under my skin. Good. That's where I want it.

I grasp his knee as I hold his gaze. "So to answer your question, selsara, yes. I am very, *very* gay."

CHAPTER 8
BEAU

The next morning, I cling to Fuoco's long, black claw as my breakfast tries to escape the confines of my sloshing stomach. My whole life, I thought coming face to face with a dragon was the most terrifying thing I could experience. Now I know I was wrong.

Flying through the air in the curve of a dragon's paw is definitely the most terrifying thing a person can experience. I grip Fuoco's claw as we soar over the syndicate, the world reduced to neat squares and thin ribbons of road beneath us. Up here, his territory looks rich and peaceful, with green fields dusted with snow. Mountains loom in the distance, their snowy caps wreathed by clouds. I huddle in my borrowed cloak, which keeps the chill at bay. But I hardly need the garment with Fuoco carrying me. His massive body is like a furnace, his scales hot to the touch. Warm and rested, I'm free to enjoy the view.

But it's not like I have a choice. Ever since I entered Lord Fuoco's castle, I've been under his command. Or as he put it, his "care."

"I can't allow it, selsara," he said last night when I asked to return home to check on my father. "Not when you're still weak from your injuries." He scooped me off the bed in the infirmary and tucked me under the blankets. He stood back, the brilliant green scales on his upper body shimmering in the light streaming through the windows. "You heard Dieter. You need rest."

"But my father—"

"Will be well. I'll send someone to check on him."

Alarm bolted through me. "A dragon?"

Fuoco gave me a tender look as he brushed my hair back from my head. "He won't be disturbed. You have my word. Now, what are your favorite things to eat?"

He ordered a feast from his kitchens. Then he watched me dine, his green eyes following every forkful until I protested that I couldn't possibly eat anymore. Afterward, he excused himself only to return moments later fully clothed and carrying a lute. He arranged his big body on the bed next to mine and strummed beautiful, haunting songs that lulled me into a peaceful sleep.

This morning brought another delicious meal—and his announcement that we would fly into the village to fetch my father.

"Would that please you, selsara?" he asked, his voice husky with dawn's first light.

It did please me. But as I followed him to the courtyard and watched him shed his clothes and shift, apprehension twisted my gut.

It twists again now, nerves joining the brewing revolt. Lord Fuoco has been nothing but courteous. But how long is that courtesy going to last? If I'm really his mate—and I have no reason to think he's lying—he's not going to be content sleeping in the bed next to mine. He's going to want us to share a bed...and do a lot more than sleep. He's twice my size. If he wants me that way, I have no hope of stopping him.

Heat blasts my cheeks, then runs a fiery path down my limbs. Memories of Fuoco's nude body fill my mind, images of his golden skin, broad chest, and pierced nipples popping into my head like they're spring-loaded. But the vision that jumps to the front of the line is his heavy, round penis. His *pierced* penis.

As blood pumps to my very ordinary, very unmodified member, I squeeze Fuoco's claw. His wings beat the air, the great whooshing sound keeping time with my heart, which pounds as I recall his long shaft and the bulbous tip decorated with a golden, bejeweled ring. More gems glittered at his wrists and in his ear, but I barely noticed. And as I drifted to sleep with the sound of his lute in my ears, my mind supplied me with other visions. Fantasies. Forbidden things I had no business picturing. Like me on my knees pressing my lips to that ring. Maybe licking it. Licking him. Would he let me do that? A whimper escapes me as I imagine taking him into my mouth and tasting all that he has to offer.

Without warning, a massive wing swoops into my vision. Fuoco's claws curl more tightly around me as he wheels in the air. His other wing beats steadily, rotating us slowly as he lowers his head and peers at me with glowing emerald eyes. As we hover in the sky, a question forms in the gem-bright depths, and the tiny row of horns above his brow lift in an arch. His expression is unmistakable, as is his inquiry. *Are you all right?*

"Yes," I rasp, then clear my throat and raise my voice over the roar of his flapping wing. "Yes! Fine!"

He huffs, sending warm air gusting over my face. His snout looms closer, making panic jump down my spine. But he merely snuffles me, sending more hot air rushing through my hair and down my neck. The sensation is mild and more than a little ticklish, and I release an embarrassing giggle before I push his snout away.

"I said I'm fine!" His scales around his snout are smaller than the ones on his flank, and I run my fingers over the rough, bumpy ridges. He groans and leans into me, nudging his face against my hand in a universal gesture. *Pet.* Laughing, I smooth my palm over his snout. When his green eyes go heavy-lidded, I do it again. And again. I spend a few moments like that, nestled in the safety of his paw as I stroke his face.

"Better?" I ask after a minute.

Green eyes gleam with gratitude that warms me more than his body heat. With another gentle snuffle of my hair, he spreads both wings and propels us through the sky. Moments later, we touch down on the outskirts of the village. He deposits me carefully, and I clutch the packet of his clothes as he lumbers away and shifts.

The transformation is magical, which makes sense considering it's pure magic. But as he rolls his shoulders and shakes out his arms, his human form seems just as magical as his beast. For one thing, he's just so *big*. Everywhere. I run my gaze over his lats and delts, heat prickling through me as I take in the thick curves of his biceps. He runs both hands through his hair, smoothing the strands that are several shades darker than mine. But when he rescued me in the courtyard, his hair was *fire*. Crackling green flames that glowed as brightly as his eyes.

Goosebumps lift on my skin as he turns and strides nude toward me, his thick shaft bobbing against his thigh.

"Here," I blurt, thrusting the packet of clothes toward him. He takes it, tosses it on the ground, and cups his hands around my jaw.

"You okay?" he asks softly.

"Me?" I blink rapidly, a hundred different emotions firing

in my brain. Shock, confusion, and arousal. More than a little stupidity. "Yeah," I gasp. "I'm good. Thank you."

His eyes stay serious. Steady. "Good," he rumbles, stroking his thumbs over my cheeks. "I'm glad." He doesn't move. Just continues gazing into my eyes, the pads of his thumbs tracing my cheekbones in tiny caresses that make me suddenly aware of every cell in my body—and *acutely* aware that he's nude in the road with the village a mere shout away.

"Um." I swallow thickly. "Are you going to get dressed?"

"No."

I blink again. "No?"

He shakes his head.

"But...why not?"

"Because I'd rather do this." He bends and slants his mouth across mine. I gasp, and he pushes his tongue into my mouth—gently at first and then deeper as I tilt my head and open under the pressure of his lips. He spears his fingers through my hair, his touch sending shivers down my spine, and then he strokes his tongue along mine in a hot, wet caress.

It's a passionate kiss. My *first* kiss. And it's everything I ever wanted. A man's lips on mine. A man's tongue in my mouth. A moan winds its way up from my throat, and I clutch at his shoulders as he answers my moan with one of his own. He slides his big hand to my nape and squeezes as he slides his tongue against mine, his strokes bold and demanding.

At last, he pulls back, sucking gently at my bottom lip before cradling my face in his hands. My heart thumps wildly as he regards me with bright emerald eyes. "Forgive me, Beau. I promised myself I would woo you properly. But you're so damn tempting I couldn't resist."

Heat floods my cheeks. I bite my tongue so I don't tell him I wouldn't mind if he kissed me again. I lick my lips, tasting mint and something dark and rich. I want to twine my arms around his neck and pull his head down so I can taste it again.

He steps back, releasing me with a sigh. "We should go before we're discovered." Humor gleams in his eyes as he scoops the packet of clothes from the ground. "We don't want to cause a scandal."

I look away as he dresses, my face flaming with a different kind of heat. It's too late to avoid a scandal. Walking through the village with Lord Fuoco at my side will start tongues wagging right away. And the second people learn I'm his mate, the whole village will know I'm—

A low noise escapes me before I can stop it.

"What is it?" Fuoco asks, instantly alert. When I press my lips together, he takes my arm. "Beau?"

"I…" Words stick in my throat, but I force them out. "Could we… Would it be all right if we wait to tell people about the selsara thing? Or at least keep it from my father for a little while?"

Understanding spreads over Fuoco's features. "Your father doesn't know you are gay."

"No," I murmur, dropping my gaze to the ground. "No one knows."

He tips my chin up, and his green eyes are soft as he says, "It's okay. We don't have to tell anyone else about our relationship until you're ready. You can take as much time as you need."

I nod, some of my anxiety ebbing away. But it rushes right back when we enter the village. As predicted, Fuoco turns heads. People I've known my whole life stop and gawk as the dragon lord prowls at my side. Several people gasp, turn on their heels, and flee in the other direction. But most simply stare as if they've seen a ghost.

I receive my share of stares, too. Eyes move from Fuoco to

me—and then over my new cloak that probably costs more than everything in my cottage combined. Shock and disapproval radiates from familiar faces. I lower my gaze, my cheeks burning.

"Steady, Beau," Fuoco murmurs beside me. He matches my pace as I hurry us through the square and down the narrow alley that leads to the bakery. When we reach it, he stops me with a hand on my arm. He looks over the storefront with its simple stone walls, wooden shutters, and thatched roof that leaks during heavy rains. Broken glass litters the sidewalk. The sheet I tacked over the broken window hangs limply, exposing the interior. Fuoco's gaze fixes on the sagging cloth. "You live here?"

"Yes." Movement inside has me starting forward again. As I cross the street, Gastonia's face appears in the open window. She gapes at Fuoco, her mouth falling open. By the time I step inside, her shock has transformed to wariness—and something that might be anger.

"Beau," she says, swallowing hastily. She sets a half-eaten pastry on a shelf behind her and dusts sugar from her fingers. "Where have you been?"

"With me," Fuoco rumbles, entering behind me and resting a warm palm in the small of my back.

Gastonia's blue eyes shoot there like a laser. Her mouth tightens as she lifts her gaze and gives me a piercing look. "Everyone wondered where you went. People have been talking." She glances at Fuoco's hand on my back and offers a tight, humorless smile. "I expect they'll talk even more now."

My gut clenches but I keep my mouth shut as I gaze around. If possible, the place looks worse than yesterday. Broken crockery litters the slime-splattered floors. Flour sifts in the air. A blue tarp stretches across the back of the shop, blocking the view to the garden.

"My father brought it over," Gastonia says, following my gaze. "He wanted to help."

"And then you helped yourself to Beau's inventory," Fuoco says, stepping forward. His boots crunch over broken porcelain, and his long cloak swings around his leather-clad legs. He's so big he takes up half the bakery.

Gastonia's cheeks color as they face off. She lifts her chin, her blue eyes defiant. "My father always said *you* were the thief."

My heart lodges in my throat. "Gastonia—"

"Your father is right," Fuoco says. As I stare, speechless, he steps closer to Gastonia, who has to tip her head back to meet his eyes. Emerald-green scales spread down his neck as he speaks in a quiet voice that's somehow more terrifying than a shout. "But Beau belongs to me now. And I don't share what is mine."

The hair on my arms lifts as his words hang in the air, the warning unmistakable.

Gastonia's nostrils flare. Just when I think she might actually be stupid enough to insult Fuoco, she turns to me. "My father's help doesn't come for free. You owe us for the tarp."

Anger kindles in my chest. I pay my bills. I might have to ask for more time, but I've never shorted anyone. And I didn't ask for her "help."

The floor vibrates. Somewhere in the bakery, dishes rattle. Fuoco leans toward Gastonia, his voice even softer than before. "If there is a fee for your *services*, madam, send the bill to the castle."

Tension fills the air. Gastonia stands her ground even as hints of fear swim through her eyes. At her side, she curls her hand into a fist. I'm not entirely certain she won't swing it. When Cory Lannigan called her "Trash-tonia" in third grade, she knocked his tooth out. But Fuoco isn't Cory. The dragon lord is utterly still, his big body throwing off enough menace to collapse the bakery's three remaining walls.

A cough echoes from behind the tarp.

Dad.

I move without thinking, crunching over pottery as I race to the rear of the shop and fling the tarp aside. Dad shuffles toward me, his head down as he picks his way across our sorry excuse for a garden.

"Dad!" I rush to his side and take his arm. His shoulders are rounded, his straight posture from yesterday gone. His worn-out sweater hangs on him, the once-brown yarn gone tan from hundreds of trips through the ancient washing machine he rigged up. White tufts of hair stick out from his head.

But his eyes light up as he places a gnarled hand over mine. "Beau! I was so worried, son."

Guilt swamps me. Out of habit, I smooth his hair back, tucking the tufts into place. "I'm sorry. I got...caught up."

Dad's smile fades as he looks past me. Surprise spreads over his features. "You've brought company."

I sense Fuoco before I see him. Heat warms me from head to ankle, the force of the dragon lord's presence cranking higher as he appears at my side and offers my father a bow straight from a medieval court.

"Fuoco of House Drakoni, sir. I am most honored to meet you."

Dad's snowy eyebrows soar to his hairline. He recovers quickly, offering Fuoco a nod as the dragon lord straightens. "Maurice Bidbury of...well, this garden. And I'm honored to meet you, as well, my lord."

"Fuoco," Fuoco corrects softly, his tone filled with the kind of respect a polite young man might offer an elder. Except Fuoco is no such thing. He has to be hundreds—maybe thousands—of years old. Which is almost as surreal as the fact that he thinks we're destined to be together.

Dad coughs suddenly, his shoulders shaking. Fuoco reacts before I can, wrapping his big arm around Dad's shoulders. I hover helplessly, equal parts worried about my father and mesmerized by the sight of Fuoco supporting him as Dad's smaller frame is racked by a coughing fit. The apples' magic should have lasted longer. Which means my father's cough isn't just a cough. I gnaw at my bottom lip as tears burn my throat.

Eventually, the rattling sound subsides. Dad wipes at his brow. "Forgive me. The winter is never kind to my old lungs."

Fuoco's voice is gentle as he eases Dad away from him. "You should see the castle healer. Dieter's gift is powerful. His services are at your disposal if you wish it, sir."

Dad looks at me, questions in his eyes. "Is that where you went last night, Beau? The castle?"

Discomfort squirms through me. "Yes," I say, feeling like a teenager who sneaked out of the house in the middle of the night. "I, um, met the healer. He—" I cut myself off before I can admit Dieter helped me after the other dragons beat me up. "He's really nice," I finish lamely.

More questions fill Dad's eyes. For a second, I think he'll demand to know just what is going on here. But then he smiles and gives a little shrug. "What do I have to lose?" He turns his smile to Fuoco. "If this healer of yours can fix me, I'd love to meet him."

Fuoco's smile is warm enough to heat the whole garden. "It will be my pleasure to fly you and Beau to the castle."

Dad gathers a few things from his bedroom. Gastonia is gone when we walk through the bakery, and there's no sign of her in the village. But as we cross the road, something makes me look over my shoulder.

Gastonia stands in the shadows under the awning of Robert's bookshop, her blue eyes narrowed. As our gazes collide, she gives me a look filled with so much malice my blood runs cold.

Then she turns and walks away.

CHAPTER 9
FUOCO

Beau's father is dying. Whatever ails him fills my mouth with a sickly, acrid taste. Air doesn't flow through his lungs like it should. They're obstructed by disease. He doesn't have long. Urgency drives me to rush Beau and his father to the closest clearing.

I throw my clothes off to shift, ignoring how Maurice stares in shock at my nude body. My dragon rises, and I let the change flow over me. When I tower over my selsara and his sire, I uncurl one claw in invitation. Beau tucks my clothing under his arm and helps his father carefully into my palm.

When I dreamed of him over the centuries, our flights together were sensual. He should be astride me now, his thighs gripping my back and his long fingers stroking my scales. The sky should belong to the two of us and no one else. Having him near and being unable to touch him the way I wish is a particularly brutal torture.

The need to pursue Beau gnaws at me from the inside out. It's selfish, but my beast doesn't care about manners. My selsara is within my grasp—literally—and I've yet to claim him. Every instinct I possess urges me to fly to my mountain lair and make the gorgeous man in my palm *MINE*. But I shove instinct away and streak toward the castle.

When we arrive, I swoop down to the courtyard and deposit Beau and Maurice on the stones. When I shift back, Beau is waiting with my clothes. He averts his eyes as I pull them on, his high cheekbones stained with pink.

Maurice studies the blackened stones where Varden's ashes have settled into the cracks. He lifts wary eyes to Beau, who glances at me.

"I burned one of my enforcers there," I say, buttoning my pants. "That's why the stones are black."

Maurice swallows but says nothing. He and Beau exchange another cautious look.

"He hurt Beau," I say, fresh anger searing my gut. "I'd burn him again without a second thought." *And zero remorse.*

Maurice pales. He opens his mouth—

"It was nothing, Dad," Beau says. "We'll talk about it later. Right now, you need a doctor."

Anger moves through Maurice's eyes as he stares at his son. "It doesn't sound like nothing." He looks at me. "This enforcer is dead?"

"Very."

"Good."

Understanding passes between us. Maurice nods, and I return the gesture as I go to him and sweep him into my arms.

His anger drops away, replaced with sputtering indignation as I stride toward the castle. "My lord, this is most unnecessary! I may be old but I can still walk."

I look down at my selsara's father. "Maurice, you're very ill. You have a disease of the lungs, and I'd rather you not strain yourself walking to the infirmary."

Beau jogs to catch up to us, his brow furrowed in worry. "You're certain that's what's wrong?"

I look at my mate and nod. "I can hear the air in his lungs." Nobody in the castle knows I'm an elemental dragon, and now isn't the time to divulge my gift. I'll tell Beau when we're alone and he's not focused on his father.

Neither man speaks, but anxiety is a cloud around us as we move through the castle. Servants catch sight of us and gasp, quickly dodging from my path and disappearing like ghosts.

By the time we reach the wing that houses the infirmary, anger dogs my steps. Anger that the humans are terrified of me. Anger that I didn't see what my enforcers were doing. Anger that I tried to rule kindly and ended up failing the syndicate despite it. Maybe because of it.

I was the weakest egg in my clutch but my mother's favorite because of my kindness. She saw it as a strength instead of a weakness. But it doesn't feel that way now. Perhaps if I'd been a little more bloodthirsty and untrusting like my father or brothers, none of this would have happened.

I'm growling by the time I shove through the infirmary door.

Dieter stands at the ready. From the look on his face, he heard me stomping down the hall. His diamond-bright eyes go to Maurice right away.

"Dieter," Beau says, worry thick in his tone. "This is my father, Maurice. He's—"

"Dying," I finish bluntly. "Please do what you can, Dieter." I set Maurice carefully down on an empty bed.

Beau rushes to his side. He grabs one of Maurice's hands and brings it to his chest.

My heart aches at my mate's distress. I want to whisk him to bed and banish his worries with my mouth. But I keep my hands to myself as I face my selsara across the bed.

As he did with Beau, Dieter explains his process to Maurice, then lays hands on the sickly man. Maurice hisses in a breath but holds steady as Dieter's magic probes.

"Easy, Dad," Beau says quietly.

After a moment, Dieter straightens and regards Maurice with serious eyes. "You have cancer of the lungs." His voice gentles. "Untreated, you won't survive the winter."

Both men gasp. Beau's eyes fill with tears.

"Selsara," I whisper, aching to touch him.

Maurice regards me with a curious expression before focusing on Dieter. His lower lip wobbles slightly. "You said untreated? Do you have a treatment? Or do I need to make arrangements—"

"Dad!" Beau rasps, clutching Maurice's hand to his chest. "Don't even say that!"

Dieter inclines his head. "I can heal your cancer, Maurice. But you'll need multiple treatments over the course of two or three weeks. If you agree, we'll get started right now."

Tears spill down Beau's cheeks. Maurice releases a shaky breath. "Of course. I'd be incredibly grateful. I'm in awe that you can do this." He frowns. "I don't know how I'll ever repay you."

"You won't," I say gruffly, and all eyes turn to me. "There's no charge for this."

Surprise covers Maurice's features. "But—"

"No charge."

Maurice studies me, confusion and gratitude in eyes that remind me of Beau's. Then he turns to his son, something like hope filling his voice. "If this works, we can go home and fix the bakery. I'll be able to help this time. And things will be different, Beau. No more experiments with magic."

Beau squeezes his father's hand. "Don't worry about it, Dad."

"But I want to…"

Panic grips me as Maurice continues, his expression earnest as he explains how he'll help Beau restore the bakery. Beau listens patiently. Receptively.

Is he actually thinking of returning to the village?

Leaving me?

Panic blooms into something thick and hot. My beast rises, fire crackling just under my skin. My selsara—the mate Fate promised me—is thinking of leaving my home. *Our* home. Doesn't he realize that everything I own is his? Every possession, every gemstone, I've procured over the centuries is for him. And now he'll walk away from the life I've built for us so he can bake apple tarts?

He can't. He *won't*. The panic claws at me, digging bloody furrows into my heart, which my selsara is doing his best to break. A growl brews in my throat. My hands curl into fists as he stares at his father with love beaming from his eyes. He's never looked at me that way. That look is *mine*. He should be lying in our bed, his gorgeous brown eyes shining with love. With obsession.

Fear beats at me, the prospect of Beau rejecting our bond washing over me in acid waves until I want to pull the castle down around us brick by brick. I can't lose him. Not for his father or any other reason. Maybe the old legends are true. Maybe elemental power is a curse. Because the horrible dread simmering under my skin doesn't give a shit about Maurice or Dieter or any of the fucking villages that dot my syndicate. It wants Beau, and it doesn't care if it has to burn the world to ash to claim him. The waves pummel me…and then shift into icy, pitch-black focus.

It centers on Beau, propelling me around the bed just as Maurice says, "We could go back sooner if—"

"Absolutely not," I snap, grabbing Beau's arm and hauling

him up. He stumbles into me, his eyes wide. Dimly, I'm aware of shocked gasps and Dieter moving out of the way. Beau gapes at me, his gaze traveling up...

"Your hair," he says hoarsely.

Flames crackle around my head. My beast moves restlessly beneath my skin. The hot, acidic panic chokes me, turning my voice to gravel as I look at Maurice.

"Beau isn't going anywhere. Dieter will heal you, and then you can go home if you wish. But Beau stays."

The old man shrinks against the pillows.

Fears me.

Beau is stiff at my side, reluctance rolling off him. He would leave me if he could. He was *planning* it.

"Come," I bark, tugging him to the door. I throw Dieter a look over my shoulder. "Heal the father. We'll be back later."

"Beau!" Maurice calls. Dieter's deeper voice rumbles assurances behind me as I clench my teeth and hustle Beau from the infirmary. It takes everything I have not to toss him over my shoulder—or shift to beast form and fly him to the mountains. I settle for keeping him locked against my side as I move through the labyrinth of corridors. Beau struggles to keep up, his breathing growing labored. I slow my strides but I don't look at him. I can't. Not until I get him alone. Not until I regain control.

But the sharp scent of his fear clogs my throat. *My fault.* He has every reason to be terrified, and I've just made it worse.

I stop before the next chamber and fling the door open. As it crashes against the wall, a maid whirls from where she stands polishing a candelabra. She fumbles the piece, almost dropping it as she stutters. "L-Lord Fuoco! Oh gods, I'm so sorry."

"Out!"

With a squeak, she rushes from the room, trailing more of that sour stench of fear. *Always* fear.

And now my selsara smells of it.

He wants to leave me.

"You *can't*," I growl, pushing him against the wall. I trap him there, my hands on either side of his head. My chest heaves as I bury my nose in his neck, hunting for his natural scent under the layers of worry and fear.

There.

Rich spices and hints of sugar. He must bake with it often. Sweetness clings to him.

He trembles against the wall, his heart a rapid beat in my ears.

"You can't leave," I croak against his skin. "I won't allow it." I drag his essence into my lungs, letting it soothe me. Slowly, the panic and the rising haze of madness recede. I keep my hands on the wall as I lift my head and meet Beau's gaze.

"Lirem is still out there. I can't let you return to the village."

"But you'll let me go once you find him, right?"

Never. I don't say it. But my silence says it anyway.

He raises his chin a fraction of an inch. "Am I a prisoner, then?"

"No." *Maybe.*

Probably.

His dark brows angle into an irritated vee. "If I can't leave, I'm a prisoner."

The panic roars back, obliterating my tenuous calm. I shove my larger frame against his lithe body, pressing him hard against the wall. Dipping my head, I brush my lips over his. "Not a prisoner." As if I'd ever lock him away. No, I want to show him everything. I want to court him properly—to guide him through the elaborate mating rituals of my people. But he's definitely not ready for *that*. Not just yet.

I move my lips to his jaw and slowly drag my mouth over his stubble. When he shivers under me, my cock goes painfully hard. "You're mine." I lift away so I can see his eyes. "And I'm yours."

He winces. "You said you wouldn't tell my father about the selsara thing. But the way you acted in the infirmary…"

Regret sluices through me, bringing clarity with it. "I'm sorry. Do you think he'll guess?"

Beau offers a wry smile. "My father is eccentric, but he's not a fool." Beau's smile fades. "Life hasn't been easy for him. I worry this will only make it worse when he returns to the village."

"Then he won't. He'll live here in the castle."

Beau frowns again, anger stirring in his eyes. "You might be able to force me to stay here, but you can't impose your will on my father. We have a life in the village—"

"Not *we*. You're not going back to that miserable place." Gods, how could he even consider it when he can live in luxury with me?

He lifts his chin, chocolate eyes sparking with defiance. "It might seem miserable to you, but it's my home. I have a business to run."

"What business?" I demand, frustration rising. "Your oven is blown to pieces. Your supplies are covered in broken glass. Tell me, what are you rushing back to? Slime-coated floors and tarp-covered walls?"

His defiance turns to anger. "The walls can be repaired. As for supplies, I'll get apples from the orchard."

"Not from mine, you won't."

His nostrils flare. "You would really do that to me? Bar me from the orchard?"

"You know the penalty for stealing." Gods, I'm such a dick. But I can't stop. Words pour from me like poison, threats spilling out as I fight the urge to do exactly what he accuses me of wanting to do and lock him away so he *cannot* leave me.

"There's nothing for you in that village, Beau. Your place is here. Your father requires my help. Stay and I'll see to it he receives it."

The color drains from Beau's face. "You're blackmailing me into staying with you? Are you serious? You'll hold the threat of my father's *life* over my head unless I do what you want?"

It's wrong. So, so wrong. But if I have to threaten him to secure his compliance, I will. Because he can't run from me. If he tries, the whole fucking world could be in danger.

From me.

"My beast is...restless," I say. *An understatement.* "I need time alone with you." I stroke chocolate waves away from his face as I scan his gaze. "Stay and Dieter will heal your father. Maurice will want for nothing."

Beau jerks his head, evading my caress.

I grit my teeth and straighten, putting space between us. "You don't need the bakery. Anything you desire, I will provide. You're my selsara. Everything I own is yours."

He folds his arms, his lean muscles bulging against his borrowed shirt. "Do most dragons capture their mates and lock them up until they agree? Is that how this is going to go?"

This is all wrong. This is how other dragons behave. I know better. I should be wooing him, not forcing him. Then again, I didn't anticipate having him inches away and still out of my reach.

"Yes," I rasp, the admission scraped from the back of my throat. "Most dragons are cruel, selfish, and possessive. I've always thought I was better than that, but the idea of you returning to that run-down cottage is more than I can bear."

He regards me with a stony expression, his jaw tight as he stands against the wall.

"Dragons dream of our selsara before we meet them," I say, hoping he can hear the truth in my words. "I have been dreaming of you for centuries. Daydreams. Dreams in the middle of the night. For so long, it was just glimpses of you from behind my closed lids. Flickers of your form in the fire. But now I see you, and I am *enraptured* by what I see."

His lips part. Slowly, he unfolds his arms.

"To have you here in my home and asking to leave is…" I grope for an adequate description. But seven hells, there isn't one. I capture his hand and place it over my heart. "This beats only for you, Beau. And for the rest of my life it will *only* be you for me. Allow me to woo you properly. We'll take it as slowly as you wish, but please don't ask me to watch you leave."

His fingers curl against my chest. Seconds pass, each one an eternity as he appears to think it over. Then steel enters his eyes. "You'll heal my father?"

"Stay with me."

"And you'll heal him?"

I nod. "I swear it."

Beau inhales deeply, then jerks his head once in agreement. "I'll stay. Just…heal him. Please."

Triumph unfurls in my chest. Humans don't make binding vows like creatures of the Myth, but I know he means it. Then again, his father is the center of his world right now.

It should be me. All in good time. Beau hasn't dreamed of me for centuries. I can tell him what he means to me, but it'll be a lot more effective if I show him. Deeds over words.

I lace my fingers with his. "Come. Let me give you a tour of your new home."

After a moment's hesitation, he nods. "All right."

The castle is quiet as I lead him through the various chambers. Servants move about, but the members of my court are absent. Of course, word of me finding my selsara has likely spread. My courtiers are creatures of the Myth. They understand how dangerous it is to get between a dragon and his mate.

When Beau and I reach the Great Hall, I gesture to the long table that sits on a dais before the massive hearth. "This is where I take my meals with the court. Everyone usually eats together."

His stomach rumbles. He slaps a hand over it, a blush spreading over his cheeks.

"Are you hungry?" I guide him to a sideboard where servants have set out trays of fruit and cheese. "Take whatever you want."

He doesn't wait. Pulling his hand from mine, he plucks a pear from the tray and takes a healthy bite. His eyes slide shut as he chews, and he gives a low groan that streaks straight to my dick. Juice dribbles from the corner of his mouth.

I can't help myself. Surging forward, I cup my hands around his jaw. Brown eyes fly open as I lick the juice away. When he gasps, I trail my lips down the column of his neck. *So fucking sweet.* I suck at his skin, groaning at the taste of him. His pulse throbs against my mouth, the beat thumping faster. My cock presses painfully against the front of my trousers.

Beau freezes in my grasp, his throat bobbing. His erection brushes mine. I want nothing more than to reach down and grip his hard length. Stroke him to release. But he's clearly starving, and I need privacy for the things I want to do to him. Releasing him, I run my fingers down his throat before stepping back.

"Forgive me, Beau. I was overcome." I gesture to the pear in his hand. "Please finish."

Once again, he doesn't hesitate. He sinks his teeth into the fruit, taking oversize bites and chewing quickly. He devours the pear and then darts his eyes to the tray.

"Another one?" I ask. I point to a platter stacked with small mountains of cubed cheese. "Or maybe some cheese?"

He gives me a grateful look and takes a cube. He eats it—then another...and another. I take the pear core from him so he can grab more food. He finishes off a cheese mountain, along with a second pear. He eats like a man possessed—or someone who's known the gnawing, aching pain of true hunger. When was the last time he enjoyed a full meal?

"Easy, selsara," I murmur as he reaches for a second cheese mountain. "You'll make yourself sick."

Beau nods, his flush reappearing as he withdraws his hand. "You're right. I don't want to overdo it. It's just... I've never seen so much food in one place."

I follow his gaze to the table. Three meager platters sit there. The servants leave the fruit and cheese for courtiers to tide them over between big meals. Few bother with it. Most of the court keep to their rooms during the day, only emerging at night to feast and make merry. *While the rest of my people starve.*

Gods, what have I done?

Choking back regret, I take his hand. It's sticky with pear juice, so I lift it to my mouth and suck his fingers clean.

Beau grunts, his pupils blowing wide as his flush spreads down his neck.

I finish cleaning him, never pulling my gaze from his. He watches my mouth with parted lips, his breaths rapid and shallow. His arousal drifts around me, the scent sweeter than the fruit.

He wants me—but he also wants to leave me. And why shouldn't he? I made his father's treatment contingent on Beau agreeing to remain in the castle.

I'm a monster.

"Beau," I murmur, nipping at one slim fingertip.

He flicks heavy-lidded eyes to mine. "Yeah?" He clears his

throat, a frown forming between his brows as he tugs his hand from my grip. "Yes?"

"Come on." I tip my head toward the big double doors on the other side of the Hall. "There's a lot more I'd like to show you."

There are tasks ahead of me that I don't relish—hunting Lirem chief among them. But for the next few hours, I'll pursue Beau. I have to make him understand why he belongs here, with me.

I show him the rest of the main castle, and then I lead him to the greenhouse. His eyes go wide as we step through the doorway. He stops and stares at the rows of fruit and vegetables like they're chests full of gold coins.

"You grew all of this?"

"The castle is self-sustaining. We grow everything we need."

"Gods," he mutters. "This is incredible. All this food."

Guilt burns my gut. "My enforcers told me the villages brought in a record harvest. I didn't know things were so dire."

Beau's expression is guarded. "You really didn't know?"

I shake my head. "When I first took over the syndicate, I attempted to rule alone. I carried on like that for almost 150 years, but the humans were terrified of me. I brought my enforcers on board because they were from lower houses. They're smaller and less intimidating. And I thought they were different from other dragons." Bitterness wells as I offer Beau a tight, humorless smile. "I was wrong."

"Is that why you burned the one and attacked the other when you found me in the courtyard?"

The guilt in my gut threatens to twist into rage. "Not entirely. They touched you." *Put their hands on what's mine.* "I trusted them, and now I know it was blind trust. That won't happen again."

Beau watches me, the sunlight streaming through the glass walls highlighting the golden flecks in his chocolate irises. "It's not a bad thing to trust, Fuoco."

"It is when it leads to abuse. I killed Nazzar after he threatened you in the orchard. I burned Varden to ash. Lirem will die for what he did to you and others. Once that's done, I can figure out how to make amends."

He gives no response, and he seems lost in thought as we wander the rows of plants. When we reach a line of peach trees, I pluck a fat, fuzzy fruit from a branch and hand it to him.

"If you'd like to bake, all of this is at your disposal. The castle's kitchen should have everything you need."

He studies the fruit, then hands it back. "Why bake if I can't sell anything?"

My heart sinks. He's still angry. And he still thinks he needs to work—that he should repair that decrepit cottage he considers his home.

His home is here. The sooner he accepts it, the better.

I tuck the peach in my pocket. "Maybe you could bake for pleasure and not because you have to in order to survive."

He holds my gaze, his brown eyes steady. "Maybe."

Tension arcs between us. Anger, mostly. But there's desire in there, too.

I can work with that.

I hold my hand out. "Come, selsara. There's one last room I want you to see."

Despite the moment's tension, he places his hand in mine. "What is it?"

I turn toward the doors that lead to my private wing of the castle. As we leave the greenhouse, I slant him a look. "Our bedchamber."

CHAPTER 10
BEAU

Fuoco's bedchamber is even more opulent than the rest of the castle. It's also the size of the village.

Well, maybe half the size of the village. I pause on the threshold, my senses overwhelmed by the decadence sprawling before me. The room is all rich, dark colors and sumptuous-looking fabrics. Heavy drapes adorn the windows. Candles flicker on various surfaces. A marble-topped vanity with an enormous jeweled mirror stands in one corner. In another corner, a grand piano with glossy black lacquer reflects the candlelight. A crystal chandelier descends from a large medallion in the center of the ceiling.

But it's the bed that makes my mouth go dry. It dominates one wall, its four posts rising like regal sentinels. A purple canopy drapes around them, the thick panels descending to the plush carpet. The black headboard is carved with symbols that lift the hair on my nape.

"Does it please you?" Fuoco asks, moving around me. He means the room but that doesn't stop my face from heating as

I tear my gaze from the bed. He's as beautiful as his bedroom, his green eyes flickering with remnants of the intensity he displayed in the infirmary. His hair is normal again, thankfully, the eerie flames snuffed out. But he's still intimidating in leather pants and a white shirt unbuttoned enough to show the emerald-green scales that cover his broad chest. His nipple piercings are shadows under the finely woven fabric.

Before I can stop myself, I lower my gaze to the thick bulge between his legs, my head filling with images of the shiny ring that adorns the tip of his dick.

"I want you to like it," Fuoco adds softly, stepping toward me.

I jerk my head up, my gaze colliding with his. The intensity is back, the green depths glittering. My heart skips a beat as I realize he's not talking about the room anymore. He moves closer, his body heat caressing mine. He's always so warm. Of course he is, I think, nervous laughter bubbling up. He's a dragon. A big, powerful dragon who says he's *enraptured* with me.

I swallow hard. "Does it matter if I like it?"

"It matters," he says, curling a finger under my chin. He tilts my head back gently. "But I don't just want you to like it, baby."

My breath shudders out, my lungs deflating as that *baby* slides under my skin.

"I want you to love it," he murmurs.

Desire beats a hard rhythm inside me. My knees loosen, fear and arousal swirling as I stare into his glittering green eyes that promise all sorts of wicked, forbidden things. Warmth spreads through me, chasing away the tight, frozen anger I *know* I should be feeling. He deserves it. He kidnapped me but says he wants to protect me. He dangles love before me when his most recent actions have been anything but loving.

And yet...

"Are you doing this?" I ask. "Making me feel this way?"

Slowly, he shakes his head. "That's not my magic, selsara. And even if it was, I would never force your hand in this."

But you'll force it in other things.

He waits, little flames dancing in his eyes. Something hot and absolutely ancient hovers there, its gaze so possessive it steals my breath. *His beast*, I realize. A dragon has me in its sights. Memories rise—snippets of passages I've read about dragons in the books Robert lends me. Dragons hoard treasure. They covet glittering, shiny things. But they reserve all their avarice for their beloved, fated mates. *And woe betide the fool who steps between a dragon and his most precious treasure.*

"Selsara," he says, the word delivered in a broken whisper. And then he lowers his head and claims my mouth. The kiss is gentle at first, his soft lips brushing against mine as if testing the waters. When I gasp, he deepens the kiss. He skims his hands up my sides to my hair as his tongue teases its way into my mouth. After a few easy caresses, he strokes his tongue boldly, his long fingers cradling my head. When I move my tongue tentatively against his, he gives a low groan—the sound undeniably needy.

He wants me. Desperately, I think of all the reasons I shouldn't want him back. He's holding me hostage. He barred me from his orchard. He won't help my father unless I stay.

He groans and sucks at my tongue. Need clenches in my belly. Dimly, I'm aware he's walking me backward across the carpet, his thighs brushing mine. His *dick* brushing mine.

And I'm hard—harder than I've ever been. I shouldn't want this, but my body doesn't seem to care that I've been blackmailed and bullied into this arrangement. Not at all. For only the second time in my life, I've got a man's tongue in my mouth and a man's body—a large, muscled body—

driving mine backward, and all I can think about is getting more.

Fuoco gives it to me, pulling me tightly against him just as my back meets the wall. His kiss turns hot and demanding, his tongue plunging deep as he grinds his erection into mine. He seizes my hips and rocks against me, letting me feel every hard inch. I grip his shoulders for balance as I melt into him, my self-control spiraling away.

His heat seeps into my skin. Sweat beads on my forehead. I'm going to burst into flames and I don't care even a little bit. My head goes fuzzy, lust and anticipation obliterating rational thought. His hand works between our bodies, and then he palms me through my pants.

Gods. Maybe I say it, the word swallowed by his tongue and the lust that's drowning me. He pulls back, and I chase his mouth, a broken whimper breaking from me as he takes his heat with him.

But he keeps his hand on my dick. He braces his other hand on the wall and stares at me with swollen lips and eyes dancing with green fire. We're both panting, our breaths mingling.

He looks at me for a long time, his big hand cupping my erection. Then he leans closer, not stopping until his lips graze mine. "Do you love it?"

The question rumbles against my mouth and streaks straight to my cock.

"Yes," I whisper, the admission wrung from the bottom of my soul. I've fought so hard not to like this, but I can't deny it. And I don't want to anymore. He moves his hand from the wall to my jaw. Easing back a bit, he trails his fingers to my mouth and presses a thumb between my lips.

I suck on his thumb, tasting salt and fire. Imagining sinking to my knees and sucking his cock this way. The mere thought of it drags a deep groan from my chest.

"Baby," Fuoco breathes, his eyes narrowing to burning emerald slits. He pushes his thumb deeper, forcing my jaw wider.

A shudder rolls through me. My heart races as I swirl my tongue around his thumb. I'm in uncharted territory and I'm probably messing this up.

But Fuoco doesn't seem to think so. His breathing grows ragged as he watches me suck and lick. His hand on my dick tightens...and then begins to stroke, his fingers digging in just enough to make me moan as he pumps up and down in a slow, steady rhythm.

"*Ungh,*" is all I can manage as I buck my hips, thrusting my dick into his hand with an eagerness I should be embarrassed about. And if he keeps touching me, I *will* embarrass myself.

He seems to understand my predicament, because he steps back and pulls his hands away. Gaze still locked with mine, he fists the bottom of his shirt and yanks it over his head. Hard pecs and washboard abs covered in dragon scale reflect the candlelight. His skin is sun-kissed, the hollows of his muscles dark spaces I want to explore with my hands and tongue. I want to touch him everywhere—to feel all that heat and muscle under my palms. Fuoco claims he's dreamed of me. Well, maybe I've dreamed of him, too. Alone at night when no one can see, I've dreamed of feeling a man's body against mine. Touching flat, broad chests. Kissing a man's stomach. A man's cock. Feeling the weight and heft of one other than my own.

Fuoco's big hands go to the button of his pants. And tires screech in my mind, spiky nerves throwing up barriers that make me suck in a breath.

Fuoco frowns, his hands stilling. "Beau?"

Words stick in my throat. My erection flags as fear and

frustration grip me. Just when I finally have an opportunity to do all the things I've fantasized about, my courage deserts me. Because I don't know what to do. I don't know the first thing about anything. Fuoco is hundreds, maybe thousands, of years old. Experienced. And I'm…me.

Fuoco's expression changes, understanding spreading through his eyes. He steps into me again and cups my jaw. "You've never been with a man."

I swallow hard. "Or…anyone."

His eyes go wide. "Never?"

"Never," I whisper, and the sound is pitiful. *I'm* pitiful—and so far out of my depth it's laughable.

Fuoco doesn't laugh. He brings his other hand to my face and feathers his thumb over my burning cheekbone. Tenderness shines from his eyes as he gazes down at me. "Beau," he murmurs, and his voice is as soft and gentle as his hands on my face. He lowers his head and brushes his lips over mine in a kiss that's over almost before it begins. But it's enough to make my heart flutter.

He brushes his nose against mine. "You have no idea how beautiful you are, do you?"

I shake my head, my face flaming. I know I'm not ugly. Plenty of women have looked my way. It would have been so much easier if I wanted to look back.

But no one has ever looked at me like this dragon.

"Let me show you," he says. Slowly, he reaches down and grasps my hand. Gaze locked with mine, he places it on his cock, which is rock-hard and burning hot through his pants. At my swift intake of air, he gives a shaky laugh. "*That's* what you do to me, Beau."

My heart pounds. Fuoco's heat sears my fingers.

"What do you want?" he asks. "Tell me and I'll help you

explore it." His thumb strokes my cheek, his touch featherlight. "You can trust me, Beau. I'll never hurt you."

He won't. I've never been more certain of something. He's violent and dangerous. He burned his enforcer before my eyes. But he'll never turn that brutality on me.

"Yes," I rasp, and I don't know what I'm agreeing to—or asking for. Maybe I'm asking for everything.

He gives me another tender smile. "Come on," he says softly, taking my hand and leading me to the bed. He pulls the bedding back and pats the white, pristine sheets. "Lie down."

Heart racing, I obey, crawling into the center of the mattress that's as big as my bakery. He follows, stretching on his side with his elbow propped and his head resting on his hand. With another smile, he extends his free hand in invitation. "Come here."

I can hardly breathe as I let him tug me against him. My head lands in the crook of his shoulder as he wraps me in his arms, holding me close against his bare chest. His scales are softer in this form, the brilliant colors ranging from the lightest green to the deepest emerald. His heartbeat thrums beneath my ear, the beat steady and strong. For several long moments, he simply strokes my hair. Then, when I sigh and settle more deeply into his embrace, he starts his exploration.

He touches me everywhere—soft brushes of his fingertips against my temple, my neck, my chest just under the collar of my shirt. He unbuttons it with quick fingers, then lifts me and whisks it away, leaving us chest to chest. My skin tingles, heat spreading through me so swiftly I wonder if *my* hair might turn to flames.

"Gorgeous," Fuoco murmurs, circling one of my nipples before pinching it lightly.

"Oh!" I squirm against him, little rivers of pleasure flowing under my skin.

Fuoco does it again, his gaze riveted on my face. He watches me closely, as if he's waiting for any sign of discomfort or regret.

But those things don't exist to me. They're impossible. And I'm *lost* in his arms, my body perched on the edge of something unknown and intense. I'm no stranger to orgasms. But this is so very different from the way I touch myself.

"You like that?" he murmurs, plucking at my other nipple.

"Yeah." I shudder and grind my hips into his, feeling his dick and needing *more* and *now*.

But he takes his time, tracing patterns that feel like he's painting stories on my skin. My dick aches as desire rushes back, and it's not long before I'm panting and aching. Then I'm begging.

"Please," I moan, my breath hitching.

He rolls me under him so quickly I gasp. My back arches as he presses my hands over my head. "Leave them there," he says, a playful smile on his face. The playfulness fades as he unbuttons my pants. He pauses, his glowing green eyes lifting to mine. "Do you want this?"

I give a jerky nod. "Yes. Yes, I want it."

He pulls my pants off, then my underwear, and then I'm nude beneath him, my dick hard and red. Moisture clings to the tip. He pushes my thighs wide and settles between them.

"I want to touch you," he murmurs, leaning in and pressing a soft kiss to the thatch of dark curls above my shaft. He nuzzles the base of my dick, and his breath tickles my heated skin. "Let me touch you."

"Yes," I croak, and I couldn't look away if I tried. I stare down my body, scarcely able to believe the sight of him between my legs. I bite my lip hard as I study the bulge straining the front of his pants. "Can I see you?"

He flashes a quick grin. Equally fast, he strips off his pants and pitches them past the foot of the bed. He resettles on his knees between my thighs, his hand on his dick. The ring in his cock head glints in the candlelight. As he gives himself a languid stroke, more metal glints under the thick shaft.

Oh, gods. He's pierced there, too.

He reaches for me, and I forget all about his piercings as his fingers wrap around my dick. He swirls them along my shaft and strokes from base to tip and back again, each pass wringing hoarse moans from my throat. It's everything, his big hand gripping me. Stroking me. He knows what he's doing. When I get too close to that shimmering edge, he eases the pressure. When I need more, he squeezes harder, tugging me up so I'm arching and moaning his name. He fondles my balls, his big hands tugging and caressing the delicate skin.

Then he goes to his stomach and sucks my balls into his mouth.

I cry out as pleasure courses through me and my hips lift off the bed. Fuoco sucks and licks, his tongue swirling around and around one tender globe...then the other. He mouths at my sack, planting soft kisses before flicking his tongue over the seam. He teases the sensitive area between my sack and my hole, sending shivers rippling through me. I bend my knees, my thighs splayed wide as the air fills with the sound of my harsh breaths and his wet kisses.

He lets my damp balls fall back against my skin, then slowly moves his tongue up my shaft. Gripping me at the base, he licks my slit, teasing the tiny opening. Lapping at the moisture with a satisfied-sounding hum. He sucks my tip into his mouth and swirls around the crown with long, slow licks that make me shudder and gasp and claw at the sheets. Green eyes sear mine as he closes his lips around my cock head and suckles me, that *hum* rumbling down my dick and into my balls. I writhe beneath him, my hips bucking as I barrel toward the edge.

Just as I'm about to plunge over it, he pulls back. "Not just yet, selsara," he rasps, stroking his big hand up my glistening length.

I thump my head hard against the mattress, both hating and loving his teasing.

With a chuckle, he bends and licks down my shaft, tracing the veins that run along my engorged length. He holds me in an iron grip as he sucks and bites gently. And I'm helpless. Trembling and desperate, I can only watch as he worships my dick with his talented, devious mouth. My muscles clench. I cling to the edge by my fingertips.

Then he swallows my dick.

"Ahh!" I shout, hips thrusting. I bite my lip, trying not to scream as he deep-throats my shaft, taking me all the way to the back of his throat and swallowing loudly around my length. Hot, wet pressure engulfs my cock. He hums around me, the vibrations making my toes curl. He bobs on my dick, sucking and *sucking* me. Swirling his tongue over my head before licking down my shaft. He slurps at my cock, letting the tip hit the back of his throat over and over until I'm reduced to guttural, incoherent moans. His hand massages my balls. And I fly apart.

My orgasm shatters through me. I shout his name and thrust into his throat, my release pumping from me. It's so much—too much—and I squeeze my eyes shut as I ride the waves. His throat works around my dick as he swallows my cum, that deep growl of his rumbling the bed. And he knows when I grow too sensitive because he takes a final lick at my cock head before pulling off and collapsing beside me.

I stare at him, panting and shivering in the aftermath.

"Gods, Fuoco..." I gulp breaths, scarcely able to believe what just happened.

He brushes hair off my sweaty forehead. "Was it okay?"

"Are you kidding? It was great."

He grins, his emerald eyes gleaming with satisfaction. "Good."

I stroke his arm, the intense warmth of his skin sending a pleasant tingle up my spine. "Could I...? Would you let me...?"

He knows what I'm asking. Satisfaction turns to anticipation as he takes my hand and presses his lips to my knuckles. "Of course, selsara. Anything you want."

Oh, I want. Nerves rising, I guide him onto his back. He watches me with hooded eyes as I kneel between his legs and wrap my hand around his dick. It's as big as the rest of him, and my thumb and forefinger don't touch as I give him a tentative stroke. The gold ring through the tip catches the light as I work him. Another piercing decorates the smooth skin under the base of his dick. A small, golden ring adorns the area between his balls and the pink, puckered skin of his asshole.

My fingers tighten around his dick. He grunts, and I snatch my hand away. "I'm sorry—"

"No." Lifting onto one elbow, he grabs my hand and guides it back to his shaft. "Keep going, Beau. You're doing good." He flashes a rueful smile. "*Too* good, if you catch my meaning."

Emboldened by this praise—and the idea that I can make him as needy as he makes me—I quicken my strokes. He grows harder under my hand. His ridged abs twitch, his green scales glittering as his breath hitches. A bead of moisture swells at the prominent slit in his cock head. Unable to resist, I lower my head and swipe my tongue over it.

His taste is exquisite. Salt and fire and man. I mimic what he did to me and fasten my lips around his tip. Immediately, more of that delicious taste fills my mouth. I swallow every drop as he begins to move, bucking his hips gently against my mouth. I take that as encouragement and suck him deeper into my mouth, licking and swirling my tongue over his shaft as I go.

"Oh, Beau," he murmurs, his voice thick with appreciation. "Yes, baby. Just like that." He threads his fingers through my hair and guides me with gentle hands as he whispers praise and encouragement. I probably don't deserve it. My moves are clumsy and uncoordinated. My jaw aches from his cock, which is far too big to fit down my throat. But my enthusiasm must make up for my lack of skill because he bucks harder against my mouth.

I keep sucking, my eyes rolling back in my head at the taste of him. He clenches his fists in my hair, and I know he's close. Saliva coats my chin but I don't stop. I want this for him. I want to make him come. I take him deeper, pushing him over that cliff. He shudders beneath me, his entire body shaking as his release erupts in my mouth. I swallow convulsively, gulping him down, my senses spinning.

I don't pull away even after he softens in my mouth. I keep kissing him, licking and nipping at his tip—at the golden ring that's warm against my tongue—until he stops shuddering and finally exhales. Then he moves in a blur, surging up and wrapping his thick arms around me. We collapse in a sweaty tangle, my head on his chest. Exhaustion tugs at me, threatening to close my eyelids.

After a moment, Fuoco shifts so he's facing me. He leans in and kisses my forehead. "You amaze me, *selsara*," he whispers against my skin. "You always have."

Impossible. He barely knows me. But if the stories are true, and he dreamed of me for centuries, maybe he knows me better than I think. But do I know him?

Can I trust him?

I must drift off because the next thing I'm aware of is a warm cloth wiping me down. Fuoco's deep voice murmurs something I don't catch, and then a sweet-smelling blanket covers my nude body. The bed is so soft—soft enough to sink into. So I do, letting the waves of exhaustion pull me under.

CHAPTER 11
FUOCO

I sit in a velvet chair next to the bed watching Beau sleep. One of his arms is shoved under the pillow, the other slung off the side of the bed. His fingers twitch now and again as he slumbers. His legs are pressed tightly together like he's trying to take up the least amount of space possible. Perhaps that's accurate. His cottage in the village was tiny. His bed was probably little better than a cot.

Regret is a heavy weight in my gut. I'm not foolish enough to believe that one well-timed orgasm is enough to make Beau drop the subject of returning to his bakery. I coerced him into staying with me. Used his father's illness as leverage. That sort of dominance can force cracks into any relationship—even a fated one. If I try to compel Beau's love, I'll break us.

I prop my elbow on the chair and rest my chin on my hand. I keep my free hand on the chair's other arm, my fingers stroking the velvet. Beau is right in front of me and yet he's not totally mine. When I dreamed of my mate, I never imagined I'd have to convince him to accept our bond. For me, our connection is clear as day—bright and beyond certainty. But Beau isn't a dragon. Maybe he doesn't feel the same pull that I do.

The panic of the infirmary is a painful undercurrent to the sated, hazy afterglow of having his mouth on me. As much as I tell myself I *shouldn't* force him, I know I'll do anything to keep him.

Treasure-hoarding thieves, the lot of you.

The words ring through my mind for the hundredth time, along with the growing realization that the old man was right. Because if Beau returns to that village, I'll find him. Steal him. Make him the jewel of my hoard.

Perhaps I'm exactly the monster that human accused me of being. I thought myself better than other dragons—certainly better than the enforcers who betrayed me.

A growl rumbles in my chest. Lirem is still out there, and that won't do. He's dangerous. He could hurt Beau...

The chair's arm creaks under my hand.

A knock at the door pulls me out of my thoughts.

My beast screams to the surface, the dragon riled at the thought of anyone disturbing our sleeping mate. I rise and cross the room, ripping the door open with a scowl.

One of the human servants flinches on the threshold, then quickly drops her gaze to the carpet. "My lord..." She gulps a breath and speaks in a rush. "I'm sorry to bother you at this late hour but there's a pixie in the Great Hall asking for an audience." She hesitates, her blue eyes darting from the carpet to my face and back again. "He said something about you missing an appointment—"

"Jasper Lilygully," I bite out. The meddlesome pixie is the very worst of his kind, always sticking his nose in other people's business. But perhaps I can use him to my benefit. Pixies always seem to know more than they should. Jasper in particular has a knack for digging up gossip.

I look down at the human. "Thank you, Tess."

Startled blue eyes lift to mine. Her cheeks go red. "You know my name?" She sounds shocked—and slightly horrified—at the prospect. Another problem I can lay at my enforcers' feet.

But...no. I'm the master of my castle. I can't blame Varden and the others for this. Gentling my tone, I offer the woman what I hope she interprets as a kind smile. "I know the name of every human in the castle. You're Tess Greenlee. Your mother works in the kitchens and your father assists in the greenhouse. You have two younger brothers." I search my memory, recalling something Dieter told me a few years ago. "The eldest broke his leg climbing a tree."

Her lips part as she places a hand over her heart.

After a moment of awkward silence, I clear my throat. "I'll find Lilygully. Was there anything else, Tess?"

Big eyes blink a few times. "N-No, my lord. Nothing else." She curtsies, then whirls and hurries toward the main castle. The stench of fear lingers in the hall, but maybe it's a bit lighter than before. That scent kept me away from the servants in the past. Another mistake.

With a sigh, I shut the door and return to the bed. Beau slumbers on, his dark lashes long and thick against his cheeks. I drink him in greedily, plans spinning through my head. I'll spoil him. Show him how much he means to me. In time, he'll understand that every decision I've made throughout my long life was with him in mind.

Unable to resist, I lean down and stroke chocolate waves away from his forehead. He's relaxed in sleep, the signs of worry absent from his face. Our bedplay was a first for him—another gift I don't deserve. But I'll take it. Cherish it. I have so many other firsts to share with him.

But right now I have to go see about a pixie.

That's enough to bring the growl back to my throat as I make my way to the Great Hall. I hear it before I reach it. A late-night party is in full swing, raucous music spilling through the Hall's massive double doors. Laughter bounces off the thick stone walls as I push through the doors and pause between them.

None of my courtiers notice my presence. Myth creatures lounge around the long tables, several in various states of undress. Pitchers of wine sit among platters heaped with food. My stomach clenches as my head fills with images of Beau tearing into a pear like he worried someone might take it away from him.

A burst of laughter rises from the head of the table.

Lilygully. The fucking pixie sprawls in my chair, his pale wings fluttering behind him. The dragon seated at his right leans in and whispers something in the pixie's ear.

A slow smile spreads across Jasper's face. He turns to the dragon and nods. The dragon's expression grows heated as Jasper strokes a hand down the male's square jaw. After a second, Jasper swings his legs over the chair's armrest. He tips his head back, and the dragon dangles a bunch of purple grapes over his waiting mouth.

Gods, he's insufferable.

Stalking up the length of the table, I kick the leg of my chair. "Get up, Lilygully. You try my patience." My beast roars to the surface, wreathing my head with green flames.

Jasper sits up, a slow grin splitting his face. Brilliant blue eyes fix on my hair. "Aww, did I upset you, flame daddy?" He plucks a glass of wine from the table and takes a hearty swig, his eyes never leaving mine. Mischief rolls off him in a thick wave that's almost tangible, the sensation like beetles scuttling over my skin.

"You requested an audience," I say. "I'm granting it."

Without waiting for his response, I turn and stride to the far end of the Hall. A chair scrapes behind me, followed by his soft footfalls and the flutter of wings that sets my teeth on edge. The sooner I get him out of the Great Hall the better. If he hasn't already noticed my enforcers' absence, he will soon—and he'll undoubtedly start asking questions. My courtiers don't know Nazzar and Varden are dead, and I'm not ready to explain it.

Plus, Lirem is still out there. He should have never escaped in the first place. He slipped away while I was distracted and desperate to tend to my wounded mate.

Jasper trails me down the darkened hall and into one of my private meeting rooms. A large, round table dominates the center of the space. A fire dances in a hearth big enough for several men to stand inside. Diamond-paned windows take up the far wall, offering a view of the moon that sits high and bright in a pitch-black sky.

Jasper sighs loudly behind me. When I turn, he clasps his hands together, a look of delight on his face.

"A private room, Fuoco? Moonlight and a roaring fire?" He moves to the table and hops onto it. "Gods, if you wanted me that badly we could have done it in the Great Hall." He winks. "You dragons are into that sort of thing, I hear." His delicate wings flutter, scattering silvery glitter onto the table's surface. He crosses one leg over the other and gives me a seductive smile. "Here I am, m'lord. Ready to be defiled."

I fold my arms. "What can I do for you, Jasper?"

He cocks his head to the side. "You're such a sweet talker, Fuoco." He glances around the room, his tone turning airy. "I do need something from you. But we'll get to that in a second. All this cloak and dagger business tells me you need something from me, too." The firelight flashes in his blue eyes as they travel down my body. "How can I be of service?" he asks breathlessly.

"My selsara sleeps in my bed as we speak, pixie." I gesture to my body. "*This* is not available to you."

He studies me. "Arrogant, but you're hot enough to pull it off." He nods to himself. "I'll allow it."

I speak through clenched teeth. "State your business."

He hops down from the table and leans against it. "The rumors are true, then? A certain pretty little baker is warming your bed?" A sigh lifts his chest. "Tale as old as time."

I give him a stony stare. Under the crackle of the fire, a snuffling sound reaches my ears.

"I met him, you know," Jasper says, examining his short nails adorned with some kind of symbol. *Hearts.* He looks up at me with a grin. "He's got gorgeous...apples."

I lean forward. "I'll ask you a final time why you and your mouse require an audience."

Jasper looks down at the pocket of his leather jacket. "You can come out." After a moment, he rolls his eyes. "Of course he heard you, he's a dragon. And no, he won't eat you." Jasper gazes into his pocket as he appears to listen intently. "Well, what do you expect? Your damn breathing is so fucking loud, Bert. It's like an elephant, honestly."

A tiny gray head pops out of his pocket. Round, black eyes peer at me.

"I never said I won't eat you," I tell the mouse.

Bert lets out an indignant-sounding squeak. He scurries up Jasper's chest and perches on the pixie's shoulder, his long tail flicking agitatedly against Jasper's jacket.

"Don't you usually travel with another one?" I ask Jasper. Immediately, I regret the question. The last thing I need is Lilygully thinking I'm interested in hearing details about his life.

But the pixie merely smiles. Bert shifts on his shoulder. The mouse's ears twitch as he releases a series of squeaks. Jasper heaves another put-upon sigh. "Fine, I'll ask him." He strolls forward, his wings batting the air lazily. "I need to go to Paris, and dragon back is the only way to get there."

"What's in Paris?" I demand. The elves maintain their strongholds in Europe but it's unlikely Jasper has business with any of the elven houses. Despite their common ancestry, pixies and elves have long harbored animosity toward each other. Like many among the Myth, the pixies view elves as stuck-up and sanctimonious. The elves regard pixies as irresponsible troublemakers.

Of course, the elves have a point...

Jasper lifts a shoulder. "I hear the men are gorgeous."

"You're going there to stir up trouble," I say flatly. "Aren't you tired of meddling in other people's love lives?"

He presses a hand to his throat. "Me? Meddling? You wound me, flame daddy."

Bert chatters in Jasper's ear, his whiskers twitching.

Jasper nods. "Excellent point, Bert." Jasper closes the distance between us, not stopping until he's close enough for me to see the tiny laugh lines radiating from the corners of his eyes. He tilts his head, his expression abruptly serious. "Now, what do you need from me?"

I debate how much to tell him—or if I should tell him anything at all. But he always seems to possess information others can't obtain. Like the elves, pixies commune with animals. For all I know, Jasper has a rodent army at his disposal. And mice can run through even the thickest castle walls, sniffing out secrets and tracking down those most determined to hide.

But more than anything, I can't help but think that Lilygully is up to something. He's been lurking around the various syndicates. *Meddling.* But maybe there's a method to his scheming. There's something in the air around him.

And I learned a long time ago to listen to what the air tells me.

I unfold my arms as I lower my voice. "I recently learned my enforcers weren't carrying out my wishes when dealing with the villagers in my syndicate. They've been terrorizing the humans, stealing and leaving my people to starve. Two of the three have paid for their crimes, but the third has gone to ground."

Jasper stays silent, his face unusually somber. On his shoulder, Bert appears just as attentive.

"It's my responsibility to fix this," I say, "but first I need to find Lirem. And quickly."

Jasper cocks his head. "Your court is full of dragons. They won't help you search?"

"My court is full of courtiers, not warriors. My enforcers earned their positions because they were skilled fighters. No one here is qualified to take on Lirem." I hesitate, then voice the second reason I haven't asked my court for help. "Lirem has friends among the Myth. It's possible some of those friends reside in this castle. If he has inside help, I don't want anyone alerting him to my plans."

"What will you do once you find him?"

"Kill him." My beast stirs as visions of Beau's bloodied face float through my mind. "I'll make an example of him so everyone in the syndicate knows humans are off-limits. They deserve to live in peace like everyone else." Heat crackles under my skin and rushes up to my head. "And *no one* will ever touch my selsara again."

Bert leans toward Jasper's ear, but the pixie lifts a forestalling hand. He glances at the flames leaping off my scalp. "We'll help you. We'll start tonight."

Relief spreads through me—and I don't know whether to be surprised or worried that a partnership with Jasper is producing feelings of well-being. "Thank you."

"No problem, flame daddy."

It's my turn to sigh. "Please stop calling me that."

He leans back, his gaze critical as he runs it down my body. "You know, you're right. It's more of a *zaddy* thing you've got going on."

"Do I want to know?"

"Probably not." He holds his palm to his shoulder. Bert hops into it, and Jasper lowers the mouse carefully to the ground. Bert scurries across the floor, squeezes into a crack in the wall, and disappears. Jasper straightens and sticks out his hand. "So I'm good for a dragon ride?"

"Yes," I grunt, not taking his hand.

He waggles his palm. "Come on, Fuoco, it's just a hand. It hasn't even been anywhere scandalous." He seems to rethink that, then chuckles. "Well, not *today* anyway."

Grimacing, I shake his hand, sealing our bargain in the human fashion even though magic bound us the moment we uttered our exchange. "Let me know when you want that ride."

His blond brows go sky high. "Flame zaddy! Aren't you the impatient one."

I grit my teeth. "You know what I meant."

"I know what I wanted you to mean."

Gods, what was I thinking, making a deal with him? "Are we finished here?"

He makes a show of looking around. "I mean, *I* didn't finish, but—"

"Never mind," I growl, turning and stalking to the door. "Come find me if you hear anything about Lirem."

"Aye aye, captain," comes his cheery reply. "Say hi to Beau for me!"

Beau. I want nothing more than to return to my bedchamber, climb into bed, and pull his warm body against mine. But as I move down the hall, I head toward the courtyard instead. Jasper will honor his word and search for any trails Lirem might have left. But it's my duty to search for Lirem—and I have an opportunity to start while Beau is asleep in the safety of the castle.

Smothering a groan of longing, I walk into the moonlight and begin stripping off my clothes. I have all night to search. Lirem is out there.

And I'm going to find him.

Chapter 12
BEAU

"Is there anything else you might like, sir?"

I look up from my plate to find the woman, Tess, hovering in the doorway of Fuoco's bedchamber. She appeared when I woke at dawn to find Fuoco absent. A note lay on the pillow that still bore the indentation from his head.

Attending to syndicate business, the elegant handwriting read. *Sleep as long as you wish. The servants will bring breakfast.*

Tess made good on that promise, carrying in platter after platter of steaming food. Apparently, "breakfast" in the castle is slang for "every breakfast food ever created." Because Tess brought enough for an army.

The table before me practically groans with an endless array of dishes. Scrambled eggs. Waffles smothered in syrup. A dozen different kinds of toast. Fluffy pancakes wrapped in bacon and sprinkled with sugar. Omelettes stuffed with spinach, tomatoes, and onions. The French toast topped with currant was too sweet for my taste. A platter of cinnamon rolls as big as my head sits untouched.

I smile at Tess as I try to ignore my rising panic. "No, thank you. I honestly couldn't eat another bite."

She worries at her bottom lip. "Are you certain? Lord Fuoco won't like it if you go hungry. He said to make sure all your needs are met."

The panic blossoms into something hot and uncomfortable. If he can't make me his prisoner, Fuoco seems determined to make me his pet. Even if I could accept that kind of arrangement, I'd never be able to show my face in the village again. I look down at my plate, where egg yolk spreads in a yellow, cloying puddle. The bacon and coffee that made my mouth water half an hour ago now sets acid churning in my gut. The breakfast before me could feed half the village.

Is it really possible that Fuoco didn't know his people were starving? How could he have spent so many years surrounded by wealth when the village had nothing?

"Sir?"

Tess's soft voice yanks my head up. I stand, rattling the dishes in the process. "Sorry," I say, steadying a coffee cup before it can tilt off its saucer. I step away from the table and tuck the chair into place. Squeezing the back, I attempt a reassuring smile. "The breakfast was lovely, but I promise I'm stuffed. And please, call me Beau."

Tess returns my smile with a hesitant one of her own. "Okay...Beau." Her blue eyes flick to the rumpled bed behind me.

Heat climbs up my nape. "Um..." I clear my throat. "Have you eaten?"

Her eyes go wide. "Me?"

I gesture to the table. "I'm not going to eat this. I mean..." Oh gods, is it rude to offer her my leftovers? "I just thought..."

She eyes the platter of cinnamon rolls. "Varden doesn't like it when the servants eat food prepared for the court."

"Well, he's not here." When she looks at me, I use my chin to point toward one of the platters. "He's as crispy as that bacon."

She slaps a hand over her mouth. *"What?"*

My stomach twists. I shouldn't have let it slip about Varden. The enforcer was an asshole, but he probably had a family. People who care about him. Maybe Fuoco doesn't want news of his death getting out just yet.

But it's too late now. As Tess gapes at me, I square my shoulders. "I can't say anything else. But you don't have to worry about Varden anymore. He's gone, and I don't think Lord Fuoco will have a problem with the servants eating this food."

Above her hand, her eyes flicker with doubt. "Truly? You don't think he'll be angry?"

Fuoco's voice runs through my mind. *"I didn't know things were so dire."*

"No," I tell Tess. "He won't be angry." And if he is, well, I'll stay until Dad is better, and then I'll figure out a way to leave the castle for good.

Tess lowers her hand. Emotions play over her pale face. Curiosity and relief and, finally, something that might be a spark of happiness. She gazes at the spread of food before lifting smiling eyes to mine. "Thanks…Beau. The kitchen staff are going to love you for this."

More heat creeps over my nape. "Do you happen to know the way to the infirmary? I'd like to check on my father."

Ten minutes and a few dead-ends and U-turns later, I find Dad sitting up in bed enjoying a miniature version of my breakfast. A smiling Dieter perches on the bed next to him, opalescent dragon scales visible under the collar of his dark sweater. The two men break off what sounds like an animated conversation as I enter.

"Beau!" My father sets his biscuit down and wipes his

mouth with a white cloth napkin. "Come in, come in." He waves me over, his brown eyes sparkling. "Have you eaten? There's more than enough here for two."

"I have, thanks." I move to his side and nod to the healer. "Good morning, Dieter."

"Morning, Beau. I hope you had a restful evening."

Memories of Fuoco's bed flood my brain. His big hands undressing me. His hot mouth on my dick. "I d-did, thank you," I say, backing to the bed behind me and sitting so hard the springs squeal in protest. As Dad's brow furrows, I squeeze my hands together in my lap and focus on Dieter. "How is my father?"

The healer leans forward and places a big hand on Dad's shoulder. "Maurice is doing even better than I expected. His lungs are clearer this morning." The dragon's smile spreads as he meets my father's gaze. "We might even try taking a walk through the gardens later if he feels up to it. Exercise is excellent medicine."

Dad laughs—the kind of deep chuckle I haven't heard him make since his illness last winter. "Just admit it, Dieter, you're tired of answering my questions about dragon magic."

The healer stands. "Never. We'll continue our discussion when we take our walk." He turns his smile to me. "I'll let you and your father catch up, Beau. Let me know if you need anything." He sweeps from the room, his long coat flaring out behind him.

Dad watches him go, then turns to me with serious eyes. "How are you, Beau? And don't give me the answer you think I want to hear."

Nerves tighten my gut. I rise and move his breakfast tray to a nearby table before sitting near his hip. "I'm fine, Dad. Really."

All signs of merriment vanish from my father's eyes. He

lowers his voice. "Did Lord Fuoco hurt you?" My father's expression darkens. "Or force you to do something you didn't want to do?"

"What? No!" I glance around the empty infirmary. "It's not like that. He didn't... We didn't..." My face grows as hot as my ruined oven. "He would never hurt me."

Dad nods slowly. "I see." He takes a deep breath, then reaches out and grasps my hand. "You don't have to hide who you are, son. Not from me."

I freeze. For a moment, words fail me. I force myself to hold his gaze. "I...don't?" I whisper.

His expression softens. "I've known you were gay since you were nine years old, Beau. And I've loved you since the moment your mother told me she was pregnant with you. Maybe before." A tear slips down his weathered cheek. "We tried for a long time, you see, and we'd almost given up hope. But then you came along, so unexpected and such a joy. When your mother saw you for the first time, she said you were beautiful. And you were. So we named you Beau." Dad squeezes my hand. "You are a beautiful person inside and out, son. I can see why Lord Fuoco is taken with you."

My throat closes as tears fill my eyes and spill over, forming hot trails down my face. "I had no idea," I rasp. "I thought I hid it so well."

My father laughs lightly. "Oh, I'm sure you did from most people. But I know you pretty well." His smile fades, replaced with a fierceness I've never seen on his face. "I don't want you to ever hide again. You don't have to be afraid of judgment or punishment—not from me or anyone. I just want you to be happy and safe. That's all that matters to me, my son."

More tears streak down my face. Dad grabs his napkin and dabs at my cheek.

I recoil as something cold and squishy drops into my lap.

"Ugh, there's egg on your napkin." We dissolve into watery laughter as I bat the napkin away. Then Dad grabs my arm and pulls me into a hug that smells like parchment and axle grease and cinnamon oatmeal cookies baking in the oven.

Home. He smells like home.

"I love you," I whisper, my chin on his shoulder.

He pulls back and regards me with love and pride shining from his eyes. "I love you, too." As he wipes the last of the tears from my eyes with his thumbs, a hint of the fierceness returns. "Dragon or no, if Fuoco ever hurts you I'll kill him with my own hands."

"I would expect nothing less," a deep voice says behind me.

I spin around to find Fuoco leaning against the stone doorway, his arms folded and a slight smile on his lips. A long, black coat stitched with brilliant green embroidery hangs from his broad shoulders. Black boots climb up his legs, which are once again wrapped in black leather. Between the halves of his coat, a shiny green corset hugs his waist. A green stud winks in his ear. He's a menacing figure of muscle and power. But his eyes are alight with amusement. And approval.

He straightens and walks to the end of Dad's bed. "I trust you're feeling better this morning, Maurice."

Dad returns Fuoco's gaze steadily. "Much better, thank you. If you break my son's heart, there will be hell to pay."

"Dad!" I half rise, ready to smother my father with a pillow.

But Fuoco bows at the waist, one hand sweeping elegantly in a courtly bow that should look ridiculous but steals my breath instead. He straightens, the look in his green eyes for my father alone. "I assure you, sir, my intentions toward your son are entirely honorable. I vow to care for him and protect him with my every breath." He turns his gaze to me, and the intensity of his stare makes my heart skip a beat. "Fate has given me the most precious gift in Beau. I'll never take him for granted. I'll make sure he has all the happiness he deserves." Fuoco turns back to my father. "And if you permit it, I would love nothing more than to court Beau. Assuming I have your blessing."

Heat suffuses my cheeks as my heart tries to beat from my chest.

My father's face creases into a smile. He glances at me, then nods. "I have faith you'll do right by my son. If that's what Beau wants, you have my blessing."

Fuoco offers another bow. "Thank you, sir. I won't disappoint you." His lips twitch. "Or provoke your ire." He moves around the bed and extends a hand to me. "Or yours, selsara," he adds softly.

My breath hitches as I let him pull me up, and my stomach flutters as he tucks my arm through his and turns to my father. "I'm taking Beau to visit the castle tailor. She's exceptionally skilled at her craft. I can have her stop by later to measure you for some new clothes."

Dad hesitates.

"She uses magical thread," Fuoco says.

Dad's face lights up. He shoots me a look.

"Go ahead, Dad," I say softly. "You didn't bring much with you from the village." *Because he doesn't own much.*

"That's true…"

"I'll send her around once she's finished with Beau," Fuoco says. He bids farewell to my father, then leads me from the infirmary with my hand tucked firmly in his elbow.

"I don't need any clothes," I say, the memory of the sumptuous breakfast spinning through my head.

Green eyes gleam as they travel down my body. "Nonsense, selsara. You need everything I can give you."

~

Twenty minutes later, I stand on a small round platform wearing an unbuttoned shirt and a pair of suit pants. A slender woman with a blond ponytail and a pair of delicately curved horns squats in front of me with several straight pins bristling from the corner of her mouth.

"Feet apart," she says through the pins. "I need to measure your inseam."

I bite my lip and do as she says. In the mirrors that line the workroom walls, a dozen copies of me do the same.

And a dozen Fuocos observe from a plush chair in the corner. In the mirror, his glowing green eyes study my ass. Then, as if he feels me watching him, he lifts his gaze to mine.

Slowly, he pulls a peach from his coat pocket.

My breath catches. Is that the same peach from the greenhouse?

"Perfect," the tailor murmurs. "Stay just like that." She lifts a hand, and a measuring tape flies from a table and into her palm, its long tail thumping against the platform. She gives it a stern look, a red sheen rolling over her blue eyes. "Settle down."

The measuring tape droops.

The tailor softens her tone. "Oh, go on, then. Do both inseams, his waist, and his shoulders. Make it snappy." She opens her hand, and the measuring tape flies out of it and dives between my legs.

"What the—?" I yelp, stumbling back.

Fuoco chuckles.

"Stay still," the tailor scolds. "He'll just be a minute."

"He?" I ask, my voice an octave higher than normal as the measuring tape wriggles around my groin, snuffling like a golden retriever.

"You can call him Gordon if you want," the tailor says,

pulling pins from her mouth. Her horns catch the light as she tugs at the cuff of my trousers.

Suddenly, the tape snaps into a straight line that extends to my ankle.

"Good boy, Gordon!" the tailor says. On the table, a feather pen springs upright and begins scribbling in a notebook. A second later, the measuring tape becomes fluid again. Tail waving, it whips itself around my waist and pauses. The feather pen continues its scribbling.

"Don't move, human," the tailor says, her tone matter-of-fact as she glances up at me. With a snap of her wrist, the pins fly from her fingers and embed themselves in a perfect circle around my cuff.

I gape at the pins, then look at Fuoco in the mirror. He grins and toys with the peach. His long fingers curl around the fruit, his thumb lodged in the crease. His movements deliberate, he drags his thumb up and down the cleft.

Heat blasts me, making sweat prickle under my arms. I jerk my gaze from his and study the workroom instead. Dad would love it. Magic practically oozes from the stone walls. Under the mullioned window, an invisible hand plies a needle and thread, the stitches neat and precise as they wind around a cloth-draped mannequin. On a distant table, a pair of scissors cut along a seam, the rhythmic sound steady and oddly soothing. Bolts of sumptuous fabrics in all shades and textures line the walls. The air is thick with incense and the charcoal-like scent of brimstone.

"Hurry along, Gordon," the tailor says, standing and giving the measuring tape an expectant look.

Snuffling and wagging, it winds around my chest and stretches across my shoulders. The feather pen scribbles, then drops back to the table. The measuring tape shivers, the loose tail beating against my hip.

"Good boy," the tailor says, extending a hand tipped with red claws the same shade as her lips. The tape shivers, then zips into her palm and curls into a coil. The tailor looks at Fuoco. "Do you want to see fabric swatches?"

"No," Fuoco says. Peach in hand, he unfolds his big body from the chair, his tall form filling the mirrors. "Just make one of everything."

The tailor props a hand on her hip. One arched eyebrow climbs high on her smooth forehead. "I have over twenty thousand bolts of fabric."

I suck in a breath. "I don't need that much!"

Fuoco ignores me as he addresses the tailor. "That will do nicely, Zara. Please deliver the garments to my quarters as you make them."

"Will do." Zara slants me a look from under her lashes. "I'll start with pajamas." Before I can say anything, she winks out of sight. A thin, black cloud hangs in the air for a moment before dissipating.

"Demons," Fuoco says, strolling to me. "Theirs is a dry humor."

I avert my eyes from the peach in his hand. "I thought they were like the cops of the Myth."

"Some are. But there are several daemonum. Zara is a *precisor* demon. Her stitches never unravel."

"Then I don't need twenty thousand outfits," I point out. Even with the platform, I have to tip my head back to meet his stare. "I don't even need a hundredth of that."

"You need clothes." His gaze roams down the strip of bare skin exposed by my unbuttoned shirt. "Although, I prefer you in nothing at all."

Desire blisters through me, tightening my dick. But I can't be distracted by lust. I tug the halves of my shirt together. "It's not fair for me to have so much when the villagers have so little."

Fuoco steps closer, his body heat searing my skin. His fangs flash as he growls, "We've already established that you're not returning to the village."

Fear and arousal twist through me. Before Fuoco, I wouldn't have found that combination particularly compelling. But it's as if the former fuels the latter. The same instinct that tells me Fuoco won't harm me also whispers that I might enjoy feeling a little afraid of him. Might revel in playing the role of his prey.

At the same time, a little voice warns me that there's a difference between sex and everyday life. It's one thing to capitulate in bed—quite another to surrender outside of it. If I don't stand up to him now, the power balance between us will be forever skewed.

I draw an even breath. "I understand that you want to give me things—"

"Everything."

"—but you have no idea what life is like in the village. If the townspeople find out how much breakfast you waste every morning, they'll storm the castle with pitchforks."

Green eyes flash. "They can try."

"They might if you antagonize them."

Exasperation flashes across his features. "I have no wish to antagonize them. I only ever wanted to help." He glances around the workshop. "I'll have Zara make them coats. She can use her most expensive fabric."

"They don't need fancy clothes." My voice climbs, and I fling an arm out, making my shirt gape wider. "They need their roofs repaired and enough firewood to get through the winter. They need to know the food they work hard for won't be snatched out of their hands by your enforcers."

Fuoco moves in a blur, his big arm snagging me around the waist and pulling me against him. His lips brush my forehead, and he breathes a word against my skin. "Done."

I put a palm on his chest and fight the urge to curl my fingers against the soft fabric and the hard muscle underneath. Drawing back, I stare into his emerald-green eyes. "You won't send new enforcers into the village?"

"Not if you don't wish it."

"I don't."

"Then, as I said, it won't happen." He slides his hand under my shirt and rests his palm over my ribs. "It's as simple as that, selsara."

My breath catches as the heat of his hand sinks into my skin. Slowly, he draws me forward, helping me step down from the platform. Then he turns us so he's standing behind me, both of us facing the mirror. Green flames dance in his eyes as he tugs the shirt from my shoulders. He wraps his arms around me, the peach still clasped in one hand that he rests over my pectoral.

"Look at yourself, Beau," he murmurs in my ear. He bends his head and drops a kiss on my shoulder, then slides his lips up my neck to nip at my earlobe. "How can I deny you anything?"

My heart slams against my ribs. I want to turn and look at him, but I can't tear my gaze away from his hands in the mirror. The air around us crackles, tiny currents of electricity licking over my skin.

He slides one hand down my abs to squeeze my aching cock, which is leaking all over the suit pants. Ordinarily, I'd be mortified but it's the last thing on my mind as he curls his long fingers around my dick and strokes. At the same moment, he lifts the peach to my mouth and whispers, "Bite."

With a whimper, I obey. Sweet, sticky juice explodes in my

mouth. More trickles down my neck. Fuoco unzips my fly and pulls out my dick.

"Look at that," he rasps, pressing a kiss to my temple as he begins working my cock. He doesn't have to tell me. Because I'm already looking everywhere. At his hands. At his big body behind mine, the contrast between my nudity and his fully clothed form so surprisingly hot I think I might combust. The trousers slip down my legs and puddle at my feet. I can't muster the energy to care. I lean into Fuoco's chest, letting him support me as pleasure pumps through my veins.

He tugs me harder against him, pressing his rigid erection into my cleft. With his other hand he lifts the peach to my lips again. "Bite," he grunts, jerking me faster.

I cry out as I sink my teeth into the peach. Juice courses down my neck and forms little rivers that traverse my chest. I let my head flop back on Fuoco's shoulder as juice trickles over my nipple, making me moan wantonly.

He sucks the peach juice from my neck, the emerald stud in his ear winking as he sinks his dark head lower and laps at the nectar. All the while, his big hand continues flying up and down my dick, which is hard as granite and shiny with precum. He grinds his dick into my ass, his thick cock rubbing up and down my cleft and the place I desperately want him to be.

"Please," I whisper.

He lifts his head and locks eyes with me in the mirror. With a grunt, he walks me forward, half-lifting me when I stumble around the trousers at my ankles. "Hands against the glass," he murmurs, tossing the peach aside and cupping my ass with both hands.

Nerves run a quick, fraught path down my spine, but I do as he says, my breath puffing against the mirror.

Fuoco drops a kiss on the spot where my neck meets my

shoulder. "Anything you don't want, you stop me. Understand?"

"Yeah," I rasp. But I want it. Whatever he's willing to give, I'll take it. I've waited so long for this.

He palms my cheeks, squeezing lightly. Letting me feel the heat of his hands. He traces light patterns over the quivering muscle, then pushes my cheeks apart and slips his fingers between them.

"Gods," I gasp, resting my forehead on the mirror.

"No, selsara," he rumbles, running his fingers up and down my cleft. He strokes around my pucker, teasing the most sensitive part of me. "No gods, my love. Only your mate."

My love. He can't mean it that way.

He pushes the tip of his finger inside me, and the thought spirals away as my spine turns to liquid. I groan against the mirror, my hips rolling and my breathing growing ragged. He pulls his finger out and rubs slow, firm circles around my entrance. His other hand finds my cock and strokes.

"Yes!" I gasp, thrusting my hips. "Please don't stop."

"I won't," he says, a smile in his voice as he brushes his lips over my nape. "Open a little more for me, Beau. I want to show you something." He works my dick faster, slicking my precum up and down my shaft. His finger against my hole disappears.

I lift my head in time to see him suck it into his mouth. Green eyes flash with heat and promise as he carries his damp finger back to my pucker and pushes inside.

My mouth opens but no sound emerges. I'm beyond speech. All I can do is watch his face in the mirror as he fingers me, filling me with delicious pressure while he strokes my dick.

"There you go," he says softly, pushing deeper. "Relax." He withdraws and then pushes inside again—and strokes something that makes pleasure crash through me in a thick, hot wave. *My prostate.* I've nudged it before when I play with myself. But my fumbling experiments have never felt like this —like everything good in the universe bundled together and injected directly into my veins. My eyes roll back in my head as I release a long, shuddering groan. My ass spasms around his finger, my muscles clenching tightly.

"That's it," he breathes against my neck, his hand flying up and down my dick. "So tight for me. Come on, baby." He pumps his finger, nailing that magical spot over and over. With each thrust, lightning shoots through my dick and balls.

The pleasure builds until I can't take any more. I cry out, my toes curling as I come, shaking and gasping against the glass. Fuoco holds me steady, one hand gripping my spurting dick. His thick finger still lodged inside me. I moan his name, shuddering with aftershocks as he slows his strokes and gently pulls his finger from my ass. When I sag, he turns me in his arms and guides my head to his shoulder.

"That was perfect," he whispers, his breath tickling my cheek. "How do you feel?"

"Tired." As his chest shakes with laughter, embarrassment floods me. I lift my head. "I didn't mean—"

"I know," he says, taking my lips in a slow, easy kiss. When he pulls back, he's smiling. "Would you have dinner with me tonight? There's something else I'd like to show you."

My face turns pink in the mirror. Even with my pants around my ankles and my leaking dick soft against my leg, I'm apparently capable of embarrassment. "Something better than that?"

Fuoco's smile grows as he strokes his knuckles down my jaw. "Oh yes, baby. Something much bigger and better than that."

CHAPTER 13
FUOCO

The Great Hall is even louder than usual. Laughter rings out, mingling with the upbeat tune the musicians play from the gallery. The full court is present, a buzz of excitement in the air. It's not every day a dragon formally takes a selsara. The *formally* part promises to be the main event of the evening.

I just have to hope it's not too overwhelming for Beau.

"Everyone is staring at me," he says under his breath, looking around the tables of dragons and other Myth creatures before pinning his gaze to his plate.

I place my hand over his on the arm of his chair, which the servants positioned next to mine at the head of the table. "Because they can't take their eyes off you." I fold my fingers around his. As he lifts an uncertain gaze to mine, I squeeze his hand. "And neither can I."

His cheeks turn pink, and my cock tightens at the sight of him clothed in a manner befitting his station. Zara outdid herself. Navy leather pants hug his lean thighs. A snowy white shirt peeks from the top of a jacket the same chocolate shade as his eyes. Twin rows of emerald-studded buttons march down his chest. Swirling green embroidery decorates his collar and flows down his sleeves, forming dragons in flight. He'd turn heads in rags. In court clothes, his masculine beauty is breathtaking.

But he's clearly uncomfortable with the attention he's receiving. If the night goes as planned, most of that attention will shift to me. My beast rises, eager to begin the ancient ritual I've waited my whole life to perform.

Beau's pulse flutters rapidly in his neck. He tugs at the collar of his jacket, exposing the hollow of his throat.

My mouth waters. I want to lean forward and lick the delicate skin at the base of his neck. Press my lips against his pulse and taste the sweetness that clings to him.

But I can't. Not yet.

"You've barely touched your plate," I say, gesturing to the dinner before us. I pick up a piece of warmed fig dripping with honey butter and hold it to his lips. "Let me help you."

His pupils dilate. The beat in his neck jumps faster, and the air seems to sizzle as he parts his lips. I slide the fig into his mouth, brushing my fingers against his tongue as I withdraw. A growl rumbles in my throat as he licks honey from his lips.

"More?" I rasp.

He nods, his dark eyes glittering with candlelight and anticipation. I bring a second fig to my own mouth and take a bite before offering him the rest. When he opens obediently, I drag honey over his bottom lip, then dip my head and lick it away before pushing the fig between his lips. When I keep my fingers in place, he whimpers and closes his lips around them.

"Suck," I murmur. Another sexy whimper breaks from him as he obeys, his dark lashes fluttering and that pretty blush stealing down his neck. Gaze locked with his, I pull my fingers away and suck my thumb into my mouth. He grips the arm of his chair, his eyes going heavy-lidded.

I reach for another fig when movement at the far end of the Hall catches my eye. Jasper appears in the doorway, his gossamer wings on full display. He's dressed to kill in a red suit that hugs his body and leaves nothing to the imagination. He's shirtless under his jacket, his smooth chest glowing faintly. The light glamour he typically wears is pulled back, revealing his tapered ears and otherworldly beauty.

He strolls through the Hall, pointing at courtiers and calling out greetings as he passes the tables. When a trio of muscle-bound ogres catcalls him, he blows them a kiss. A second later, one of the horned males yelps as red spots spread rapidly over his skin. His buddy next to him shoots Jasper a menacing look.

"You're asking for trouble, Lilygully!"

Jasper smirks. "You asked first, Krug the Ballbiter."

"It's Warhammer!"

"They both sound stupid."

At my side, Beau stiffens. "I've seen that man before," he says under his breath. "He came to the bakery."

I grunt, irritation prickling over my skin as I observe Jasper's progress. "He's a pixie," I mutter. "And a pain in the ass."

Jasper makes his way to the head table, where he sweeps me an insolent bow. He winks at Beau as he straightens, then looks at me and pulls his lapel aside, exposing his nipple bisected by an emerald-studded barbell. "I asked that dreamy jeweler in your basement to make me something special." He angles his head down and stares at his nipple, his brow furrowing. Almost to himself, he murmurs, "Although, maybe it's taboo to wear green piercings tonight?" He looks at me, his frown firmly in place. "I don't want to upstage your big, sexy dragon strip tea—"

"Get lost, Lilygully," I growl, my voice dipping lower than any human could speak. At a table under a row of banners, a group of centaurs launches into a rowdy song. A chimera seated behind them turns and spits fire over her shoulder, searing the beard of the loudest reveler.

"Oh, I would, flame zaddy," Jasper says, strolling forward. With a quick gust of his wings, he sails over the table and plops into the chair next to mine. As the unfortunate centaur's companions pour a pitcher of wine over his smoking face, Jasper lowers his voice. "But if you recall, you asked me to gather certain information."

It's my turn to stiffen. Slowly, I lift my goblet and speak behind the rim. "And do you have information for me?"

"Mmm." Jasper keeps his gaze on the centaurs as he says, "The male you seek has been sniffing around a certain bakery in the village."

I tighten my fingers on the goblet. Taking a sip, I swallow the rage that rises in my throat. "You're sure of this?"

Jasper slants me a slightly offended look. "My sources are solid." His blue eyes flick to Beau, who's a still, watchful presence on my other side. Across the Hall, the centaurs break into another song. Jasper pushes back from the table. As he rises, he speaks just above a whisper in my ear. "I'd keep my baker close if I were you."

My blood turns to ice in my veins. Jasper rounds the table, his wings scattering pixie dust as he reenters the throng of food and merriment. He flings his arms wide. "Somebody get me a drink!"

Cheers go up. The music continues to pump. Wine flows as the party continues, my courtiers unaware of the danger flowing like poison around us. At least, it appears that way. I sip my wine and let my gaze wander over the crowd, my senses primed for hints of treachery. Any sly looks or covert glances.

But there's nothing. Just bawdy laughter and colorful celebration. One of the centaurs snags Jasper around the waist and pulls the pixie into his lap. Jasper laughs and runs his hand down the male's broad chest, his sober expression from a moment before replaced with his usual insouciance.

"Fuoco?"

When I turn to Beau, worry brims in his eyes. He glances at Jasper and starts to say more, but I lean in and kiss him. He hesitates for a second, then opens under me with a deep moan that rumbles against my lips. I slide my tongue over his, tasting figs and honey, and then I move my mouth to his ear. "Later," I murmur. We'll have no secrets between us, but this isn't the right time.

Suddenly, the music changes. The strings go silent, leaving a rolling, rhythmic drumbeat. *Boom. Boom. Boom.* It shivers around the Hall, the sound primitive and impossible to ignore.

Beau pulls back as all eyes turn to us.

To me.

I stand and gaze down at my uneasy-looking mate. "When a dragon finds his selsara, there is always rejoicing." I turn to my court and lift my voice. "Am I not right?"

Shouts of affirmation rise from those assembled, the cheers echoing off the stone walls and momentarily drowning out the sound of the drum. When the noise dies down, I leap onto the table. "But we don't leave it at that," I say.

"Take it off!" someone yells from the rear of the Hall. Laughter follows. The heckler's tablemate smacks him good-naturedly on the back of the head.

"Patience," I admonish, smiling as I nudge platters of half-eaten food out of the way with the tip of my boot. Servants spring forward and help, quickly clearing a space. When they retreat, I turn to Beau, who stares up at me with wide brown eyes. The pulse in his neck flutters more rapidly than ever.

"We don't leave it at that," I repeat softly, unlacing my corset. A dragon rises from a nearby table and moves to help me.

Beau sucks in a breath.

"When a dragon takes a selsara," I say, "his selsara must take him, too."

Anticipation ripples through my courtiers, but I pay them no mind as my corset drops to the table. Beau's brown eyes follow the path of my fingers as I unbutton my shirt.

The drumbeat rises around me, vibrating across the stone floor and shaking the table beneath my feet. I slip my arms from my sleeves and toss my shirt away. Scales shimmer over my chest in a hundred shades of green. The bars through my nipples wink in the candlelight. Murmurs rise behind me as the drumbeat grows faster. Wilder.

Beau's lips part. He grips the arms of his chair, his knuckles going white.

I bend and remove my boots. The murmurs swell, becoming chants. Magic crackles in the air.

Ritual.

Beau swallows hard as I unbuckle my belt. I fling it aside and unlace my pants, my dick straining against the leather. My selsara's dark eyes go to my groin. He licks his lips.

My dragon hums in my chest as I push my pants down my hips, freeing my shaft that leaks for him. It bobs, my Prince Albert catching the light as I step out of my pants and stand nude before my mate.

The drumbeat pulses around the Great Hall. The courtiers' chants climb higher and higher. Beau's chest rises and falls faster as his gaze roams my body, returning again and again to the golden ring through my glistening cockhead. Precum beads at my slit and drips onto the table.

"I'm dripping for you, selsara," I purr. "Touch me. Accept me. Allow me to be yours."

Beau bites his lip, his white teeth digging into pink skin. Gods, I want to bite him there. Bite him everywhere.

I lift my arms away from my sides. Pitching my voice low, I look into my mate's eyes. "What do you say, selsara? Will you take me?"

CHAPTER 14
BEAU

I can't breathe. I can hardly think as I stare at Fuoco standing above me. His shaft sticks out from his hips, the thick, round head dripping with arousal. The drumbeat stops abruptly. Silence reigns.

Will you take me?

The Great Hall seems to hold its breath—the various monsters of the Myth waiting for my answer. Thank goodness my father isn't present. The shock might actually kill him. Hell, the shock might kill *me*. My heart thumps wildly, each beat echoed in my dick, which is embarrassingly hard. This scenario shouldn't be enticing. It should be scandalous.

And it is...but it's also titillating in a way I can't deny. Fuoco stands before me, completely unashamed of his nudity. Tiny flames dance in his eyes as he holds my stare. His body is perfection, every line taut and powerful. Broad, thick shoulders. Trim waist and rippling abs. His biceps flex as he holds out his arms, his palms turned up. Brilliant green scales cover him from neck to thigh, his golden skin still faintly visible underneath. It's like the two halves of his spirit mesh and coexist within him—and his beast is never too far from the surface. His beautiful cock thrusts proudly in my direction, the thick length curving upward. The head is deep crimson, the wet slit pierced cleanly by the golden, emerald-studded ring that fills me with a mix of lust of apprehension.

"Beau," he rasps, stepping forward, his feet as elegant and perfectly formed as the rest of him. For a moment, visions flood my head. Me on my knees pressing a kiss to one of his high arches. Me sprawling in a big chair with my legs flung apart, Fuoco dragging his bare foot up and down my dick...and then delving lower, his strong toes wriggling under my sack to stroke the sensitive skin around my hole. Me crawling up the foot of an oversize bed and playfully nipping at his ankle.

My breath catches as I blink rapidly, banishing the images from my mind. But the reality before me is just as riveting. Fuoco waits. Behind him, the whole court waits.

"Selsara," Fuoco murmurs, lowering himself to his knees. His scent—fire and spice and man—spins around me, invading my lungs. The piercings through his nipples and cock head wink in the Hall's soft light. "Say you'll take me, selsara. Say yes."

Time stops. The world stands still, the only two beings me and the dragon lord kneeling before me. Slowly, I nod. "Yes."

The Hall erupts into chaos. Cheers split the air. The musicians strike up a new song, this one fast and boisterous. Chairs tumble backward as Myth creatures stand and pull partners into a dance. Others pour wine. Jasper Lilygully throws his head back and laughs as a male with shiny black horns leans close and says something in his ear.

These things happen in some distant universe. Because the only thing I see is Fuoco's grin. It spreads wider as he rises, steps down from the table, and pulls me to my feet.

"What are you—?" My question ends in a gasp as he swings me into his arms. Hoots and applause follow us as he strides down the rows of tables to the big double doors.

"I can walk," I protest, fighting the urge to squirm. Something tells me that'll only make things worse. Knowing Fuoco, he'll simply toss me over his shoulder and keep going.

Green eyes gaze down at me with satisfaction—and a healthy dose of lust. "I'm aware, selsara. But you'll have to indulge me, because I like carrying you. And I'm too impatient to wait."

Wait for what? The question hovers on my tongue, but I hold onto it. Because I already know the answer, and it sets my heart fluttering as I settle deeper into his arms.

He walks quickly, the castle walls blurring as we wind our way through corridors and chambers. Within moments, we enter the courtyard. The stones are soaked in moonlight, the dragon statues around the perimeter stretching toward the night sky.

Fuoco sets me down and gives my forehead a quick peck. "Wait here." He strides a few dozen steps away and shifts, the transformation no less spectacular than the first time I witnessed it. His tail sweeps over the stones, striking sparks as he lumbers back to me. His glittering scales rival the moon. His claws are longer than my body.

But his eyes are gentle as he lowers his head and gently thumps his snout against my stomach. Warm breath puffs from his nostrils. He draws back, then offers an upturned paw. When I scramble into it, he nuzzles the top of my head and curls his claws around me protectively.

Then he launches us into the sky.

We soar high above the castle grounds, the cold wind whipping my hair. Once again, his body heat prevents me from getting too chilled. Below us, the village sparkles, its lights twinkling in the darkness. Fuoco spreads his wings wide, turning us and flying North. We cross rivers and streams, passing through fog banks and clouds. I cling to his claw, my heart racing as we climb higher and fly faster.

Finally, after what feels like hours of flight, a mountain range appears, its slopes shrouded in mist. Fuoco circles twice, then lands in a narrow valley tucked between two peaks. As he shifts, I drag crisp mountain air into my lungs, my head tipped back as I take in the blanket of stars winking overhead.

"It's beautiful," I murmur as Fuoco returns to my side.

"It's yours," he says, taking my hand and leading me to a stone door hidden behind a cluster of boulders. The door swings open at his touch, revealing a large corridor carved from the rock. Crystals as big as my fist sparkle from the floor to the ceiling, where chandeliers dance with blue flames. Fuoco tugs me inside, his hand warm in mine. "Everything here is for you, Beau. Come see it."

He leads me deep into the mountain, but it doesn't feel like we're underground. The air is warm. The ceilings soar overhead. The crystals in the walls turn to gemstones—rubies and garnets and sapphires as blue as the ocean. After several minutes, the corridor opens into a sprawling chamber.

And I freeze in place, my jaw dropping open as I look upon splendor that's like a gateway to another world. The walls shimmer with ribbons of silver and gold. More sparkling chandeliers hang overhead. In the center of the room, a massive fountain carved from black marble spouts crystal-clear water toward the ceiling. Plush rugs cover marble floors. Chairs and sofas are arranged in groups around tables carved from stone and studded with gems. High overhead, a window reveals the sky with its blanket of stars. A roaring fireplace crackles, its blaze setting all the gems in the room twinkling.

It's a room fit for a king—or a dragon lord.

"Come over here," Fuoco says, leading me to a sunken sanctuary of enormous silk and velvet pillows. His bed, I realize, goosebumps lifting on my skin. He's still nude and aroused, his cock bobbing as we descend to a cushioned platform softer than a cloud. Tiny diamonds sparkle along the golden ring that dangles from the tip of his dick.

"Your piercings..." I clamp my mouth shut before I can voice my errant thoughts.

But it's too late. "What about them?" Fuoco asks, pulling me down to the pillows. A smile plays around his mouth as he brushes his fingertips over the blush I can feel in my cheeks. "Let me guess, you noticed they disappear when I shift?"

"Yes," I rasp, trying not to stare at the monster between his legs.

"It's dragon magic. The metal is spelled to adapt to my beast form. It doesn't truly disappear. Just grows small enough to tuck behind my scales." His eyes shimmer with amusement as he eases me onto my back and comes down beside me. "And if you're wondering, my curious little selsara, my cock retreats into a sheath when I take dragon form. If it didn't, I'd probably have a hard time flying."

"I—" I gasp as he flips the button of my trousers and slips his hand inside to grasp my dick. "I wasn't wondering."

"Liar," he whispers, smiling.

I bite my lip. "Why do you have it?" I clear my throat. "That, um, piercing."

His smile spreads. He rolls me under him and grinds his dick against mine. "Because it feels fucking amazing."

"*Oh,*" I gasp, my hips lifting on their own, my body eager for more friction. More *him*. "That's a good reason."

His laugh puffs over my face. "Indeed, it is," he murmurs, then lowers his lips to mine.

The kiss is slow and languid, as if we have all the time in

the world. He teases me with his tongue, exploring my mouth until pleasure eddies through me in dizzying waves. His big hands roam everywhere—stroking my sides, pulling me closer, tugging at my beautiful clothes like they're rags instead of precious leather and silk.

My trousers go first, followed by my jacket and shirt. Then I'm nude beneath him, my feverish skin pressed against his. He kisses his way down my body, dipping and swirling over each nipple before moving to my abdomen and tracing feathery lines along the ridges of my abs. When he reaches my cock, he grabs my hips in both hands and sucks my cockhead into his mouth. He tongues my slit, dipping into the tiny opening over and over before taking me straight to the back of his throat.

I moan loudly, my head thrashing back and forth as he bobs up and down on my dick. He caresses my thighs, pushing them up so I'm splayed open, my knees pulled to my shoulders. Then he shoves them higher and buries his face in my ass.

"Fuoco!" I gasp, lifting my head as the exquisite and unfamiliar sensation barrels through me. His eyes glint with heat—and hints of mischief—as he pushes my cheeks wide and laps at my rim. It's slippery and hot and so, so good. "Fuck," I whimper, my head flopping back.

His chuckle drifts up to me as he teases my hole, swirling his tongue around my entrance. Pushing it inside me and getting me so wet his saliva drips down my crack. I rush toward that bright edge of bliss, my toes curling as he works me, thrusting his tongue so deep I claw at the pillows and scream his name. He slides a hand between my legs to cup my balls as he pumps his tongue, driving it into my hole over and over.

"You—" I writhe, panting and struggling to string words together. "You have to stop!"

He pulls back, rising to his knees and flashing a teasing smile as he wipes the back of his hand over his mouth. "You really want me to stop, baby?" He flops on top of me, his hips snug against mine. He rolls them against me, grinding our dicks together. As I shudder, he brushes my hair off my sweaty forehead. "No," he whispers gently, "I don't think you want me to stop."

I groan, rutting against him because I can't stay still. Not when his dick is so hard and perfect between us. "No," I say in a ragged voice. "I don't want you to stop."

"Do you want me to make love to you?" he murmurs, brushing his lips over mine. The look on his face is so tender that tears burn my eyes.

My heart hammers in my chest as I nod, unable to form words around the lump in my throat. He smiles against my lips, a satisfied sound rumbling from his chest as he captures my mouth in a slow, easy kiss. He rummages under a pillow and produces a little bottle of lube, then grins when I fail to muffle the mortified sound that escapes me.

"Do you know what this is?" he asks, drizzling moisture on his fingers.

I give him a look. "I'm not *that* inexperienced."

His soft laughter vibrates my chest as he tosses the bottle away and slicks himself. As he settles back over me, he fingers the rest of the lube into my hole. He kisses the tip of my nose. "Well, you're about to be a lot less inexperienced, selsara."

I stroke his shoulder, anticipation making me bold. "Get inside me."

"Yes, sir," he murmurs, rocking his hips against mine as he nips at my bottom lip. He slides a hand between our bodies and lines up the head of his cock with my entrance. He hesitates, his eyes soft. "The piercing won't hurt you. I'll go slow."

He plants a gentle kiss on the curve of my eyebrow. "Do you trust me?"

I nod, breathing him in. Feeling the slick head of his cock poised at my quivering entrance. I'm soaked and open, my most private muscles twitching from the things he did with his tongue. I spread my legs wider, drawing my knees to my shoulders. "I trust you."

"Good boy," he whispers, and those two words strike like a bolt of lightning, hot forks of electricity licking through me. I cling to his shoulders as he starts to push inside. I expect pain, but it never comes—just a slow, delicious pressure as his cock stretches me. Then the blunt edge of his piercing brushes the spot that makes me see stars.

I moan and dig my fingers into the muscle of his shoulders as he rocks in and out, giving me shallow thrusts. "More," I beg, needing it. I want to be filled.

"Beau," he rasps, rising to his forearms and rolling his hips. He slides deeper with each thrust, filling me inch by glorious inch. I gasp and tremble, my eyes squeezing shut as he pushes all the way inside. He bottoms out, his warm, heavy balls snug against my ass.

He pauses, giving me a moment to adjust to his size. But I don't need to adjust. It's like I was made for him, my body designed to accommodate his. He must know it, because he pulls back and thrusts into me again, nudging my prostate and sending a burst of ecstasy pinwheeling through me.

"Yes!" I cry, opening my eyes. We stare at each other, and I see my wonder reflected in his green irises. "Fuck, yes," I breathe.

A shaky laugh warbles from him. "Selsara," he whispers, his voice reverent. He repeats the movement, withdrawing until only the head of his cock remains inside me before ramming himself home once more.

I moan loudly, my ass clamping hard on his dick. Acting on instinct, I throw my legs around his waist, hooking my ankles together and digging my heels into his back so I can pull him deeper. Pleasure blisters through me, and we both groan.

Bracing himself above me, he closes his eyes on a long blink. "You feel so good," he says, his voice shaking. "Gods, Beau, I don't know how long I can hold out."

Pleasure and astonishment mingle in my veins. He's the most powerful being I'll probably ever meet, but right now he's helpless.

Because of me.

Swallowing hard, I brush my fingers over his cheek. "Then don't," I say. "Don't hold out. And don't hold back."

His lips seek mine for a deep kiss. And then he *really* moves, letting himself off whatever chain he kept himself on. He drives his hips against mine, fucking me harder with each thrust. He moves faster and faster, our bodies slapping together as he pumps his length in and out of me.

My orgasm tightens in my belly—a tempest poised to unleash. And he must sense I'm close, because he reaches between us and strokes my dick, jerking me in time with his thrusts. "Come for me now," he says, his voice husky with desire.

That's all it takes. Half a dozen strokes and I'm done, a hoarse bellow ripping from me as I clutch his shoulders and spurt all over my stomach. Streaks of cum lash my chest, one splashing as high as my chin.

He gives a shout and thrusts a final time, pumping hot cum deep inside me. We stay like that for a moment, my legs locked around his waist and his spent cock twitching in my ass. Then he pulls out carefully and rolls us so we're chest to chest, our legs tangled together.

"Are you okay?" he asks, stroking his thumb over my cheek.

"Mmm," is all I can manage, my limbs weak with pleasure. His cum seeps from me in a hot slide. Sweat cools on my skin. Sleep tugs hard at my lids. Once again, he's worn me out. I'm going to be sore as hell tomorrow. But I loved every minute of it. Already, I can't wait to be filled again.

He kisses me softly on the forehead. "That was everything I dreamed of."

A response floats in my consciousness—words that bob gently as I drift off, warm and secure in Fuoco's embrace.

It was everything I dreamed of, too.

THE NEXT TIME I WAKE, IT'S MORNING. FUOCO SLEEPS ON HIS stomach next to me, his arms hugging a pillow and his face turned away. Light streams through the window in the ceiling and plays over his body, highlighting the elegant dip of his spine and the firm, round curves of his bare ass. His long legs are slightly spread, giving me a glimpse of the piercing behind his heavy sack.

I rise, my face heating as my body aches in places that have never ached before. Taking care not to step on Fuoco, I clamber nude from the sunken pit. My clothes are folded neatly on a nearby chair. Pulling on my pants and shirt, I take a minute to gaze around at Fuoco's hideaway. It's no less spectacular in the daytime. Gemstones wink at me from a variety of surfaces. The marble veining in the walls glitters in the sunlight. The fountain splashes gently, water bubbling toward the vaulted ceiling before falling into the large bowl at the base.

And on the far side of the chamber, a stone archway offers a glimpse of something that makes my heart rate pick up.

Books.

I'm across the room and through the archway in seconds,

and I stifle a gasp at the sight that greets me. Not just books—a full library. Bookcases climb up the walls, every shelf lined with leather-bound volumes. I run my fingertips down one row of spines, then turn and admire the rest of the room.

And there's a great deal to admire. Colorful tapestries hang in the spaces between the bookshelves. A large mahogany desk sits near one marble-veined wall, its surface piled high with papers and parchment. A globe with a carved dragon curled around its base perches on the corner. Several plush armchairs scatter through the room, each one inviting me to curl up and lose myself in a story.

Heavy footsteps vibrate the floor under my feet. A second later, Fuoco bursts through the archway and staggers to a halt.

"Beau!" Instantly, green flames wreath his head. Tension radiates from him. The dragon scales across his chest gleam as he heaves a breath. He steps forward, his eyes narrowing. "You left without telling me."

I back up, my shoulders bumping the bookcases. "I d-didn't—"

"You can't do that." He slashes a hand through the air. "You can't *leave*."

Confusion swamps me. I point to the archway behind him. "I came from the—"

"What were you thinking?" The flames around his head leap higher. "You could have been hurt! Don't you ever do something like that again, do you understand?" He leans forward, his fangs showing between his lips as his voice climbs to a roar. "If you don't go places with *me*, you don't go places at all."

In a flash, anger replaces my confusion. My feet carry me forward until I'm close enough for the heat of his flaming hair to warm my skin. My voice is deadly low in my ears as I stare up at him. "What did you say to me?"

His eyes go wide. For a moment, he seems speechless. And maybe I'm imagining it, but I can almost swear that fear flickers in his eyes.

But my blood is pumping too hot for me to care. "I asked you a question," I say quietly.

The flames around his head dim. He drags in a breath, his big chest swelling. As he releases it, he rubs a hand over his mouth. "You're right," he mutters behind his palm. When he lowers his hand, his voice is tight with regret. "I had no right to speak to you that way. It's just that..." He stares at me, and flames flicker among the dark waves of his hair. "You mean more to me than you know. My dragon is...unsettled by any threat to you."

I glance at the main chamber through the arch behind him. "It's a threat when I walk from one room to another?"

"I woke and you weren't there," he says tightly. "I couldn't find you." He sucks in another deep breath. "Last night at dinner, Jasper Lilygully told me he scented Lirem around your bakery."

Memories surface—Lirem's grating laughter as he slammed his fist into my jaw. "You think he wants to hurt me?"

"I think he wants revenge." Fuoco clenches his fists. Then he seems to catch himself, because he forces his hands open. Anguish fills his green eyes. "Lirem knows you're the most important part of my life." Fuoco's gaze searches mine. "You *must* know that by now, Beau." He rubs the center of his chest, wincing as if his heart pains him. "I can't breathe without you."

Fear and wonder tangle within me. All those years denying who I am and what I want. I never thought I'd find someone to share my life with, let alone someone who wants me as much as Fuoco does. But he wants so much...

"Dragons are possessive about their mates," he says, "but

my beast is even more so when it comes to you." He takes another step, closing the distance between us. "My magic is powerful, and it produces powerful emotion in those who wield it."

Despite the weightiness of the conversation, curiosity sparks. "What is your magic?"

"Everything," he rasps, taking my hand in both of his. "I'm an elemental, Beau. I command earth, air, wind, and fire."

My heart beats faster. "What do you mean by command?"

"I can manipulate the elements around me. Speak to them in a fashion. Bend them to my will. I can make it rain when I want. Make the wind blow as hard as I wish. And I can bring fire to life with a thought." As if to demonstrate, he slides his hand up my arm, leaving a trail of heat in his wake. "But the emotions that come with my gift are overwhelming. If I'm not careful, they'll consume me. If that happens, it won't take long for my mind to break."

The hair on my nape lifts. "And what happens then?"

"The world burns."

Coming from anybody else, such a statement would sound grandiose or even a bit silly. But seeing him now—his eyes wide and stark—I know he means it. He's capable of burning everything down.

He stares at me a moment longer before stepping back. He draws an even breath, and the flames in his hair wink out. "My gift is both a blessing and a curse. I have to keep my emotions in check, especially now that I've found you. Even the *thought* of losing you could tip me over the edge. And now that I know Lirem seeks you, my need to protect is overwhelming."

"Okay, but do you really need to protect me from your library?" I wait for him to deny it—maybe laugh and dismiss such a notion as absurd. Instead, he says nothing, his gaze deadly serious. Alarm bells clang in my head. "Fuoco, I can't live my life glued to your side."

"Would it bother you to spend that much time with me?"

"Honestly, *yes*." I gesture at the books around us. "I want to be with you, but I have interests of my own. I love reading—"

"Which you can do here."

"—and baking. I have a business I worked hard to build."

He folds his arms, his expression mulish. "I've spent centuries amassing wealth. You don't have to work anymore."

"I *like* working. And I don't just bake for profit, Fuoco. I enjoy it."

"You can bake here," he insists, frustration lacing his tone. "Or in the castle. You can have anything you want. Anything." His fingers twitch at his sides like he's just barely managing to keep himself from reaching for me. His voice climbs again. "I want to give you the world but I can't do that if I can't keep you safe, and I can't keep you safe while Lirem is out there!"

"So you'll tether me to your side until you find him?"

"If that's what it takes."

"What about after?"

His jaw is tight, the look in his eyes so stubborn and unyielding I want to slap him just to shock him out of this ridiculous mindset. How can I make him understand that I need more than nice clothes and pretty books? The apprehension I felt over breakfast in his bedchamber resurfaces.

"I can't be happy as a pet," I say firmly. "A gilded cage is still a cage." I square my shoulders. "I'm not a warrior. Not even close. But I'm not a coward, either. I don't want to be coddled, Fuoco. I need to be able to make my own decisions, and that includes taking risks. I'm not saying I want to run into the village and wait for Lirem to find me. But I need freedom of movement. If you lock me in your castle and dress me up in outfits, it'll wear me down until there's nothing left of me. And then you won't have me at all."

"Don't say that," he whispers, pain flitting through his eyes.

"Then don't treat me like a piece of jewelry you own. Treat me like an equal."

He takes my hand. "You *are* my equal. All I've ever wanted was for you to rule by my side."

I exhale slowly, the tension in my chest easing a bit. If he wants me to rule with him, maybe I should show him what that looks like. "As a ruler, what's the most pressing issue in front of you right now?"

"Protecting you," he says without hesitation.

I fight the urge to punch him. "Okay, the thing after that."

"Finding Lirem."

I smile and squeeze his hand. "Let's start with that. We should probably go to the village, right? If Lirem was around the bakery, we should check it out."

He frowns, clearly not liking the idea of me anywhere near a spot where Lirem might be lurking.

"You'll keep me safe," I say. "You're the only dragon shifter in the syndicate, right? The other dragons can't best you in a fight."

He grunts.

"Does that mean yes?"

"Yes," he says, his expression so sulking I could almost laugh. Then inspiration strikes. "We can take food from your greenhouse to the village. I've distributed bread for years. If the people see you doing it, it'll go a long way toward shifting their opinion of you."

Surprise—and something that might be respect—flares in his eyes. "You really think so?"

"It's worth a try."

He hesitates for a moment before finally nodding in agreement. He pulls me against him, his mouth inches from mine. "We'll go, selsara. But you are never out of my sight."

"I wouldn't dream of it," I say, and then I melt under his kiss.

CHAPTER 15
FUOCO

I swoop over Beau's village, my emotions rocketing back and forth between dread and hope. Beau perches carefully in my claw, looking out at the world below us. In the other claw, I carry a large wooden wagon laden with all the things he thought the humans might want—cured meats, canned and fresh fruit, salted seeds, and plenty of freshly baked bread.

His insistence on being by my side for this visit has my dragon simmering just under my skin. I imagine Lirem around every corner, although I don't think he'd be foolish enough to target Beau in front of me. But the idea of it has me bristling, fire building and curling in my throat. I huff out a stream of smoke to dispel it. I've got a lot to make up for when it comes to the humans. Setting their village aflame wouldn't be the most auspicious start.

I glide swiftly down to the village square, dropping Beau and the wagon to the ground and shifting fast. He hands me clothing and I yank the pants and shirt on before swinging a dark cloak around my shoulders. Faces appear in windows. Astonished eyes goggle at us.

An odd sensation flutters in my gut, like butterflies struggling to fly out of my mouth. Am I...nervous?

I'm ready for whatever response the villagers throw at me. Anger, fear, accusations. Not that my preparation will make today any easier. I've avoided humans for over half a century. Aside from Beau, I have no clue how to interact with mortals.

"Remember what we talked about," Beau says softly at my side. "Just be yourself. Talk to them." He brushes his hand against mine as if he can sense my discomfort. As villagers emerge from the buildings, he waves at a small girl peering at us from a window. A few men step into the street, their gazes wary and their bodies tense. One grips a pitchfork in a tight fist.

"A little on the nose," I say to Beau under my breath.

"Behave," he murmurs back, a smile in his voice. Then he lifts a hand in greeting. "Henry! Bartholomew! Join us. We come with aid."

Slowly but surely, the square fills with villagers. The little girl from the window darts out the door only to be yanked back inside by a heavily pregnant woman.

Tangible tension floats over the group. It's in the men's tight shoulders and the women's hostile stares. I remind myself what Beau told me before we left the castle—winning the people over isn't going to be easy, but each town we visit and every step we take to mend past wrongs will help.

Clearing my throat, I shove my hands into my broad cloak sleeves, doing my best to appear smaller and less threatening. "Beau and I have brought food and supplies. I recently learned that my enforcers were stealing from you. For too long, they terrorized the people of my syndicate. I didn't know, and I'm deeply sorry for what happened. I've come to make amen—"

"You expect us to believe that when all you've done is lie and steal?" The harsh feminine voice cuts across the courtyard. A second later, a young woman steps out from between two buildings and stops at the edge of the crowd. Her dark curls gleam in the sun. Bright blue eyes narrow as she looks from me to Beau.

It's the woman who helped herself to Beau's pastries when he wasn't around to stop her.

She accused me of thievery then, too.

I hold her stare. "As I was saying, I've come to make amends."

"What have you done to Beau?" she demands. "Just days ago he hated dragons the same as the rest of us. Now, he stands by your side. This reeks of dark magic."

A chorus of shouts rises among those assembled. The man with the pitchfork tightens his grip around the handle.

Elemental power stirs in my chest, sharpening my senses. Chilly air curls against the stones. The water in the fountain behind the woman trickles through old, leaking pipes. The earth below the courtyard calls to me, ready to do my bidding. It would be so easy to answer its call—to command the ground to open its jaws and swallow her whole.

Beau puts his hand on my forearm as he addresses the crowd. "Two of the three enforcers are dead. The third is in hiding. Lord Fuoco killed the others for their crimes against us. I saw this with my own eyes. He killed them the moment he found out what they were doing." Beau gestures at the wagon behind us. "This isn't enough to make up for the years we endured Lirem, Nazzar, and Varden, but it's a start. Please, take what you need."

Pride blooms in my chest. The elemental madness recedes as the heat from Beau's hand seeps under the sleeve of my cloak and into my skin.

"Is it poisoned?" someone shouts from the back.

"No," Beau calls out. He gazes around the crowd, meeting villagers' eyes one by one. "You all know me. Trust me when I tell you there's nothing to fear."

A man in the front looks at the wagon. Then he turns to the people around him. "We could use the food."

Several villagers nod. Rumbles of agreement move through the crowd.

I lift my voice. "There is more where this came from. If you give me a list of what you need for the winter, I'll bring it from my own stores."

"Been hoarding it, have you?" It's that fucking dark-haired woman again, shoving through the crowd to glare daggers at me. The cloying scent of rosewater sears my nostrils as she props her hands on her hips. "You took it from us and now you'll give it back?" She releases a short, bitter laugh. "How generous."

My beast moves under my skin. At the same moment, Beau tightens his grip on my arm. His touch steadies me, soothing my dragon and curbing my tongue.

I offer the woman a stiff nod. "You're right. My enforcers stole from you. I take responsibility for their actions, which is why I'm here. I want to give back."

The tiny girl from the window darts through the crowd and runs up to me, skidding to a stop. Several villagers gasp.

I drop to a knee so I'm closer to eye level with the child. "How may I help you, little one?"

"I saw you before," she whispers. "Your hair was green!"

I smile. "That's right." I gesture toward the wagon. "Is there something special you'd like from what I brought?"

She holds her arms out in the age-old gesture demanding to be picked up. More gasps ascend from the crowd as I lift her. Swinging her high, I place her on the wagon.

"Pick anything you want," I tell her, and she flashes me a bright, gap-toothed smile as she perches on the edge and surveys the goods within. After a moment's consideration, she chooses a giant loaf of pumpkin bread and clutches it to her chest. I help her down, and she darts back into the crowd.

For a moment, the square is silent. Then an elderly man steps forward. "Got any meat in there, Beau?"

Beau is quick to help the man, reaching into the wagon and withdrawing a shoulder of cured pork bundled in twine. "Here, Archibald. Enough for a roast and then some."

The man dips his head as he accepts the meat. Then he turns to me, his gaze wavering between distaste and watchfulness. Eventually, he offers a curt nod before shuffling back into the crowd.

A few beats pass. Then the floodgates open. Villagers surge forward, calling out requests. Beau and I busy ourselves hunting for items and parceling them out. The dark-haired woman retreats into a store, where she stands at a window and glares at us with folded arms. I receive plenty of glares from other villagers, but I grit my teeth and stay the course.

As I work across from Beau in the bed of the wagon, he meets my gaze, his eyes shining with affection. "You're doing a wonderful job," he murmurs. "I'm proud of you." The words are so low they're scarcely audible, but they ring loud as a bell in my chest. He's proud to be here. With me.

He's worth every moment of discomfort.

When the last of the food is gone, the villagers disperse. Several clap Beau on the shoulder as they depart, offering gratitude and a smile. The smiles fade as their eyes stray to me, but a few mutter "thank you" before they walk away. Then Beau and I stand alone beside the wagon.

He slips his hand into mine. "I think it went well. How about you?"

"They don't like me." The words sound sullen, and I smile ruefully as I lift Beau's hand and place a quick kiss on his knuckles. "Not like you do."

His cheeks turn pink, and he glances around like he's making sure no one heard. "It'll get easier." Chocolate eyes reflect the green flames in mine as he smiles up at me. "One step at a time, right?"

I nod. "One step at a time."

A week passes in a blur. Every day, Beau and I deliver food and goods to the towns in my syndicate. Some are less welcoming than others, but we always promise to return with the things they need. Beau keeps a running list, and watching him diligently add to it thaws something cold inside me.

He answers every question and listens to every request. He handles complaints with incredible grace. He's a natural with the people, who flock to him as soon as he flashes his warm smile.

I'm another story. Most of the villagers are still wary of me. Some are outright hateful. At best, they're indifferent. But they're all smitten with my selsara.

At every stop, we hear stories about what my enforcers did to my people. In a village in the far north, Beau asked a farmer what he needed to get his farm back on track.

"A new windmill," the man grumbled. "Varden set mine on fire for not paying taxes, 'cept I had paid them. He just wanted more, always more."

I placed my hand on the man's shoulder and turned him to face me. "I'll return every coin he stole with interest, and I'll see about getting a new windmill built immediately."

Fear sparked in the man's gaze. He stepped out of my grasp, but nodded and offered a clipped "thank you."

And so it's gone on for a week. Nazzar drowned someone's cow. Lirem broke all the windows in a tailor's shop and the man's leather-making supplies were ruined in a rainstorm. Varden took all the gold from one village's bank, loading it into big sacks and disappearing.

My enforcers' crimes make my stomach churn with shame. My dragon paces constantly in my chest, desperate to rip Lirem to shreds for his treachery.

Jasper checks in several times but offers no substantive updates on my missing enforcer. If the pixie's mice can't find Lirem, then he's gone so deeply to ground it could be years before he shows his face. I can't let that stand. So I begin every evening by pleasuring my mate—and afterward, while Beau sleeps, I take to the sky and scour my territory, hunting for any sign of Lirem.

As the days wear on without progress on that front, my mood sours.

Like tonight. Beau sits at my side in the Great Hall, his spicy-sweet scent doing nothing to chase away the stench of failure that burns my nose. My court is as rowdy as ever, but I can't seem to muster the energy to join in their revelry. A week of seeing hatred and disgust on the humans' faces sits like a weight around my shoulders. I'd love nothing more than to grab Beau, shift, and spin up through the clouds to leave my problems behind.

But that won't solve them.

I pick at the food on my plate, pushing it around before shoving it away. Maurice Bidbury's rich laughter brings my head up.

Beau's father sits beside my selsara, his wrinkled face glowing with good health. Maurice is clearly enamored with my court. He's constantly introducing himself to any magical creature who will speak with him. Fortunately, the courtiers reciprocate his interest. It turns out my selsara's sire is as endearing as my mate.

"Yes, Maurice," the dragon on Maurice's right rumbles with a throaty chuckle. "It's simple enough magic. The cobbler suggests what the tools should do, but they carry out the work themselves."

Beau turns to his father. "I've seen it, Dad. You should visit the cobbler to watch for yourself. And you could use some new shoes. I'll go with you if you want."

Maurice smooths his wisps of white hair. "I might take you up on that, son. Although, the ladies around here can't stop complimenting me on my new clothes. If I add shoes, they won't be able to keep their hands off me."

"Dad!"

The dragon who spoke of the cobbler gives a hearty laugh.

I toy with my wineglass as I observe them, my rings winking in the candlelight.

Beau meets my gaze, and his smile falters a little. *You alright?* he mouths.

I nod, forcing a smile. I didn't expect to fix everything immediately, but it's clear now that making inroads is going to take a very long time. The bright light at the end of my tunnel is Beau.

"As long as I have you, I'm perfect, selsara." I reach under the table to squeeze his knee. He ducks his head—but he also spreads his legs, allowing me to slide my hand all the way up his thigh. I grip it tightly, thankful I've got him by my side to sort through the messes I've made. "You amaze me," I murmur.

He's been tireless this week, never once complaining about the hard work of traveling from village to village.

My equal.

Chocolate eyes crinkle at the corners as his smile deepens. It's the seductive smile of a lover becoming comfortable. He no longer cares if someone sees that smile, or if his father observes us holding hands.

On Beau's other side, Maurice launches into an animated conversation about some fresh topic, waving his hands around as he illustrates a point.

But when I hear Lirem's name, I snap my head up to eye a dragon sitting farther down the table.

"What was that?" I demand. "What did you say about Lirem?"

The dragon gives me a wary look. "Just that I haven't seen him around in a few days." His brow furrows as he appears to contemplate it. "I haven't seen Varden or Nazzar either, come to think of it. Gods, they've missed out on quite a bit, but I suppose they're busy."

Maurice and Beau freeze.

Across the table, a pretty female dragon named Riselle sits forward, her amethyst eyes serious. "There's been talk, Fuoco. Rumors about why the enforcers aren't here."

Jasper hasn't uncovered anything to indicate Lirem has allies here in my court. And I can't keep Nazzar and Varden's deaths a secret forever. If anything, coming clean will lift one of the burdens that plague me.

Rising, I plant my hands on the table. "Nazzar and Varden are dead."

The dragons closest to me gasp, then a flurry of rushed murmurs carries the news down the tables. I draw myself up, letting my voice boom through the Great Hall. "They're dead for the crimes of theft and torture. They were stealing from the humans, hurting them and worse."

Another round of gasps peppers the air.

"What about Lirem?" someone calls from a nearby table.

A growl rumbles in my throat. "Lirem escaped after attacking my selsara." Every head swivels to Beau, who presses back into his chair, his throat bobbing.

Riselle stands. "He touched your selsara? He hurt Beau?" The look on her face tells me she finds it as shocking as I do. Harming another dragon's mate is a crime punishable by instant death. She tosses her hair over her shoulder, danger glinting in her purple eyes. "What's our next move, my lord?"

"I'll hunt him and then I'll kill him," I say, flames wrapping around my head. "And we're finished with enforcers. From now on, I'll work with all of my people directly."

Around the Great Hall, every human servant stands rooted to the ground. The familiar scent of fear fills the room.

Riselle gazes around at them. "This is not our way. Dragons didn't come to this plane to hurt people. I'm sorry."

For a moment, no one speaks. Then the dragon who spoke to Maurice stands. "Riselle is right. We aren't here to take advantage." He touches his fist to his broad chest and bows his head. "I'll do whatever I can to right this wrong."

One by one, dragons stand, their eyes gleaming as they echo the sentiment. After a moment, other Myth creatures join in.

Awe spreads through me as my court of partiers and merry-makers put down their wineglasses and commit to serving the people.

Riselle turns glittering amethyst eyes to me. "How do we get started, my lord? Tell us what you need and we'll do it."

Before I can answer, Tess crosses the Hall with a serving platter in her hands. She pauses before my table, her cheeks brilliant red as she darts a quick look at Riselle before staring at the ground. She speaks in a hushed voice that nevertheless echoes around the quiet tables. "Lord Fuoco and Beau have been delivering supplies to the villages. They've been making regular trips, but the people still need food and firewood to get through the winter." Tess tightens her fingers around the platter. "I just thought... Maybe you could..." She trails off, a mottled blush spreading down her neck.

Beau stands, rounds the table, and goes to Tess. He takes the platter from her and puts his other arm around her shoulders. They stand among my court of Myth creatures, both mortal and seemingly powerless. But their courage shines as brightly as any gem.

"Tess makes a great point," Beau says. "Fuoco and I have made a lot of progress, but we could use more help. I've got a list of items each village needs. Perhaps we can split up the responsibilities to distribute them more quickly."

The screech of chairs being pushed back fills the hall. As one, my courtiers raise their glasses.

"We are with you," Riselle declares. She swings toward me and inclines her head. "Whatever you require, my lord, we'll make it happen."

"I'll help, too," Tess says, her voice stronger as she looks at me from under Beau's arm. "If it pleases you, my lord."

I nod. "It would please me very much, Tess."

Her smile transforms her pale face from meek to lovely. Beau releases her, and she slips among the tables, her steps lighter than before.

As Beau returns to my side, Maurice rises and puts a hand on Beau's shoulder. "Your mother would be so proud of you, son." Eyes brimming with tears, he pulls Beau into a hug.

"I love you, Dad," Beau says. Around the Hall, courtiers glance their direction and smile. At a table near the double doors, Jasper catches my eye. The pixie winks, his wings flicking silvery dust into the air as he stands and walks from the Hall.

Probably up to something. I try to scowl after him, but I can't stop the smile that insists on spreading over my face. The atmosphere in the Hall is more subdued now, the wild carousing replaced with earnest conversation as courtiers discuss plans for taking food to the people. The transformation is so complete, it's like a spell descended over the court.

But as my gaze settles on Beau, I realize that's not quite right. The change is magical, but it's not a spell.

It's Beau. *He's* the magic. He's bringing humans and dragons together. He's flourishing by my side, not locked up in a glittering tower like my most prized possession. He's nothing I expected and everything I needed.

I'm going to tell him that tonight as soon as we're alone.

Maurice wipes tears from his face as he eases away from Beau. "It's been a wonderful evening, but I need to get to bed." Maurice's brown eyes twinkle as he looks from me to his son. "And I think that's where you two need to go, too."

"Oh my *gods*, Dad," Beau says, burying his face in his hands.

Maurice grins at me. With a chuckle, he claps Beau on the back before heading for the doors.

Smiling, I pull Beau's hands away from his face. "You heard your father." I tangle my fingers with his, then lift our joined hands to my mouth and bite his knuckle. "Bedtime."

We set a record getting to our bedchamber, and we stumble through the door locked in each other's arms. I stroke my tongue deep into his mouth, shoving my hips against his as he rips my shirt from my shoulders.

We fall into the bed and I yank his pants down, tossing them to the floor. He climbs on top of me with a big smile, then gasps when I flip us, flinging him to his back and pushing his legs up. With a wicked smile of my own, I dip down and suck his balls into my mouth, swirling my tongue around one swollen globe, then the other. I reach up and find his cock, which already drips for me.

"Fuck, Fuoco," he moans, gripping his knees and pulling his legs higher. "Don't stop."

Chuckling, I trail my tongue down to his pucker. I lap at his quivering hole as I stroke his hard length, teasing him until he's panting and rocking his hips to meet my mouth. When his thrusts grow wild and desperate, I sit back on my heels.

"Nooo," he whines, shooting me a faux glare from eyes gone glassy with lust. "Teasing was never part of our bargain, my lord."

"That bargain is finished," I say. I'll never threaten him again. My beast curls in my chest, content in the knowledge that I don't have to worry about Beau leaving me. He's *chosen* to stay, which is more precious to me than any treasure.

The lust in his eyes flares higher when I reach under a pillow. But as I withdraw two brilliant green gemstones, he sits up with a gasp.

"These are beautiful." He strokes the stones with careful fingers. Their light plays over his chest, scattering green sparks across his skin and making me bite back a groan.

"They're mating jewels." I give him one, and his hand dips under the gemstone's weight. "Dragons consider them sacred. If you accept mine, I'll bind it to your chest. Then I'll bind my own and our mating bond will be sealed."

He looks up at me, his chocolate eyes wide. "And what happens once we're bound?"

"We live together for eternity," I murmur, anxiety stirring. I'm asking for everything. What if he's not ready to give it? "This binds us soul to soul. If one of us dies, the other will as well. There is no greater bond among creatures of the Myth."

He studies the jewel, brushing his thumb over the glossy green surface. Just as my anxiety threatens to blossom into full-blown panic, he looks up and gives me the brightest, most beautiful smile. "I'd be honored, selsara."

Pleasure frazzles through me. My dragon roars under my skin. "You called me selsara," I rasp.

Beau hands me his gemstone. "Claim me. I accept."

Growling, I grip his shoulders and flip him into the pillows. Straddling his hips, I rub at a spot in the center of his chest. "I'll place this here while I take you. And when we come together, the jewel will bind itself into your skin."

A hint of unease enters his eyes. "Will it hurt?"

"No." I smile. "You'll come harder than you ever have."

Humor and heat shine in his eyes as he bites his lip. "That's hard to believe."

"I swear it. Are you ready?"

He nods, and the humor in his eyes fades, leaving only heat. "Yes."

I place his jewel carefully in the divot just under his pectorals. Then I hand him my stone and show him where to hold it against my skin. "Don't let go."

"I won't."

I grab the lube and drip a sticky string onto his bobbing cock. Then I toss the bottle aside and stroke moisture over his shaft. Precum beads at his slit as I coat him from base to tip.

He grunts, rocking his hips and bowing his spine.

"You need more, selsara?" I tease, slipping my hand down to his sack and slicking his balls. When he's shuddering, I work a finger into his hole. His cock leaks all over his rippling abs. "It's a wonder you need lube at all," I say. "You always get so wet for me."

"Fuck," he whispers, clenching so hard around my finger I almost lose my grip on his jewel. "It's too good." He groans when I push a second finger inside. "I'm losing my mind."

Smiling, I play with his hole a bit longer, stroking and

teasing in and out of his tight heat as I work him open. Then I grip my cock and slap it playfully against his before taking both of our dicks in hand. I rock my hips, stroking us together. Gripping our shafts, I fuck his cock with mine until we're both panting. As Beau cries out, I know I don't have long. My mate is ready.

"I've waited for you my entire life," I say, guiding my cock to his entrance. I push inside slowly, perfect heat and pressure engulfing me.

Beau's cries stretch into a full-on wail. He squeezes his eyes shut, but his hand pressing the jewel to my chest remains steady. "Fuuuck," he groans, the tendons in his neck taut.

I jerk my hips, burying my dick to the hilt inside him as white-hot pleasure streaks down my spine. Under the jewel, a burning sensation like a thousand tiny pinpricks stabs at my skin. I rock out of Beau, then slam back inside, jolting his body against the pillows.

"The jewel," he bellows, dropping a startled gaze to his chest. Just as quickly, his eyes roll back in his head and a wanton moan escapes him. "Gods! Fuck!"

I thrust harder, pumping my hips faster. My breaths come in short gasps as I lose all sense of time and place. The intensity between us mounts. With every thrust, the jewels glow brighter.

Beau opens his eyes, his gaze wild as he stares up at me. His breath is ragged, his skin flushed and slick with sweat. The jewel sears my chest as we approach our peak together. I push and pull in time with Beau's choked cries, sweat sheening my skin as the stone grows even hotter.

My vision tunnels, focusing solely on Beau as pleasure builds like a wave inside me. The burning sensation intensifies, and I keep going, my thrusts jerky and uncoordinated as my balls tighten and the bright, shiny edge of release speeds toward me.

Beau gets there first. He convulses, his cock spurting across his heaving abs. My mouth hangs open as I watch cum paint his skin. Then I'm coming, too, a scream ripping from my throat as I line Beau's ass with my release. I roar, the sound somewhere between my human voice and the animalistic, predatory bellow of my dragon.

Red and green galaxies burst behind my eyelids as I ride the wave of ecstasy with my mate. He writhes beneath me, his hand never moving from the jewel he presses to my chest. The crescendo ebbs and rises again, and I'm obliterated from the inside out, my orgasm so powerful my teeth gnash together, my jaw locking tight as I curl over him, shuddering so hard I swear I can feel my bones grinding to dust.

Long minutes later, I blink my eyes open. Beau pants beneath me. His lips are parted, his chest rising and falling as he takes great, gasping breaths. In the center of his chest, his mating jewel glows as if lit from within.

My mouth falls open as a cascade of green light shines from the gemstone, illuminating his face and bouncing off the walls around us. I pull out and fall onto my ass, tears pricking my eyes as I gaze at my mate.

Beau sits up. As he looks down at his chest, I brace myself for the worst. I wait for him to panic or demand I remove the bond, which I can't do. We're locked in this together now.

He lifts his head, his eyes shining with unshed tears as he gazes at the matching jewel in my chest. Going to his knees, he brushes his fingers over my pecs and the glittering edge of the gemstone. "This is the most beautiful thing I've ever seen."

A split second later, he gasps as I tackle him to the pillows. I stretch my body over his, my hands pinning his wrists next to his head. "I love you," I blurt. "I've loved you for my whole life, but having you here with me..." I drag in deep breaths as I struggle to finish the sentence. "I can't imagine anyone else I'd want this with, Beau. Selsara." My voice breaks as emotion overtakes me. So I stop talking. Burying my nose in his neck, I suck in deep breaths of him. Cinnamon. Sugar. All the smells of his bakery are imbued in his skin.

"I love you, too," he says.

"I will always protect you," I vow. "No matter what comes."

"I know," he says, rubbing a hand over my back. He turns his face into my shoulder and smiles against my skin. "I'll protect you, too. You're mine, Fuoco."

Bound for eternity.

I've never been happier.

Chapter 16
BEAU

Fuoco's light snores fill the room. As usual, he lies on his stomach with his legs flung apart. Smiling, I stroke my fingers through his hair. Poor dragon. I wore him out.

For once, I'm too worked up to sleep. But maybe that has something to do with the jewel embedded in my chest. Its green light is dimmer now—because Fuoco is sleeping. My selsara. After our second round of lovemaking, he explained that my gemstone will always reflect his state of mind. Likewise, his will echo mine. When he's at rest, the jewel in my chest will rest, too. *"And when I'm aroused, selsara, you'll feel it everywhere."*

He wasn't kidding.

Moonlight pours through the window and splashes over the bed, joining the light cast by my jewel. *Bound for eternity.* Fuoco and I didn't exchange vows in the traditional sense, but we're as good as married now. Maybe *more* than married. It's not like I can divorce him.

My heart thumps faster, and something that feels a little bit like panic scrabbles down my spine. I didn't hesitate when Fuoco presented me with the mating jewels. But maybe I should have? How many people marry the first person they fall for? Fuoco is immortal, and now that my life is linked with his, I'll live as long as he does. What happens a hundred years from now? A *thousand* years from now?

Fuoco stirs, the muscles in his back rippling as he snuggles the pillow more tightly. I hold my breath while he moves, then slowly release it when he finally settles down. Slipping from bed, I go to the big wardrobe and pull on the first clothes I find. There's one person in this castle who knows me better than I probably know myself. Maybe he can give me some advice.

Ten minutes later, Dad offers me a startled smile as he opens his door. "Beau! What are you doing up at this hour?" His snowy brows pull together. "Is everything okay? Are you sick?"

"No," I say quickly. "I'm totally fine. But I need to talk to you about something."

He nods and steps back so I can enter. A familiar whirring sound greets me as he shuts the door. A large worktable sits against one wall, its surface covered in test tubes, mechanical contraptions, and other equipment.

"You've got a whole lab in here," I say, wandering toward the display.

"Isn't it great?" Excitement bubbles in my father's voice as he steps beside me. "Fuoco had everything delivered this morning. Dieter gave me a clean bill of health, so I can start inventing again."

Gratitude swells my chest. Fuoco didn't mention any of this to me. He just did it—he took care of my father because that's what he does. My *husband* takes care of the people he loves.

"Beau?" Dad moves in front of me, concern in his eyes. "What did you want to talk to me about, son?"

I take a deep breath as I struggle to find the right words. "Fuoco and I... We're together now. Permanently." I tell my father a censored version of what happened this evening, explaining the jewels and how Fuoco and I are bound. "It all happened so fast, and now I wonder if I rushed into it?" I shove a hand through my hair, my heart thudding in my chest as doubts ripple through me. "I mean, Fuoco has been dreaming of me for longer than I can wrap my head around, but I don't know. Maybe I'm just infatuated. It's not like I've dated—"

"Beau," my father says, interrupting my rambling. Smiling gently, he tips his head toward the balcony. "Why don't we go outside and get some fresh air, hmm? I have some thoughts on your predicament."

We step into the brisk night and sit at the table and chairs by the railing. Dad takes a moment to look at the stars, and I can almost see his thoughts turning as he gazes at the sky. Finally, he turns his attention to me.

"I remember when your mother and I first met. I felt like I'd been knocked over." He flashes me a self-deprecating smile. "I'm sure I acted like a fool. But she never seemed to mind. Or maybe she felt just as ridiculous and out of her depth as I did. This is a tired cliche, but we were like two magnets drawn together by invisible forces neither of us could control."

"Sound like Fate," I murmur.

"It was." Dad's eyes go soft, his face suddenly years younger. "I knew Evangeline was special from the very start. My gut told me this was it, that I was going to love this woman forever." He pauses, studying me for a moment before continuing. "Not everyone has the privilege of finding the person they're meant to be with. It's an uncommon gift. Those old wedding vows say it all, really. You're with them through good times and bad, sickness and health."

A low sound breaks from my throat. I reach across the table and grab his hand. "Dad…" I say softly.

He places his other hand atop ours on the table. "Love isn't always easy, son. In a lot of ways, it's a leap of faith. A great deal has happened to you in a short period of time. But I think if you listen closely enough, you'll hear your heart speaking to you. It has a way of cutting through all the noise in your head. It'll tell you what's right."

I smile, remembering how I felt the first time Fuoco and I met in the apple orchard. "Yeah. My heart has already spoken."

Dad grins and squeezes my hand before releasing it. "Anyone who looks at you and Fuoco together can see you're meant for each other. But what I told you in the infirmary still stands. If you ever feel like your heart is telling you something different, I'm here for you."

I swallow a lump in my throat and nod. "Thank you, Dad. I'm so grateful that you—" My throat closes up, tears burning my eyes. "I used to worry…"

"Beau," he says gently, taking my hands again. "No matter who you love, I will never turn away from you. You can trust me in this for the rest of your life. That's a promise from your father to his son, and it can never be broken."

Throat burning, I can only nod. Dad might not possess dragon magic, but his vow is just as powerful as the one Fuoco and I made.

He stands and ruffles my hair the way he used to when I was a boy. "I think I'll make a few notes before I turn in. And you should probably go find your husband before he comes looking for you."

I snort. "He's out cold. Snoring." Abruptly, I realize I'm absolutely right. The jewel in my chest is subdued—almost drowsy. And somehow, I know that if I focus on it, the drowsiness will spread through my limbs.

Dad chuckles. "Well, that's marriage for you."

"Do you mind if I sit out here a bit longer?" I want to study the feeling hovering in my chest, to explore whether it changes depending on how far away I am from Fuoco.

"Stay as long as you like." Dad kisses me on the forehead and disappears inside.

Alone, I close my eyes and focus on my chest—on the feeling of Fuoco inside me, connected to me through our bond. It's like a steady heartbeat, each thrum warm and reassuring. I bask in the feeling, letting it chase away the chill of the winter night. My father is right. Love is an uncommon gift. I'm not a dragon, but I've found a treasure all the same.

A faint, sweet scent rises in the air. Rosewater.

Startled, I open my eyes just as a cloud of glittering dust fills my vision. It rushes up my nose and into my lungs, squeezing them tight. Clawing at my neck, I flail, tipping my chair back.

A hooded figure leaps over the balcony railing. I get a glimpse of glittering red eyes before the figure throws an arm around my neck and drags me over the edge and into the night.

THE NEXT TIME I OPEN MY EYES, I LAY ON MY SIDE ON THE GROUND with my wrists bound in front of me. As I struggle to get my bearings, boots crunch. A second later, a hooded figure emerges from the gloom and thrusts a torch in my face. Heat sears my cheek, and flames sizzle in my ear. I recoil, wriggling backward as best as I can. "Hey! What—" Pain explodes in my side, and air leaves my lungs in a whoosh.

Torch in hand, the hooded figure kneels in front of me and throws back the cowl.

My heart races as I take in Lirem's glittering red eyes and mangled face. Healing burns cover him from forehead to shoulder, the skin on his left side red and waxy. Tufts of blond hair sprout from his blackened scalp like new vegetation struggling to grow. On his right side, his blond hair dangles to his chin in dirty, matted clumps.

Lirem stares at me, the disgust in his eyes so potent I can't stop myself from cringing away. His lips twist into a sneer, one side of his mouth curling higher than the other as scar tissue stretches. "You think you can escape me, you worthless little shit? I don't even need to tie you up."

"Then why did you?" I ask before I can think better of it.

His hand flies out, tangling in the front of my shirt. He yanks me roughly off the ground and onto my feet. Dizziness swamps me, and I stumble, wincing as the rope around my wrists abrades my skin. Lirem jerks me against him, his fist digging into my throat. My stomach churns as the stench of charred flesh invades my nostrils.

He leans in close, his breath hot and foul on my face. "Because I like it," he growls. "I like watching you weak, disgusting mortals struggle in the dirt where you belong."

Contempt gleams so strongly in his eyes, it loosens my knees. He wants to kill me. The desire is there right alongside the contempt. Fear grips me as the memory of Fuoco's voice flows through my head. *Even the* thought *of losing you could tip me over the edge."* Oh gods, what have I done?

Lirem's red eyes narrow. Abruptly, he thrusts me away just enough to claw my shirt open. Green light spills from my chest, illuminating the small clearing and drowning out Lirem's torchlight. He stares at the jewel, then gives a low bark of laughter. "Fuoco certainly didn't waste any time. I guess congratulations are in order, baker."

A gasp sounds from somewhere, followed by rapid footsteps. Gastonia emerges from the darkness and stops at Lirem's shoulder, her gaze glued to the jewel.

"Gastonia?" My voice is a thread of sound. Confusion pummels me even as my heart thumps harder. I look between her and Lirem, who maintains his stranglehold on my shirt. Why is she with him? Her normally immaculate appearance is the worse for wear. Dirt smears her forehead. A twig pokes from her dark hair. Did Lirem kidnap her from the village before coming for me?

But she doesn't appear under duress. She continues staring at the jewel, her creamy skin bathed in its green glow. Then she lifts hard eyes to mine. For a second, something that might be pain glimmers in her blue irises. But it vanishes so quickly, I wonder if I imagined it. "So it's true. You let Fuoco bind you."

My confusion turns to shock. "How...?" I swallow against a dry throat. "How could you know that?"

Lirem's laugh is cruel. "You should see your face, baker. Did you really think a village blacksmith could afford the kind of lifestyle Old Man Legum enjoys?" He jerks his head toward Gastonia. "She knows plenty about dragons. She and her father have been in league with us for years. They fleeced your people like sheep."

"And turned the profits over to you!" Gastonia protests, clenching her fists at her sides.

"You profited plenty, too." Lirem keeps his gaze on me as he taunts her. "Sadly, Miss Legum, it appears your luck has run out. Your pretty boy here is very much taken. I tried to tell you. Fuoco's reaction in the courtyard made it clear what the baker is to him. But you wouldn't listen. Just like a human."

Gastonia vibrates with obvious fury. "I've had enough of your insults." Viciousness laces her tone. "You've always loved talking about how powerful you are. Where was your mighty dragon's strength tonight when you forced me to scale the side of the fucking castle?"

The torch bobs dangerously close to my face as Lirem swings toward her. "You know the rules, you spoiled little bitch. *You* serve *me*. Not the other way around. You wanted the baker, so you helped me get him. You could have saved yourself the trouble if you'd listened to me." The scars on his face pull taut as he grins at her. "But I enjoyed watching you struggle up that rope." As rage boils in Gastonia's eyes, his grin widens. "I hoped to watch you fall but, alas, it wasn't meant to be. Just like your romance."

"Get fucked," she spits.

"Gastonia," I gasp, desperation cutting through my fear. "Please, don't do this." I hesitate, not even sure what I'm trying to stop her from doing. But if she's with Lirem, her plans can't be good. "If we could just talk—"

"Shut up!" She turns to Lirem. "Kill him."

My stomach drops. I struggle against Lirem's grip. "Gastonia—" My plea ends in a pained grunt as Lirem drives his knee into my stomach. When I double over, wheezing, he seizes the scruff of my neck and yanks me right back up.

"You heard her," he growls. "Keep your mouth shut."

"Kill him," Gastonia repeats, her tone ice cold. "You said killing one soul-bound mate will kill the other." She glances at me like I'm a bag of garbage. "If you want Fuoco dead, you should slit his throat and be done with it."

"Not yet," Lirem says, his grip on my neck like iron.

"You're a fool," Gastonia says, venom in her voice. "There's no reason to wait."

Lirem lunges toward her, dragging me with him. "I've done nothing *but* wait, woman. For *decades*, I've bowed and bent, babysitting humans because Fuoco was too much of a coward to rule as he should have." Lirem's red eyes glow as he stares Gastonia down. "Fuoco is going to pay for what he did to my friends and my face. Before he dies, he's going to hurt. So we go to the mine first, where we'll take care of your boyfriend."

"He's not my boyfriend," Gastonia says, giving me another cold look. "He's nothing to me."

"Glad to hear it," Lirem says. "Now shut up and don't fall behind." He tosses the torch to the ground, then stomps out the flame. Tightening his grip on my neck, he marches me across the clearing. When we reach the tree line, he hauls me against him, his arm banded around my throat. My feet barely touch the ground as he plunges us into the woods. Branches whip my face and yank at my clothes.

"How far is the mine?" Gastonia demands, scrambling after us.

What mine? I've never heard of any mines in the syndicate. Questions spin through my head, but I can hardly concentrate on them as I struggle to stay upright. If I go down, I have no doubt Lirem will make me sorry.

"Don't fucking worry about it," Lirem growls. "Just move faster."

"I'm moving as fast as I can," Gastonia fires back, panting as she struggles over a fallen tree. Worry enters her tone. "You said Fuoco won't be able to feel him underground, right?"

Lirem grunts. He tightens his grip as he splashes us into a ravine. With my hands bound, all I can do is stumble along with him, freezing water filling my shoes. Moonlight pours down on us, giving me glimpses of Lirem's scarred face tight with determination.

Terror drags an icy claw down my spine. Tears sting my eyes. I should have listened to Fuoco. He warned me it was dangerous to stray from his side. But I was too stubborn. And now Lirem is taking me underground. With every step, he carries me farther away from my mate.

Please, my love. Find me.

CHAPTER 17
FUOCO

Urgent knocking at my door rips me out of a sensual dream about my selsara. I shoot upright in bed, reaching for Beau.

Instead, I grasp his empty, cold pillow. He hasn't been here in a while.

Pain lances through the jewel buried in my chest—a knife blade so hot and sharp that I arch in the bed, screaming as rhythmic waves of agony radiate from my sternum. It takes everything I have just to force oxygen into my lungs.

Beau is in danger.

Choking for air, I lurch out of bed and stagger toward the door, jerking my pants on as I go. I don't need to look around the room for Beau. Because he's *not here.*

And wherever he is, he's fucking terrified. That terror throbs in the jewel—a horrible, raw feeling like a predator stripping my flesh from my bones. But that terror isn't mine—it's his.

Bellowing at the pain, I rip the door open to find Maurice

on the other side, his features twisted in desperation. "She took him! Gastonia! Beau was with me and—"

"Come!" I command, gripping his wrist. Another sharp stab of pain hits me square in the chest and I stumble against the wall, crying out.

Maurice hovers, his voice vibrating with worry. His eyes fall to where I clutch my mating jewel. "What's wrong? Do you know where Beau is?"

"She's hurting him," I gasp. *The dark-haired woman from the village.* "We've got to find him!" I straighten, shoving the agony away as I grip Maurice's arm and hurry him toward the courtyard. "Tell me everything!"

Maurice wheezes as he runs to keep up with me. "Beau and I were talking on the balcony in my room. When I went inside, Gastonia appeared. She had a hooded figure with her. I didn't get a good look, but whoever they were, they were bigger than a human."

"Lirem," I snarl. I whisk Maurice into my arms and run faster. The frantic need to find Beau slices through my pain like a lance through a festering wound. Cool tendrils of power snake through my veins, my gift rising like a leviathan spiraling up from the depths. Wind whips behind me, shoving at my back and speeding me forward. The ground trembles as I fly over the flagstones. Doors loom ahead.

OPEN THEM, I tell the currents that flank me. Wind screams down the corridor and flings the doors wide. Clutching Maurice to my chest, I burst into the courtyard and collide with Jasper.

The pixie flies backward, his wings fluttering wildly. He catches himself in mid-air and crashes to the ground. Chest heaving, he points in the direction of the village. "They've got Beau in a cart. They're taking him through the woods outside the village. I've got Bert following them but I have to stay close or I'll lose my connection."

I move in a blur, setting Maurice down and sprinting away. I shift in a flurry of shredded clothing before returning to Maurice and Jasper. They scramble into my paw, and I leap into the sky.

"Hurry!" Jasper shouts from inside my grip. "They're moving fast. Get me close so I can hear Bert and the others!"

Some part of my brain acknowledges what I've long suspected —Lilygully has more than one animal helper. But that's a mystery for another day. Right now, my only concern is finding Beau and *annihilating* those who dared to touch him. I streak toward the village as Maurice fills Jasper in on the details of Beau's kidnapping. At the mention of Lirem, my outrage sizzles higher.

But confusion joins my wrath. Lirem despises humans. Why would he work with one to take Beau?

The jewel in my chest burns like it's trying to burrow through my skin into my chest cavity. Rage and regret swirl in a toxic cloud in my mind. If only I'd been selfish. If I'd kept Beau locked away, Lirem could have never gotten to him.

Even as I think it, I know I could never do that to Beau. My sweet, independent selsara would never stand for it—and I couldn't live with myself if I trampled his spirit.

Pain hits swiftly, spearing my chest like a sword burying itself through the center of my heart. It comes so suddenly, I falter in the air, plummeting forty feet before thrusting my wings wide and righting myself.

Jasper and Maurice cling to my claws.

"Fucking hells, Fuoco!" Jasper hollers. "Keep it together!"

I scream into the night, releasing a stream of fire I can't hold back. Lirem and the human are hurting Beau. Possibly, Lirem wants my mate as a way of getting to me. Now that Beau and I are soul-bound, his death would also be mine. And without me to rule, Lirem would undoubtedly attempt to take over the syndicate.

Rage coils around me, wrapping tight as the elements respond to my fury. The air goes hot and stifling. As I streak over the forest, trees fall flat in great rows behind me. Water bubbles up from the ground, creating pools of steam that follow us toward Beau's village.

"Circle!" Jasper shouts from my claw. "I need to find Bert!"

Panic chokes me as the ground underneath Beau's village quakes.

"Calm down, Fuoco!" Jasper orders, leaning out from between two of my claws to scan the woods. "You're going to flatten your mate's village!"

STAND DOWN, I urge the soil. I claw back my anger as I widen my circle. If they fucking hurt him—

"There!" Jasper points to a small footpath that cuts through the woods. A tiny pinprick of gray scurries up the trail. "Bert has an update! Get me closer!"

I wheel in the sky, swooping over the footpath. Jasper cocks his head to the side as if he's listening. Desperation claws at my throat as I wait for the pixie to receive word.

"Straight ahead!" Jasper points in front of us. "There's a series of caves that used to be mines. Bert says they went in there!"

The jewel in my chest throbs. As I streak forward, I focus on my connection with Beau. *Pain. Terror. Fear.* His emotions pour through the link, each one stoking my rage higher. *I'm coming, selsara.* I can't speak to him through our bond, but I try to channel comfort back to him. If he can just hang on…

But in the span of a second, the connection snuffs out.

The bond is gone.

CHAPTER 18
BEAU

We don't walk long. Within minutes, Lirem drags me into a dark cave with a ceiling supported by thick wooden posts that march down a narrow tunnel. Moonlight spills into the entrance, illuminating a rusted set of tracks that snake into the distance. My jewel casts a dull, emerald glow. Several large, wooden carts with equally rusted wheels sit on the tracks. Others huddle against walls dripping with water.

Gastonia swings toward Lirem. "*Now* will you kill him?"

I struggle against Lirem's grip, then cry out when he cuffs me against the side of my head. My vision blurs, and my ears ring as nausea burns my throat. As my stomach threatens to revolt, Lirem produces a knife and cuts the rope that binds my wrists. Before I can process my newfound freedom, he drags me to one of the carts that sits on the tracks. He shoves me hard, and the world tumbles over itself. I crash into the bottom of the cart, striking my shoulder and elbow as I land in a heap. The stench of rotting wood invades my lungs. My stomach pitches, and I swallow bile as I struggle to rise.

"Stay down," Lirem barks, shoving me. My forehead scrapes the wood, and I tuck my chin in case he strikes again. "We're not killing him yet," he mutters. "I want Fuoco to feel it."

"This is stupid," Gastonia says above me, derision in her tone. "You have a chance to kill Fuoco, and you're wasting it —" Her sentence ends in a strangled scream. Choking sounds and the crunch of stone echo around the cave as Lirem forces her away from the cart.

"Fuoco won't survive this night, bitch," Lirem snarls. "Make no mistake about that. But I've waited a long fucking time for this." The choking sounds grow louder. "Fuoco will feel everything I do to his selsara, and he'll die with his mate's agony in his chest. And that's exactly what Fuoco deserves for being a traitor to his own kind. So unless you want to join the baker in the cart, keep your mouth shut and do as I say."

The choking sounds cut off. Gastonia's labored gasps reach me, along with the crunch of stone as Lirem moves around the cave.

RAGE. Out of nowhere, black fury fills my chest. It obliterates my aches and lingering dizziness, leaving only cold, calculated anger. The emotion is so thick I could almost choke on it. But it's not mine.

Fuoco. Tears prick my eyes as I cup my hand over the jewel in my chest. *He knows.* My mate knows I'm missing, and he's furious.

"And what happens then?" I asked him when he spoke of the danger of losing control.

"The world burns."

But the rage in my chest isn't hot. It's icy cold. My vision clears, and I swear I can see my breath puffing against the wood in front of me. Some instinct compels me to hold my hand over my jewel, muffling its light.

Stone crunches, and then Lirem looms over the side of the cart. His red eyes glitter as I dare to turn my head and meet his gaze.

"You look lonely, baker. It's a long ride to our destination." His lips curve, his scarred cheek pulling in a grotesque parody of a smile. "But I'm a kind male. I've brought you some company. They're dying to meet you." He lifts a wooden crate. Faint scrabbling sounds emanate from the interior. "You might even say they're hungry to make your acquaintance." Just as fresh terror squeezes my heart, he tips the crate, spilling its contents.

Hot, furry bodies rain down on me. As I scream, my new companions scream, too. Lirem has filled the cart with rats.

"No!" I cry, slapping the wriggling bodies away. "Please!"

Lirem disappears, then returns a second later with something big and wooden in his hands. *A lid.* He slams it onto the top of the cart.

Plunging me into blackness.

Pain. Movement. Darkness.

I don't know how long these things last, only that they've become my world. I claw at the box and the rats claw at me, digging into my skin as I thrash. Their teeth nip and pinch. Fur fills my mouth. Tails whip my legs and flick against my skin. High-pitched screams fill my ears. Some are mine. Some belong to the rats, which dig at my flesh like they're trying to burrow down to my bones.

The wooden cart creaks and shakes, its wheels squeaking as I roll toward some unknown destination. I can only assume Lirem set it on the tracks, but I'm not entirely sure—and I'm not sure I care. All I know is pain, movement, and darkness.

The latter bothers me the most. At some point—and I can't remember when—the jewel's light dulled to almost nothing. And now I fight so hard I'm not sure I see it anymore. Shadows squirm over my eyes, which I try to squeeze shut as I flail against the teeth and claws that writhe and scratch mercilessly. I scream again and again, pounding against the wood as I try to dislodge my tormentors.

But they won't let go. Tears wet my face. Or maybe it's blood. As soon as the thought enters my head, the coppery scent registers in my nostrils. The rats are shredding my flesh. If this goes on much longer, they'll kill me.

Sorrow wraps around me, and it's worse than the pain and the darkness. *"If one of us dies, the other will as well. There is no greater bond among creatures of the Myth."*

If I die, Fuoco will die, too.

No. The thought rises in my mind as clear and bright as a shooting star. Fuoco will *not* die. It's not happening, not even if Lirem dumps a thousand fucking rats on my head.

Gritting my teeth, I pound on the side of the cart. Claws dig more frantically into my back as I bellow so hard my throat aches. "Let me out, you fucking coward!" I rock back and forth, throwing my shoulder against the rotted wood. My thoughts run in circles as I grope for the insult most likely to get under Lirem's skin. "You're so afraid of a human you have to put me in a box! Face me like a man, asshole!"

No response. Just pain, movement, and darkness. I kick at the side of the cart, rage building in my chest. And this time, the rage is *mine*. My whole life, Lirem has stolen from me and the people I love. I won't let him steal my future. Fuoco said he spent his whole life looking for me. Now I know I was looking for him, too. I won't let him go.

I kick harder, grunting with my efforts. The cart continues rolling and creaking. And then, finally, it stops. A second later, the cart tips violently. Light floods my vision as I tumble onto the ground. Wood splinters, and rats scatter in every direction. Squinting against the harsh light, I struggle to my hands and knees. Stinging pain covers me from head to toe. Blood seeps from dozens of wounds on the backs of my hands. More blood drips from my chin to form tiny red craters in the dirt.

"Not so loud now, are you?" Lirem asks, his boots appearing in front of me. One flies in a blur, catching me under the chin and sending me sprawling onto my back. A soaring ceiling spreads above me. Then Lirem blots it out, his scarred, twisted face even more shocking in the harsh light. He steps on my shoulder, grinding it into the ground. His red eyes gleam like rubies. "What was that about facing me like a man?"

My jaw throbs, which makes it easier to keep my mouth shut. He didn't kick me as hard as he might have. He held back, which means he's not ready to kill me just yet. The longer I can delay, the more time Fuoco has to find me.

I cringe away from Lirem, doing my best to appear cowed and meek. It's not much of an effort with pain stabbing at me from all angles and the stench of my fear thick in my nostrils.

DESPERATE. The emotion comes out of nowhere, nailing me in the center of the chest. It frazzles through me, the feeling so powerful and frantic it's a struggle to lie still. Fuoco is searching for me. But I have no idea how to tell him where to find me. Tears burn my throat as I picture his green eyes that crinkle at the corners when he teases me. Green eyes that burn with possessiveness when he lowers his mouth to mine.

I hold his image in my mind as I stretch my senses toward him. *Come find me, selsara.*

Lirem's lips pull in a sneer as he presses his boot harder into my shoulder. "You're like the rest of your kind," he says, contempt coating his tone like oil. "Weak and worthless."

My heart thumps hard. Sweat stings the cuts and bite

marks that cover me. I swallow the urge to point out the hypocrisy of calling me weak when he's got his boot on my shoulder. And anyway, I want it there. I want his eyes on my face. Anything to keep him from looking at the jewel in my chest. If Fuoco is connecting with me, the gem's light is probably growing brighter.

"Please," I croak, injecting as much obeisance into my voice as I can muster. I blink rapidly, letting tears spill down my temples. "Please don't hurt me."

"Get up!" Lirem steps back, and I roll to my side and struggle to my feet before he can kick me into doing his bidding. Gastonia stands a few steps away, her arms folded and her blue eyes cold and flat. As I look past her, I forget how to breathe.

We stand on a cliff in an underground cavern twice the size of Fuoco's Great Hall. A narrow rope bridge spans the width of an inky black chasm that appears to have no bottom. On either side of the rift sit riches almost too vast to contemplate.

Torches line the walls, the firelight dancing over the enormous hoard. Marble statues of gods and goddesses stand among chests piled high with glittering coins. Gilded weapons lie across tables inlaid with mother of pearl. Jewels, crowns, and necklaces sparkle in a rainbow of color. Everywhere my gaze lands, priceless treasure greets me. Silver goblets, golden trinkets, tapestries, and paintings worth more than a small kingdom.

Or a village.

Because it's not just gold and gemstones. Sacks of grain sit among the riches, the burlap bags so fat the seams strain to contain their contents. Rocking chairs and plain, sturdy farm furniture peek from among the austere Chesterfields and elegantly sculpted tables. Lirem's hoard is a storehouse of the villages' wealth.

I look at Gastonia. "You knew he was taking all of this. You helped him steal from us."

She holds my stare, her gaze unflinching. "It was my only way out." Her voice is tight, her tone as frosty as her eyes. "You could have come with me, Beau. Together, we could have escaped and lived a *real* life."

My heart drops into my stomach. I knew she wanted to leave the village, but not like this—not by stealing from everyone she knows and loves. She saw what the enforcers did to people. She watched the theft and abuse up close. Broken windows and broken bones. Children so hungry the teacher had to send them home because they couldn't concentrate on their lessons.

"People were starving," I rasp, disbelief pounding through me. But no, it's not disbelief. The proof of her betrayal glitters all around me. Her guilt is written across her face—and in her actions tonight. No, what I feel isn't doubt. It's anger.

Her lips curve in an acid smile. "So earnest, Beau," she says softly, strolling toward me. "Such a *good* son, always doing the right thing. Taking bread to hungry kids in the village." She reaches me, and the malice in her eyes glitters as brightly as the plundered riches around us. "But that didn't stop you from running to the castle at the first opportunity. And when the dragon lord summoned you to his bed, why, you jumped right in."

Heat suffuses my cheeks. "That's— It wasn't like that—"

"It wasn't?" She tilts her head. "Tell me, then. How was it?" She runs a scathing gaze down my body, her eyes lingering on the jewel visible between the two halves of my shirt. "You mean you and Fuoco sit around and play chess?" She throws her head back and laughs, the brittle sound bouncing around the cavern. But when she lowers her chin and meets my gaze once more, her eyes are devoid of emotion. "I would have taken good care of you. But that's over." She drops her voice to a hiss. "You missed your chance."

I draw a deep breath and step forward. "Gastonia, please. It doesn't have to be this way. There's still time to do the right thing."

She shakes her head. "It's too late. I've made my choice, and you've made yours. There's no going back now."

"Please think this through—"

"I am *tired* of thinking!" she screams, her face twisting with so much abrupt rage, I suck in a breath. She advances on me, blue eyes blazing. Spittle flies from her lips. "I'm tired of waiting and hoping for things to be different! I'm done with the fucking village, and I'm done with you!"

Madness dances in her eyes. I stumble backward just as Lirem clamps an unforgiving hand on my shoulder. He steers me around and propels me forward.

"Time to go, pretty boy. You and I have unfinished business." He pushes me to the rope bridge. A rat streaks from the splintered remains of the cart, its beady eyes reflecting the torchlight. Lirem snarls and kicks the rodent, sending it screeching into the abyss.

A whimper escapes me before I can stifle it.

Lirem chuckles as he forces me onto the planks, which creak and sway immediately. "Face you like a man, huh?" He digs his fingers into my shoulder, pressing hard into the bite wounds that throb in sync with my racing heart. "We'll see how long that tough guy act holds up once we reach the other side." He leans close, his hot breath searing my nape. "Nazzar left a lot of knives behind. I think I'll carve out your liver first."

As we make our way across the bridge, my gaze is drawn to the fathomless gorge beneath us. There is no bottom in sight, just impenetrable darkness. Sharp gusts of frigid wind buffet my face. If I fall, nothing will catch me. And once Lirem gets me to the other side, he's going to make me regret my words in the cart. I focus on my jewel, straining for any glimmer of Fuoco. But there's nothing.

Only silence.

CHAPTER 19
FUOCO

Gone. Beau is gone.

I bellow my fury at the sky. The air responds, whipping violently as I bullet in the direction Jasper points me.

Can't feel Beau.

Can't feel Beau.

Can't feel Beau.

The desperate refrain beats in time with my heart, which threatens to pound from my chest. Power surges through me, tearing away layers of reason until all that's left is the unyielding drive to find my selsara. It speeds me forward—faster, faster, faster—as Jasper shouts directions.

A ravine twists and curves like a snake below us, moonlight sparkling over the water. As I pump my wings, Lirem's scent slams into me so hard I tumble in mid-air. Clenching my paw tightly around Maurice and Jasper, I quickly right myself. With a roar, I dive for the ground, my wings flat against my body. As the trees rush up, I fling my wings wide and land, depositing Jasper and Maurice at the edge of the ravine.

"Follow Bert!" Jasper shouts, pointing to a trail of mice and other rodents who scurry along the embankment. They're all headed in the same direction.

Lirem's scent is everywhere, his anger and frustration soaking the air. Underneath that cloying, tart stench is something light and sweet. *Beau.* As I drag his essence into my lungs, I sense a third scent signature—rosewater, fear, and bitterness. *Gastonia.*

Nostrils flared, I lumber forward, careful not to trample the mice as they lead me up the edge of the ravine. Maurice and Jasper hurry in my wake. For five harrowing minutes, we race along the leaf-strewn water's edge, the scents growing stronger. Yet my jewel remains dull and silent. That can only mean one of two things—Beau is so deep underground that I can't feel him, or he's locked behind iron where Myth magic can't reach him.

Or both.

But my beast scents him, and that keeps me moving until the mice lead me around a bend to find a dark tunnel tucked among fallen trees and tangled brush. It would have been invisible from the sky. The opening is supported by twin wooden beams. A rusted sign over the entrance marks it as a former mine. The opening is far too small to accommodate my beast. Frustration rises hot and fast as I pace, my tail swishing and my talons clawing up the soil. The ground shakes, the earth itself responding to my anguish.

"Easy, Fuoco," Jasper says, his eyes flashing in the moonlight. "If you collapse the cave, we'll never get to Beau."

Grunting, I shove my head into the cave's entrance and suck in a deep breath. The sickly scent of Beau's fear fills my nostrils. But there's something else.

His blood.

I shift so quickly I'm still a dozen feet above the ground

when I take human form. I hit the dirt already striding forward, rage bubbling so close to the surface I can almost taste smoke in my mouth. Flames wreath my head, and green scales descend from my shoulders to my knees. When Jasper and Maurice jog inside, I round on them.

"You can't follow. Lirem won't hesitate to kill you."

Maurice lifts his chin, determination shining in his brown eyes. "If he hurts my Beau, I'll kill him first." He draws himself up to his full height, which is more than a foot below mine. But he seems taller as he defends his son. And it's clear he won't be pressured into staying behind.

Jasper steps forward. "We should go with you." A mouse skitters past him and scurries down a set of rusted tracks. Water drips down the mine's walls. The wind buffets the flames dancing around my head.

My power slithers under my skin, the elements ready for my command.

"Stay close," I tell Maurice and Jasper. "And if I tell you to run, you do it."

We follow the tracks, which lead us deep into the darkened mine. Empty sconces line the walls, any torches they held long gone—or removed by Lirem. A few dozen feet into the tunnel, Jasper stops me with a hand on my arm.

"Maybe we should do this with the lights off." He gives my head a pointed look. "If Lirem has any kind of lookout posted, they'll see you a mile away."

The pixie is right. But my dragon is so close to the surface, I'm not sure I can rein it in.

"It's for Beau," Jasper says softly, squeezing my arm. "You'll do anything for him."

My throat tightens. "Anything," I echo hoarsely. And holding onto my temper is the least I can do. Gathering every bit of self-control I possess, I close my eyes and drag in a deep breath. Then another. After a moment, the heat licking around my head goes cold. When I open my eyes, my night vision kicks in, revealing Jasper and Maurice. Behind them, tiny, furry bodies hurry up the tracks.

Without another word, I rush after them. Power hums under my skin. The elements answer, racing alongside me as I move faster and faster. Dripping water and the crunch of dirt. The chilly breeze that swirls around my feet and ruffles my hair. Embers whisper from the empty sconces, begging to be coaxed into flame.

The ground dips, the tracks marching down an incline. The mice scamper over the rails, little feet flying. Behind me, Maurice's breathing grows labored. But Beau's sire doesn't fall back. He and Jasper stick to my heels as I surge forward, following the mice. The dark plays tricks on my mind, sending phantom voices bouncing off the rocky walls as I rush through the tunnel's twists and turns.

But then I hear it. Lirem's sneering baritone echoes down the tunnel, followed by a woman's angry shriek. A second later, a masculine whimper reaches me.

Beau.

They've hurt him.

Cold, black fury fills my mind. My beast thrashes against my ribs, struggling to break through flesh and bone to rain fiery vengeance on Lirem and Gastonia. But I can't shift in this tunnel. I'll cave the whole thing in.

As I race forward, a small circle of light appears in the distance. I run at it, urgency pounding harder as the circle grows broader. The mine track veers off to one side and ends in a cluster of wooden carts. The light swells. I speed toward it, and now it's so bright it hurts my eyes. But the pain is nothing. Beau is *everything* as I push myself to run faster, faster, faster, finally stumbling to a halt as the tunnel opens upon a vast cavern. Panting, I gaze over the largest dragon hoard I've ever seen.

The cavern is huge, its walls lined with torches. The light dances over chests spilling with gold and jewels. Marble statues of kings and goddesses stand amid the treasures, their expressions passive. And directly ahead, Lirem drags Beau across a swaying rope bridge suspended over a black chasm. The human woman, Gastonia, follows, her dark hair tangled down her back.

Rage builds in my chest, the pressure so intense it overshadows all other emotions—and likely my connection to Beau. But that's probably a good thing. If I sense his pain right now, I'm not sure I'll be able to keep my power in check.

My beast pushes harder, straining to break free. The cavern's ceilings have to be at least a hundred feet high. Plenty of clearance. Stepping farther into the cavern, I let the shift take me. In dragon form, I look back to see Maurice and Jasper huddled at the mouth of the tunnel.

I peer at them, doing my best to convey my wishes through my expression. *Stay put.* Swinging back around, I snake forward, my gaze pinned to Lirem as he pulls Beau farther across the bridge.

The hoard's scents fill my sensitive nostrils. Gold and furniture and expensive perfumes. The earthy aroma of grain. But the strongest scent is the one that makes my lips peel back from my fangs.

My selsara's terror.

Ahead, Lirem and Beau reach the end of the bridge. Lirem grips Beau by the hair as he forces Beau onto the rocky cliff that juts over the chasm. Piles of treasure rise around them. Gastonia picks her way across the last few wooden planks and exits the bridge.

Hold on, selsara.

Moving as soundlessly as possible, I unfurl my wings as Lirem reaches for a long ax handle sticking out of the pile of treasure in front of him.

He turns.

Not an ax.

A lever.

"Hello, Fuoco," he snarls, jerking the lever down. The biting scent of iron fills the air as forty-foot spikes rain down from the ceiling, slicing through my left wing and burying themselves in the rock beneath me.

Agony obliterates conscious thought as I lunge forward, only to come up short. I'm pinned in place, trapped by the metal impaling me. Worse, it's iron. My magic dims, power slipping away.

Beau screams, but the sound is distant and muffled, like someone tossed a thick blanket over my senses. The iron seeps into my body, stealing my magic and sucking it into a void so depthless I can barely sense the elements. My bond with Beau stays dark even as he shouts for me across the cave. With every breath, pain skewers my wing and ripples through my body in sickly waves.

Across the bridge, Lirem wrenches Beau tightly against him, Beau's back to Lirem's chest. My former enforcer reaches into a chest of weapons and withdraws a long, jagged knife. He flips it once, then places the tip under Beau's chin.

I roar, struggling against the stakes impaling my wing. But every move tears muscle. With each labored breath, more iron seeps under my skin.

Beau. My Beau.

My hind legs give out, straining my trapped wing more tightly. My power drifts farther away. Huffing out a pained breath, I push forward, testing the iron, but it doesn't give.

Across the chasm, Lirem twists the tip of his blade. Blood rolls down Beau's neck.

Roaring, I pull harder. Blood pours down my wing, sticky rivulets coating my scales.

Lirem thrusts Beau away from him, then grabs him by the shoulder and spins him around. As Beau staggers, Lirem backhands him across the face. Beau flies into a pile of treasure, smashes his head against a wooden chest, and crashes to the ground.

Red covers my vision. I open my jaws and roar, the vibrations shaking the ground. As dust sifts from the ceiling, Lirem grabs Gastonia. He shoves her toward Beau, barking instructions to keep an eye on him.

Then Lirem whirls and stalks to the bridge. His red eyes glitter as he crosses, his gaze locked with mine. He stops just out of my reach, his lips curving in a cold smile that pulls his scars taut. "You're fucked now, Fuoco," he murmurs, twisting the tip of his blade into his thumb. He watches the blood drip down his finger, then licks it off and smiles up at me. "You killed Nazzar, didn't you?"

When I don't answer, he shrugs. "No matter, all the more treasure for me."

I surge forward, snapping at him, but the iron stakes hold me tight. I can't shift—not with iron sapping my magic. I am, as Lirem says, fucked.

"That last man you burned called us thieves," Lirem says, studying his blade. "I don't think of it as thievery, though. We deserve everything we take from this godsforsaken plane. We sacrificed our world for this one, and you want us to serve the vermin who inhabit it? You're out of your fucking mind." He spits the last word, his ruined features twisting into rage.

In my peripheral vision, Maurice and Jasper sneak around

the outer edge of the cavern, hugging the shadows among the treasure.

Beau's moan echoes across the chasm, pulling my attention back to him. Gastonia stands over him, her fists balled at her sides. When he tries to sit up, she delivers a swift kick to his shoulder. He cries out and falls onto his back.

I bellow and jerk against the spikes, gritting my teeth when agony halts me.

Lirem watches Gastonia over his shoulder for a moment, then turns back to me with an acid smile. "She thought she could help me snatch him and then she'd actually get to keep him. Stupid cunt." He tilts his head. "What's it like, knowing you'll never taste him again? I think I might like a little taste before I rip that fucking jewel from his chest."

Mine.

Beau.

Selsara.

I stretch my neck out, snapping at my former enforcer. He sidesteps easily, raising a blond brow as he offers another mocking smile.

Just don't look back, I pray. *Keep your eyes on me, you fucking asshole.* Over his shoulder, Jasper flies across the chasm with Maurice in his arms. The pixie's wings beat the air as Beau's sire clings to his neck. Gastonia catches sight of them. Before the men land, she screams and sprints to the bridge.

Lirem whirls around. "No! You useless fucking bitch!" Knife in hand, he charges across the bridge.

Beau. He's going to kill Beau.

I need my magic. I've got to get to Beau.

Lirem reaches Gastonia. He tries to shove past her, but the planks are too narrow. The bridge sways wildly. Jasper touches down with Maurice.

Lurching forward, I screech, agony blooming as the spikes

tear through my wing. Muscles and tendons rip from bone, iron cutting through me like a blunt knife. My wing snaps, the momentum almost sending me sprawling. The wing dangles uselessly. But I'm free.

Lirem tangles with Gastonia, shoving her down and stepping over her. She screams, grasping at the ropes as the bridge swings from side to side. As Lirem scrambles onto the cliff, Jasper steps in front of Beau. The pixie grips a knife, his expression deadly cold as he faces off with Lirem.

Agony lances me, my wing hanging limply. Now that I'm free of the iron, my power rushes back. In a flash, I shift into human form and stalk across the bridge. Gastonia scrambles her way to safety, but I pay her no mind. No, I only have one quarry at the moment.

"Lirem!" I shout, leaping over the last few planks and onto the cliff.

He spins. Red eyes go wide.

"It's over," I say, power surging through my veins and closing the wounds on my arm. "You were a dead man the moment you touched my selsara. But you also tortured and stole from the people you swore to protect. You betrayed your vow. And for that, you must die."

Lirem raises his knife. "You are the betrayer! We are meant to rule this plane! But you were too weak to see it!"

"Perhaps," I say, power spiraling higher. It climbs up and up, filling me as I hold Lirem's stare. "But I'm stronger than you." I lift my arms out to my sides and let my power spill over.

EARTH, COME TO ME. Instantly, the ground shakes. The piles of treasure tremble, jewels spilling onto the ground and shivering to the edge of the chasm. Coins tumble and bounce. Lirem gasps as a ruby-studded diadem falls into the chasm and winks out of sight.

WATER, JOIN US. Steam hisses above our heads. A second

later, water shoots downward in great streams that soak the tumbling, bouncing coins. Little rivers form, ferrying more of the hoard into the abyss.

"No!" Lirem shouts, panic twisting his features as he watches his treasures stream toward the edge and disappear. "Stop it!"

FIRE. With a flick of my hand, I summon it from the torches. Plumes form a line at the edge of the cliff, cutting Lirem off from the rivers of flowing treasure. *MORE,* I command, and another round of flames leap from the torches and into my hands. They warm me. Soothe me. Old, familiar friends. Power I've spent my whole life keeping at bay. But no more. Now, I embrace my power—and I have one final friend to call.

"AIR!" I roar aloud, my bellow toppling treasure. In a blink, wind whips through the cavern, screaming around the walls like a hurricane. In some corner of my mind, I'm aware of Jasper and Maurice helping Beau to his feet. The men cringe against a large chest, their hair tossed around their heads. *Selsara.* I should go to him.

Lirem staggers, jerking my attention back to him.

I step forward, wrath forking like lightning over my skin. "You touched him!" I shout. "And now you die! Nobody will ever know where your bones lie. Your name will be wiped from the history books."

"No!" Lirem cries. He falls to his knees.

Reaching a hand toward him, I call the air from his lungs. It whooshes from his lips in a great rush of breath. He claws at his throat, his eyes rolling wildly.

My power climbs to new heights, fury curling into madness. "YOU FUCKING TOUCHED HIM!"

Lirem's mouth stretches on a silent scream. The cliff rocks, boulders tumbling from the walls. Water flows around Lirem's knees. Wind roars, streaks of fire joining the maelstrom that spins around the cavern.

I stand in the center of it all, the cavern coated in the red haze of my fury.

NOW, I tell the air.

Lirem's lungs implode. His body jerks, back arching. His skin wrinkles and splits as I suck every bit of air from his body. I call it until there's nothing left of him but a dried husk. It drops to the ground and explodes into fine powder.

Satisfaction thrums through me—a shivering note in the jangling, swirling power that spins faster around the cavern.

Good, I tell the elements.

More, they respond.

Yes. I tip my head back and close my eyes. Red paints the inside of my lids.

Yes. *More.*

CHAPTER 20
BEAU

I gape at Fuoco as I struggle to stay on my feet. He stands in the center of the inferno that surrounds us, his arms outstretched and his face tilted toward the ceiling as if he's basking in the sun. But the sun is a distant memory in this place. Now, there is only screaming wind and flashes of fire. A tempest whips around the cavern, scooping up coins, jewels, and pieces of furniture. Weapons clatter over the trembling ground, knives and swords tumbling like driftwood. Sofas and statues join the fray, spinning in an ever-faster moving circle.

"He's lost it!" Jasper shouts, his blue eyes narrowed against the wind. His wings tremble violently as we cling to the side of an oversize chest. Dad huddles at my back. Jasper grips my shoulder. "You have to talk to him!"

"What? How?"

"Show him you're safe! Make him see reason, Beau. You're the only one who can."

My heart stutters. Drawing a shaky breath, I push away from the chest. I stagger toward Fuoco, my progress sluggish like I'm moving through water. Sweat drips down my back, stinging my myriad cuts and bite marks. With every step, a thousand aches and pains assail me. But I keep moving, side-stepping coins and jewelry that fly over the ground.

Behind Fuoco, the rope bridge swings, wood creaking as the wind tosses it from side to side. Movement on the ropes catches my eye, and I stop as I try to puzzle out what I'm seeing.

Mice. Over a dozen of them scurry up the ropes. A few drop to the planks and begin chewing at the knots that hold the wood in place.

What the…?

"Selsara?"

I jerk my gaze to Fuoco, who stares at me with glowing green eyes. Green flames leap around his head. But nothing gleams as brightly as the jewel in the center of his chest. Its glare flashes across my vision, and I gasp as my jewel throbs hard enough to make my breath hitch. As connection sizzles between us, I raise my voice over the storm.

"It's me, Fuoco! It's Beau!"

The wind ebbs. Around the cavern, coins and furniture crash to the ground. Fuoco holds my gaze, blinking as if waking from a trance. He takes a step toward me, and then another. The flames around his head shudder, waves of his dark hair flickering among the fire.

"Beau?" he rasps.

"Yeah." Joy bursts like a firework in my chest. I swallow against a suddenly thick throat. "It's me, baby."

Tears fill his eyes. His big shoulders slump as he draws a ragged breath. With a hoarse cry, he reaches for me.

At the same moment, Gastonia streaks out of nowhere, a jeweled broadsword in her hand. Her face is a mask of fury as she pounds toward Fuoco, who's angled away. He can't see her coming.

Everything slows down. I move without thinking, launching my body across the short distance separating me from Fuoco. With a bellow, I hurl myself in front of him, my muscles screaming. The blade grazes my shoulder, and then clatters to the ground as Gastonia slams into me. We flail, our limbs tangling, as she claws at my face.

"How dare you!" she screams, dark hair flying. "How could you want someone like *him* when you had someone like *me*?"

My lungs burn. Everything hurts, but the pain is nothing compared to the anger that punches through me. It lends me strength, and I growl as I fling her away. She goes flying, landing with a grunt on the first few planks of the rope bridge.

Chest heaving, I stalk forward and stand over her. "I never had you," I snarl, "and you certainly never had me."

For a brief moment, her face crumples. Then she hauls herself to her feet, murder in her eyes. The bridge sways as she claws her way toward the cliff, her dirt-streaked hands on the rope railing. "No one humiliates Gastonia Legum! You and your *beast* will pay—" She shrieks as a mouse scampers over her hand. As more mice race along the ropes and leap onto the cliff, she yanks her hands close to her body. "Get the fuck away from me, you disgusting rats!"

An ominous groan swells, echoing through the cavern.

Gastonia freezes, fear flashing in her eyes. "What—?"

The bridge snaps. For a fraction of a second, her terrified gaze collides with mine. Then she plunges into the abyss.

Silence reigns. Jasper appears at my side, his wings gently waving as he cuddles his mouse close to his chest. Stroking the creature between its pink ears, the pixie directs a mild look into the chasm. "Bert's a mouse, not a rat."

I get one second to stare at Jasper. Then strong arms seize

me, and I'm spun around and pressed against a sweaty, bare chest.

"Beau," Fuoco breathes above me, and then his mouth is on mine, his kiss wild and desperate. The world spins as we cling to each other, our tongues exploring hungrily. He slides his hands down my back, gripping my ass and pulling my hips into his. He deepens the kiss, ravishing my mouth.

Eventually, we break away, both gasping for air. Tears fall unchecked down Fuoco's cheeks as he grips my arms. "I couldn't feel you. I thought I'd lost you."

"Right back at you," I say through my tears.

His eyes go stark. "You...did. I lost control, selsara." He swallows hard, and then he frowns, confusion entering his green eyes. "I'm not sure why, but I feel like that won't ever happen again."

"It won't," Jasper says beside us. When Fuoco and I both look at him, he smiles and gives a little shrug. "Beau broke the curse."

Stunned silence rolls off Fuoco. Then he straightens. "What are you talking about, Lilygully?"

Jasper gives Fuoco an exasperated look. "The *elemental* curse." An unspoken *duh* hangs in the air as he looks down at Bert. "These dragons really are as thick as fence posts."

Tension ripples through Fuoco. "That's a legend."

Jasper cants his head up, a smile playing around his mouth as he meets Fuoco's gaze. "Is it?" Bert wriggles into Jasper's front pocket and disappears. The pixie's smile blooms brighter as he looks at me. "I knew you could do it, Beau."

It's my turn to be confused. "Uh...thanks." I clear my throat. "What, exactly, did I do, again?"

"You stepped between Fuoco and the sword. The blade wouldn't have killed him, but it doesn't matter. The point is, you were willing to give your life for his. An act of true love is old magic. When it's done right, it can be powerful enough to break a curse." His smile softens. "Even a very, very old one."

Fuoco stares at Jasper. "How do you know this?"

For one brief moment, it appears like Jasper might say something profound and earth-shattering. But then his lips quirk. "That's what I do, flame zaddy. I'm hot, and I know things."

A muscle twitches in Fuoco's jaw. "Being hot isn't something you do."

"It is when I do it."

"Listen here, Lilygully—"

"We should get moving, my lord." Jasper casts a dubious look at the ceiling. "I'm not feeling an abundance of confidence about the structural integrity of this cavern after you played hurricane in here." He rolls his eyes as he looks between us. "You two are probably going to make out again, and then Beau really needs to hug his dad. After that, we can head back to the castle, where I intend to drink myself into the lap of the first strapping centaur I see."

The mention of my father has me whirling around. He stands a short distance away, his hair sticking up at odd angles and a patient smile on his face.

"Dad!" I rush into his arms, inhaling his familiar scent. "Are you all right?"

"Never better, son. And never more proud." When we ease apart, wonder moves through his eyes. "You were like a warrior."

My face heats. "I don't know about that..."

"I do," Fuoco says, taking my hand. "You were magnificent."

We hold hands the whole way out of the mine, only breaking apart when we emerge to find most of Fuoco's court —and more than a few human servants—waiting at the entrance with weapons in their hands. Tess meets my gaze from the back and gives me a little wave.

The female dragon Riselle steps forward, relief in her eyes as she looks from me to Fuoco. "Oh, thank the gods you're safe!" Her purple eyes sharpen. "Is Lirem dead?"

"Very," Fuoco says.

A cheer goes up among the crowd, shouts of "let's party!" and "drinks are on me!" rising from the chorus of jubilant celebration. "The drinks are free, you idiot!" someone calls out. Two ogres attempt to high-five and miss. Riselle winces, then offers us an apologetic look. "They're a little drunk."

"It's fine," Fuoco murmurs, his eyes shining as he gazes over his court. "They came."

Riselle smiles. "We could start a training program, my lord. You don't have to defend the syndicate all alone."

I slip my hand into Fuoco's. As he looks at me with love in his eyes, I squeeze his fingers. "She's right, selsara. You don't have to do anything alone anymore."

He lifts my hand to his lips. Just before he presses a kiss to my knuckles, he murmurs, "Not with you by my side, I don't. You're a dream come true."

EPILOGUE
FUOCO

Early spring

I swoop through the greenhouse in dragon form, Beau riding atop my back with a sack of seeds in his hand. He dumps them in a steady stream, hanging onto my neck spines as I wheel and fly down the row we just planted. Crackling power surges through me, and I call the earth to cover the seeds by just a few inches. By the time we reach the end of the row, the seeds are warm and snug in their spots.

In the next field over, I sense the seedlings straining to rise from the ground. I'd help them along, but the struggle seems to make them stronger. Just because I can control them doesn't mean I should.

Beau taught me that.

Everywhere, plants and people thrive. As I wheel in the air, Tess looks up from a row of tomatoes and waves. Beside her,

Ellen does the same. Her cap is gone, her hair swept back into an elegant bun. Soft tendrils frame a face that's now rounded with good health.

I trumpet a greeting, smoke rolling from my nostrils. The women laugh as I soar toward the front of the greenhouse, my selsara's happiness humming in the jewel in my chest.

My wing twinges, and I wince as I descend and land. The wing is fully healed, but still aches on occasion, especially when the weather changes. Dieter has done what he can, but dragons heal more slowly when we're injured in beast form. I stretch the wing once before folding it close to my body.

The front wall of the greenhouse is gone, the space open to the outside. Humans and creatures of the Myth work alongside one another to expand the fields and erect a new wall. When they finish, the greenhouse will be triple the size it is now.

Beau slides off my back with a quick stroke down my scales. "This place will be amazing next winter, my love." He plants his fists on his hips and looks around, pride shining in his dark chocolate eyes. "Think of all the seeds we can give the farmers in another month or two." He tips his head back, meeting my gaze with one of his soft smiles. "You're changing lives with this, Fuoco."

I shift into human form and loop an arm around his waist, pulling him close. "This is all your doing, you know. I wanted to throw the people a party."

Beau rolls his eyes good-naturedly. Parties are the one thing we disagree on. I always want a party—it's the perfect chance to show off my beautiful mate. But I'm the first to admit that my selsara's idea of opening the greenhouse to the whole syndicate was a stroke of genius. The more time people from the villages spend around me, the more at ease they are in my presence. I've been getting my hands dirty helping to grow food. Even better, I've been getting to know the humans who depend on me to lead them. Already, I can sense them shifting from depending on me to trusting me.

"Did somebody say party?" Jasper strolls in from outside, his wings shimmering in the sun pouring through the glass walls. He stops and gives my hips a pointed look. "Oh, *that* kind of party. I should have known."

Beau tosses me a pair of pants with a laugh.

"Didn't you say you had somewhere to be?" I ask Jasper, pulling the leather over my hips. The meddlesome pixie has been a permanent fixture in the castle since Beau's rescue.

Jasper shrugs noncommittally. "I suppose I could claim my dragon ride now. I'm overdue at court."

My senses sharpen. "And what court would that be?" There are only so many "courts" among immortals. If Jasper is overdue for an appearance of some kind, he's most likely visiting the pixie court. Its location is one of the best-kept secrets of the Myth. Queen Mab might be as mischievous and wayward as her subjects, but she takes security seriously. On the other hand, there's a decent chance the pixie monarch simply enjoys keeping people guessing.

Jasper winks at me. "Wouldn't you love to know, flame zaddy."

"For the last time, Lilygully, I asked you not to call me—"

"I can leave as soon as tomorrow if you two think you can manage without me." He gestures around the greenhouse. "I mean, it looks like you've got things well in hand." He waggles his brows at Beau.

"Very well in hand," my selsara says with a laugh, taking Jasper's teasing in stride.

Jasper returns Beau's smile, the expression softening as it reaches the pixie's blue eyes. "It's good to see you happy, Beau. You deserve it."

"What about me?" I grumble, folding my arms.

"You too, of course, my lord. You two are couples goals for sure."

Beau bumps Jasper with his hip. "Wanna see something? It might change your mind about sticking around a few more weeks."

Jasper's lips curve in a devious grin. "Show me everything, cutie."

I glance at the ground under Jasper's feet. A small hole opens, and he lets out a startled yip as he drops into it up to his ankles. He flutters his wings furiously, shooting me an exasperated look. "Are you really that possessive?" When I raise an eyebrow, he waves a dismissive hand. "Yeah, yeah, stupid question."

I jerk my head toward my selsara. "Beau's been excited to show you this. Get out of my hole and—" I clamp my mouth shut as Jasper bites his fist, devilry dancing in his eyes. "Forget I said that," I growl.

The pixie makes a strangled sound.

"Lilygully..." I warn.

"All right, all right!" With a flick of his wings, he clears the hole and flits to Beau's side. My selsara just shakes his head, a smile twinkling in his eyes as he leads Jasper through the greenhouse.

Pleasure lights up the mating jewel in my chest. Beau's happy, so incredibly happy. I trail him and Jasper as they round a field of half-grown corn. At the end of the row, a piece of wooden machinery sits in a small clearing. A metal tube pokes from underneath the contraption, leading to a large wooden bowl.

Maurice appears around the side of the machine, Riselle close behind him.

Beau goes to his father and places a hand on the older man's shoulder. "Well? Is it working, Dad?"

"Like a charm," Maurice says, beaming. He turns his bright smile on Riselle. "But only because of Riselle's advice. I couldn't have done it without her."

Riselle pats the side of the machine. "Nonsense, Maurice. It's your fuel that powers this, and hopefully many more like it." She winks at Beau's sire. "We're good partners."

The tips of Maurice's ears turn pink. Jasper looks from Maurice to the female dragon, silvery dust falling softly from the edges of his wings.

Beau gestures toward the big wooden machine. "Well, Dad, tell everyone what you've invented."

Maurice claps his hands together, pride shining from his eyes as he gazes at the machine. "It's a wine press! Fuoco is already growing grapes on the other side of the greenhouse. By the end of the summer, we should have a full production line going."

For the next half hour, I listen as Maurice explains the inner workings of the press, along with the magical fuel that powers it. But I reserve the bulk of my attention for Beau. He watches his father, and I watch him, my selsara's joy tangible in my jewel. The powerful emotion spreads through me, warming me from within.

Eventually, Maurice and Riselle wander to the rear of the machine, their voices animated as they debate the merits of adding some kind of filter before the press fills the final bowl.

Beau grins as he turns to Jasper and me. "We can probably head back to the castle. They're going to be at this for a while."

A tiny head pops up from Jasper's shirt pocket. The pixie stares down at his mouse as it releases a long stream of chatter. "How in the world do you know that, Bert?" Jasper demands. When the mouse's chirping grows louder, the pixie throws up his hands. "Okay! I'll tell him." He looks at me. "Bert says you should use that press to make elderberry wine. It'll speed the healing of your wing."

I blink. Then I meet the mouse's dark eyes and offer a bow. "Thank you."

Beau reaches out, and Bert hops into his open palm. "Thank you for everything, friend," Beau murmurs, stroking the top of Bert's head. "I wouldn't be here without you. I'm forever grateful."

Jasper sniffs as he retrieves Bert and tucks the mouse carefully back into his pocket. "I hate goodbyes."

"Is that why you've moved into my castle?" I ask.

"Fuoco!" Beau scolds. "We owe Jasper as much as we owe Bert."

As usual, my selsara is right. Softening my voice, I place my hand over the jewel in the center of my chest and bow over it. "My apologies, Jasper. You have my thanks…and my help if you should ever require it." When I straighten, Beau gazes at me with love shining in his eyes. I make a mental note to apologize to Lilygully more often.

Jasper smiles. "You'll probably regret that."

"I don't doubt it," I say, returning the expression.

We stay like that for a moment, friendship and affection swelling among the three of us. Well, four of us, I mentally amend with a glance at Bert. Then Jasper flutters his wings.

"Gotta run. I need to pack." He blows us a kiss and heads toward the front of the greenhouse.

My heart sinks. "He's got *so* much luggage."

Beau laughs and links his arm with mine. "You can handle it, selsara."

I snag him around the waist and bury my face in his neck. "I never get tired of hearing you say that." I bring my lips to his ear and nip his lobe, then trail a row of kisses down the vein throbbing just under his skin. Dragging his collar aside, I kiss my way to the hollow of his throat. "You taste like the most sumptuous of wines, selsara," I murmur. "Have dinner with me tonight."

Beau's laugh rumbles against my lips. "I have dinner with you every night, my love."

"But tonight I want to show you off."

He tangles gentle fingers in my hair and forces my head up. "You got new jewels, didn't you?"

I pretend to be affronted, but I can't keep up the appearance. "I'm not the least bit sorry for lavishing you in riches, Beau Bidbury. Now come, I want to show you what I got you."

His plump lips curl into a smile as he follows me to our bedchamber. When we reach it, I grab a stack of clothes Zara delivered earlier.

Beau smiles. "Another corset. Color me surprised."

Grinning, I place the clothing in his arms and grab a blood-red collared shirt off the top. I slip it over my shoulders, then step back to give my selsara an eyeful.

Pink steals across his cheeks as he sets the clothing down and plucks the corset from the pile. "Face the mirror." His husky command sends a trill of anticipation down my spine. Beau and his commands are something new we're trying in the bedroom. Turns out my sweet baker has a deviant streak. Exploring it has been so much fucking fun.

Literally.

"Hands on the mirror," he murmurs. When I obey, he slips the corset over my shirt and makes quick work of the laces at the back. As he yanks them tight, I meet his eyes in the reflective surface.

"Perfect," I whisper.

His smile grows bigger, and he ties the laces at my lower

back. The mirrored tie comes next, and he turns me to face him, his fingers working deftly to knot it around my neck.

And I can't stop looking at him.

"You're fucking beautiful, Beau," I murmur. "As beautiful as the day we met."

"You're not too bad yourself." He chuckles, one dark brow rising. "You planning on wearing pants? I didn't see any in that stack."

I grumble. "They're not ready yet, so I'll wear something I have." I gesture to an ornately jeweled box on a stand by our door. "Open the box, Beau. Your present is inside."

He tosses a flirty look over his shoulder as he goes to the door. When he opens the box, his gasp fills the room. "It's beautiful," he breathes, turning the vambrace in his hands.

I cross the room and take it from him. Flipping it over, I show him the scrolled design on one side. "The House Drakoni crest, my love. I had this made before I ever met you."

Eyes bright with tears, he leans forward and places a tender kiss on my lips. When we part, he strokes the glittering metal. "I love it."

"I want you in nothing but this after dinner," I say, slipping the vambrace around his forearm. As he shivers, I pull the laces tight and knot them.

Beau turns his arm over, the vambrace's metal surface catching the light. When he lifts his gaze to mine, his expression is so open and loving it steals my breath. "You ready to go see our people, my lord?"

Our people. I love the sound of that. I stroke my fingers along his stubbled jawline. "Yes, selsara. But you're the only thing I'll see."

"I love you," he murmurs, dark eyes shining. He reaches up and brushes the back of his hand over my cheek. "But you know you don't have to get me things. I already have everything I need."

I pull him against me. "Well, that makes two of us, selsara. I've got everything I need right here."

Happily ever after.

I can't imagine a more perfect ending.

About Anna Fury

Anna Fury is a North Carolina native, fluent in snark and sarcasm, tiki decor, and an aficionado of phallic plants. Visit her on Instagram for a glimpse of the sexiest wiener wallpaper you've ever seen. She currently lives in North Carolina with her Mr. Right, a tiny tornado, and a lovely old dog.

Keep up with new releases by visiting annafury.com

Sign up for her newsletter to get access to most of her books spicy epilogues, including hours of free audio!

BOOKS BY ANNA FURY

DARK FANTASY SHIFTER OMEGAVERSE

Temple Maze Series

NOIRE | JET | TENEBRIS

DYSTOPIAN OMEGAVERSE

Alpha Compound Series

THE ALPHA AWAKENS | WAKE UP, ALPHA | WIDE AWAKE | SLEEPWALK | AWAKE AT LAST

Northern Rejects Series

ROCK HARD REJECT | HEARTLESS HEATHEN | PRETTY LITTLE SINNER | SALVAGED PSYCHO | BEAUTIFUL BEAST

Scan the QR code or visit www.annafury.com to access all my books, socials, current deals and more!

@annafuryauthor
liinks.co/annafuryauthor

ABOUT AMY PENNZA

Amy Pennza is a USA Today Bestselling Author of steamy paranormal and contemporary romance. After stints as a lawyer and a soldier, she discovered her dream job is writing about stubborn alphas and smart heroines. She lives in the Great Lakes region with her husband and five children.

Keep up with new releases by visiting amypennza.com

Sign up for Amy's newsletter and get a FREE scorching-hot paranormal romance!

www.amypennza.com/subscribe

ALSO BY AMY PENNZA

Check out all my books by visiting my Amazon author page or my website.

The Bitten and Bound Series. Dark Fantasy MMF Menage:

Given

Stolen

Kept

The Dragon Lairds Series. Paranormal Romance MMF Menage:

Kiss of Smoke

Dark Fire Kiss

Kiss of a Dragon King

Lux Catena Wolf Shifters Series:

What a Wolf Desires

What a Wolf Dares

What a Wolf Demands

What a Wolf's Heart Decides

Made in the USA
Coppell, TX
12 July 2025